Fionn: Stranger at Mullán Bán

The Fionn mac Cumhaill Series - Book Four

BRIAN O'SULLIVAN

D1462611

Irish Imbas Books

Also by Brian O'Sullivan

The Beara Trilogy:
Beara: Dark Legends

The Fionn mac Cumhaill Series:
Fionn: Defence of Ráth Bládhma
Fionn: Traitor of Dún Baoiscne
Fionn: The Adversary
Fionn: Stranger at Mullán Bán

The Irish Woman Warrior Series
Liath Luachra: The Grey One
Liath Luachra: The Swallowed
Liath Luachra: The Seeking
Liath Luachra: The Metal Men

Short Story Collections
The Irish Muse and Other Stories
Celtic Mythology Collection 1
Celtic Mythology Collection 2
Celtic Mythology Collection 3

Fionn: Stranger at Mullán Bán

BRIAN O'SULLIVAN

IrishImbas Books

ISBN: 978-1-99-115814-7
ISBN: 978-0-9951079-1-5

DEDICATION

This book is dedicated to Jonathan O'Mara.

ACKNOWLEDGEMENTS

Special thanks to Marie Elder.

Many ancient Fenian Cycle texts were essential for the completion of this work. These included Macgnímartha Finn (The Boyhood Deeds of Fionn), Acallam na Senórach (The Colloquy of the Ancients), Fotha Cath Cnucha (The Cause of the Battle of Cnucha) Aided Finn meic Chumail (The Death of Finn Mac Cumaill) and many more.

Glossary

Some of the Irish terms/concepts used frequently in this novel are listed below. For those readers who would like to know the correct pronunciation, an audio glossary is available at the Irish Imbas website.

Aintín – Aunt
Amadán – Idiot/fool. (Plural: *Amadáin)*
Ar aghaigh linn – Let's go
Bandraoi – Female druid
Beacáin scammalach – Literally, 'cloudy mushroom'. A fungus with hallucinogenic properties.
Bod – A penis
Brocach – A den
Brón – Sadness
Buachaill – Boy. When speaking to a boy it's expressed as *'a bhuachaill'*
Buaile – A feeding or milking place for cows. Usually refers to the transfer of cattle to summer or winter feeding areas.
Cabóg – A clumsy/awkward person
Conradh – A champion/ battle leader
Derbfine – Member of a patrilineal group
Díbhearg – A band of warriors, usually a raiding party or reavers
Draoi – A druid
Dún do chlab – Shut your mouth (beak)!
Éclann – Clanless state. A person not affiliated to any particular clan
Fadharcán – A troublesome individual
Fian – A band of warriors or war party (plural *'fianna')*
Fidchell – an ancient board game used in Ireland believed to be similar to chess
Gaiscíoch – a hero warrior, a fighter of great prowess
Garsúr – Boy. When speaking to a boy it's expressed as *'a gharsúr'*. It's actually a more modern term but used in this novel for variation.
Gléas Gan Ainm – Literally 'Tool Without a Name'
Imbas forosnai – A divination/prophetic ritual
Lamraighe – Name of a tribe
Léine – Ancient shirt-like garment
Lis – Circular courtyard of a *caiseal* or *ráth*
Óglach – A young, unblooded warrior (plural: *Óglaigh*)
Ollamh – Chief/Head Druid

Plámás – Soft talk or sweet talk

Ráméis – Nonsense talk

Rechtaire – A title for someone acing as an administrator/ steward

Rí – Literally translated as 'king' but generally refers to a tribal leader

Rígfénnid – Leader of a *fian*

Síd – Ancient burial mound

Slat – Slang word for penis (cock/dick)

Tánaiste – Successor to the rí or leader

Techtaire – Messenger/envoy

Tíolacadh – A paranormal gift or skill

Uí Cuaich – A tribe

Uí Barraiche – A tribe

Uisce beatha – Water of life. Modern-day translation is 'whiskey'

Chapter One

It was a death-sun that revealed the strangers' tracks, south-east of the Bládhma mountains. Sliding in on the heel of dusk, its slanted glare cast a bloodstained hue that clearly illuminated the broad spread of footprints. Liath Luachra, the Grey One of Luachair, regarded them in silence, her expression grave and hard as stone. In all her years travelling that isolated territory, she'd never once encountered evidence of another person's passage. To come across a trail with such a number, and such a diversity, of tracks all at once, made her stomach muscles clench in unease.

Kneeling beside the nearest footprints, she chewed on the inner tissue of her left cheek and glanced warily around at the surrounding forest. The dense vegetation meant there was little enough to see: a series of endless dark walls where tall oak trees layered the ridges to the north and south, the distant blur of the Bládhma mountains peeking above the canopy to the east. Within that landscape however, there was no sign of movement or anything else out of the ordinary.

Reassured by the absence of any immediate danger, the woman warrior bent closer, probing one of the footprint's shallow depth with the fingers of her right hand. Conscious that the early evening sunlight would soon be fading to grey, she scraped a piece of dirt free, raised it to her nose and sniffed.

It smelled, naturally enough, of earth.

Of the Great Mother's moist and muddy breath.

Tossing the gritty residue aside, she wiped her hand on the leather leggings that hugged her haunches and considered the two boys who stood nervously to her right. Bran, with almost seventeen years on him, was more youth than boy and by nature tended to solemnity. That sombre temperament was evident now in the furrows that lined his forehead and the nervous manner in which he chewed at his fingernails while studying the erratic mesh of tracks. The youth was visibly troubled by the prospect of strangers in Bládhma territory. He might not have been able to remember the full detail of his parents' brutal murder at Ráth Dearg fourteen years earlier, but he was certainly old enough to realise that incursions like this didn't bode well for anyone.

1

'Who are they, Grey One?'

The younger boy, the dark-haired Rónán, had little more than seven years on him but was markedly more upbeat than his friend. Despite being burdened with a wicker backpack full of pork and venison cuts – the prize from a successful hunt in the Drothan valley – he stared down at the scattered tracks with unbridled excitement.

The woman warrior shrugged dispassionately. 'Read the story in the Great Mother's mantle. Read what the earth tells you and tell me what you see.'

The dark-haired boy reacted to the suggestion with his usual animation, nodding fervently as he moved closer to the tracks. Ever keen to accompany the woman warrior on her forays into the Great Wild, he invariably responded to such tests with enthusiasm. Crouching alongside her, features fixed into a frown, he chewed on the inside of his own cheek in unconscious mimicry as he studied the tracks. His long hair was held from his eyes by a leather headband, but several strands had worked free, and he brushed them away with an irritated gesture.

Liath Luachra watched as his gaze fixed on the single footprint in front of him before transferring to the jumbled network of other tracks that surrounded it.

He's just like Bearach. Happy, eager as a puppy.

She suppressed that thought immediately, burying the accompanying hurt deep in a dark place where she rarely chose to venture. Some memories were best embedded in dark caverns, places best avoided, crannies where it was wiser not to light a torch for fear of what you'd see.

'There's five or six sets of tracks,' noted Rónán. 'The prints are spaced wide apart so they're travelling fast.'

She nodded, pleased by the keenness of his observation.

'Yes.'

'They're headed east.'

She inclined her head to her left shoulder but made no response. That fact was plain enough to see from the direction in which the tracks were pointing.

Sensing that he'd disappointed her, the boy tried again. 'They're men,' he said warily, as though not entirely convinced of his own conclusion.

Again, easy enough to work out from the breadth of the imprints and the depths of their impressions.

'Yes,' she pressed. 'But what else? What's the pattern?'

Rónán looked down at the prints once more. Unable to distinguish any obvious configuration, he threw an anxious glance towards Bran, but the youth had already turned away, focussed on other, more distant tracks.

Realising there was little succour to be had from that quarter, Rónán turned back to scrutinise the nearest imprint, bending to examine it more closely in the fading light. Despite further study however, his efforts garnered no fresh intuition. Finally, raising his eyes to the woman warrior, he conceded defeat with a frustrated shake of his head.

By then, Liath Luachra had already changed position, moving away to lean against a holly tree, her backpack pressed against the coarse trunk to take some of the weight from her back and shoulders. She was looking towards the dying sun when she caught the movement of his head from the corner of her eye and, squinting against the ruddy light, turned back to consider him with an impassive regard.

'It's a *tóraíocht*. A pursuit.' She shifted to adjust the balance of the backpack against her shoulders. 'A group of men is chasing a single man, a solitary traveller from the looks of it.'

She gestured towards a particular line of tracks that had a visibly different appearance to the others.

'See how those footprints look older? The edges of the prints are friable, the flat sections drier. All the other tracks are still damp because they haven't fully dried out. That means they were made more recently, probably just a little earlier this afternoon.'

Rónán thought that explanation through for several moments before raising his eyes to look at her, his lips turned down in a frown. 'Why are they chasing the single traveller?'

The woman warrior shrugged. 'I don't know. The Great Mother only ever reveals part of the story of those traversing her mantle.'

Bran, who'd turned back to observe their interaction in silence, cleared his throat and shifted his weight awkwardly from one leg to another. 'Grey One. If they're travelling east, they'll strike Ráth Bládhma.'

Liath Luachra rubbed her nose and sniffed.

3

'Perhaps. Perhaps not. Just because the tracks here show them moving east, that doesn't necessarily mean they'll continue in that direction.' She gestured loosely towards the forested ridges north and south of where they were standing. 'In the confines of this landscape, it makes sense for the intruders to travel east but they might well drift to a different course once the ridges drop and the land opens out.'

Bran kept his eyes lowered and he made no response, but she sensed he was unconvinced by the argument.

Sighing, the Grey One stepped away from the tree, grunting as the full weight of the backpack settled back down on her shoulders. 'Rest easy. Our own course to An Poll Mór follows their trail for a time yet. If they veer off the eastern path, we'll know they're no threat to Ráth Bládhma.'

'What if they don't veer off?' asked Rónán.

'That ...' The woman warrior gave another noncommittal shrug. 'That's an issue we'll address if we come to it.'

***

The intruders didn't veer off the eastern path. Although they followed the trail until the fading light prevented any further pursuit, the tracks continued resolutely eastwards, bypassing several openings in the forested terrain that offered ample opportunity to change direction.

Pulling the boys off the trail, the Grey One led them up the shadowed profile of the low hill where the cave known as An Poll Mór was located. An L-shaped cavern on the hill's north-eastern slope, its narrow entrance was concealed by a screen of dense bush that made it a secure refuge. It was also a comfortable one, aided in no small part by the supply of dry wood and kindling maintained by Ráth Bládhma hunters who frequented it on occasion.

Inside the cave, Liath Luachra divested herself of the heavy backpack and left the boys to prepare the evening meal while she exited once more, working her way around to the hill's northern slope. Taking up a position in the lee of a large boulder that offered shelter from the breeze, she stood quietly and stared east. In daylight, the site was high enough to offer an unrestricted view of the forested terrain spreading out from its base. On a cloudless day, the Bládhma mountains, three or four days' march to the east, could also be distinguished. Tonight however, the gloom presented nothing but grainy darkness and she couldn't see even the flicker of a campfire.

The woman warrior clicked her tongue in agitation. The situation in which she found herself made her increasingly uneasy. With the incoming darkness, the strangers – both the original traveller and his pursuers – would have been obliged to halt for the night. As a result, she'd expected to see at least one campfire on the terrain below. It was possible – even likely – the single traveller was too far ahead for his fire to be seen, but the fire of the pursuing group should have been visible by now.

Unless they were canny enough to conceal it.

Liath Luachra stared out at the darkness once more, troubled by her lack of certainty about the *fian's* position.

Who are you?

She chewed nervously on the inside of her cheek. While following the intruders' trail, she'd noted a number of sporadic, circular indentations in the earth alongside the tracks of the pursing party, which had concerned her deeply. She was still glumly mulling over the ramifications of those marks when Bran arrived around the side of the slope and took up a position alongside her.

'The evening meal's done,' he informed her. Message delivered, he lapsed into silence, his eyes following hers out into the darkness. Despite her own focus on the eastern shadows, Liath Luachra could sense the tension emanating from him, the rigid tightness in his stance.

'Have you seen a fire?' he asked.

She shook her head.

'I know what they are.'

This time the Grey One glanced sideways at him. Although tempted to ask him what he meant, she decided to turn her attention back to the darkness instead. The youth clearly had a need to talk, and she didn't want to put him off with questions.

'The pursuers,' he persisted. 'I know what they are. I saw the sign of their spears. The indentations in the earth where they used the hafts for balance or for leverage when they were climbing.'

He turned so that he was facing her, his expression grim, as though challenging her to deny that fact.

'They're a *fían*, Grey One. A war party. Warriors travelling with their weapons at the ready. No-one else would travel set for battle like that.'

'It could be a *díbhearg*,' she countered.

'Raiders?' He shook his head. 'They've been following him too long for simple raiders. No *díbhearg* would waste so much effort on a single person.' He shook his head. 'I think there's some tribal enmity between the pursuers and their quarry.'

Despite her own restrained disquiet, Liath Luachra found herself impressed by the boy's reasoning, the clever way he'd used the skills she'd been drilling into him over the years to assemble his observations and piece together the correct conclusion. She also felt an unfamiliar sense of pride at his accomplishment, but it was a pride tempered somewhat by the perilous circumstances in which it had been revealed.

'Have you told Rónán?'

The sudden change in topic seemed to take the youth by surprise. He took an involuntary step back and regarded her with an arched eyebrow. 'You think we should tell Rónán?'

'I think he has a right to know.'

Bran chewed on his lower lip and his eyes took on a faraway look. He was, Liath Luachra suspected, recalling that moment from his childhood when he'd learned of his parents' bloody slaughter and comprehended the true meaning of fear and loss. No doubt he was also wondering whether this was truly something with which he wanted to burden his younger friend.

'I'll tell him,' the Grey One said at last. 'As elder, that task falls to me. You go back to camp. I'll follow along soon enough.'

Relieved to have the weight of that decision lifted from his shoulders, Bran nodded sharply and made to go. He'd only taken three steps however, before he halted and turned to look back at her.

'Those intruders, Grey One. They intend to kill that traveller. They mean to murder him out here in the Great Wild.'

Liath Luachra nodded slowly. That had always been her assumption. She wondered quietly what point the boy was trying to make.

'We should warn him. Help him.'

Liath Luachra's response was a single, decisive shake of her head. 'That traveller's made his own choices and it's by those choices he'll live or die. Whatever he's done to draw the ire of those who pursue him … that's none of our concern. Our responsibility's to fetch Rónán home safe, to alert our people and help protect them if there's a need.'

He looked at her in shock. 'But they'll kill him.'

'He's not our responsibility.'

'But …'

Her brutal indifference had clearly shaken him. Shocked though he was, he still attempted to convince her otherwise.

'He's a lone man, Grey One. Out here in the Great Wild he has no support to call on, no safety to fall back on. You've followed the warrior path. People still sing of your battle exploits around the fires at night. You could … we could … save him.'

She stared at the boy in stony exasperation, forcing herself to take a deep breath before responding. 'My *fian* days are done, Bran. And that traveller's not one of ours. Why would you risk your life for someone you've never laid eyes on, someone who's never done anything for you?'

'Because …' he said. 'Because …'

Bereft of a response, the boy went silent.

Because a fian just like this killed his parents.

The Grey One felt her chest tighten as Bran stood in numb confusion, his thin frame swathed in silence and untouchable layers of grief. She shifted awkwardly, unsure how to comfort him. She'd always felt a connection to the silent youth, an odd bond of kinship or empathy because of the traumatic childhood events they shared. That had never made it any easier to articulate it, of course.

When she did speak again, her voice was soft even if her words were characteristically frank.

'Turn your concerns to those dearest to you, Bran. Save your strength for the ones who touch your heart and who need it most.'

When the youth made no reaction, she hesitantly reached over to lay a hand on his shoulder. The gesture was stiff and clumsy, for such open displays of physical intimacy were a rarity for her.

'Let's return to An Poll Mór and take our rest,' she said to fill the silence. 'We'll have a challenging day tomorrow. I'll explain the situation to Rónán in the morning. For tonight, he can sleep an untroubled sleep.'

Using the hand on his shoulder, she directed the desolate youth back in the direction of An Poll Mór. This time he went without argument.

And did not look back.

**

A small fire within the inner curve of the cave illuminated that section of the narrow cavern where the boys had prepared the camp. Three bedrolls were spread out on mattresses of bracken and fern and a small meal of reheated pork stew had been poured into three wooden bowls by the fire.

Settling with the boys on the cold stone floor, the Grey One grabbed one of the bowls and started to eat. The stew was lukewarm but that didn't overly bother her as she consumed it with stoic practicality, chewing rapidly and barely taking time to enjoy the flavour. Raising the bowl to her lips, she swallowed the remaining morsels, wiped one finger around the inside of the container and sucked the last of the juice from its tip.

It was only as she replaced the container on the stone that she realised how slowly and quietly her companions were eating. Bran was chewing mechanically, staring wordlessly into his bowl. Rónán was also uncharacteristically restrained, a clear indication that he'd picked up on the earlier tension between them.

Rising brusquely to her feet, the woman warrior grabbed the strap of her wicker backpack, hauled, it onto one shoulder and then made for the cave entrance. 'Fetch the other baskets and bring them out when you've done,' she instructed them. 'I'll start on the hole.'

The boys looked at her blankly.

'To bury the meat,' she explained.

Their sustained air of bewilderment made her frown.

'The strangers lie between us and the mountains. We'll need to move deftly to get past them unseen, and we can hardly do that if we're weighed down by backpacks. The meat stays behind.'

The boys' confusion showed little sign of clearing. The Grey One snorted impatiently and, shaking her head, she moved to leave. They could work it out for themselves.

Pushing through the foliage at the cave entrance, the woman warrior emerged into the open. Darkness had already fallen and the night sky was almost obscured by a thick layer of cloud. Fortunately, there were enough slivers of moonlight seeping through to light her way back to the northern slope.

Arriving at that gentle incline, Liath Luachra paused to make sure the area was clear, then used one of the javelins to break up the earth by a nearby ash tree. Once the upper sod had been scraped away, she used her hunting knife and a loose piece of deadwood to deepen it. By the time the boys came out to join her, she'd already managed to create a shallow depression and, working silently alongside her, they helped widen it until she was satisfied.

Liath Luachra winced as she emptied the contents of the backpacks into the resulting hollow, overlaying the meat with the upcast earth and an additional layer of stones to prevent wild animals from digging it back up. The waste of good meat annoyed her; particularly given the effort required to obtain it. Tossing it, unused, into the earth, also conveyed a lack of respect – albeit unintentional – for the animals they'd killed and that didn't sit easily with her.

Brushing the dirt from her knees, she considered her two young companions. Bran stood stiff and withdrawn but Rónán was shaking from fatigue. It was obvious he'd need a good night's sleep if he was going to make it through the exertion of the following day.

'Go back and rest,' she instructed him. 'Bran and I can stand guard tonight.' She glanced at the waiting youth. 'I'll take the first watch and wake you to relieve me later.'

Consumed in his own thoughts, Bran nodded absently, following in the footsteps of his younger companion as he headed back to the cave. The Grey One watched him go, her eyes trailing his thin frame until it faded into the gloom. She waited a few moments longer before she, too, started back towards An Poll Mór, settling into position at a vantage point outside the entrance that overlooked the land to the north-east. Below her, the forest was a dense black mass, offset by a sky that was only slightly less murky. Despite the occasional flicker of moonlight, it was almost impossible to see further than ten paces from where she was sitting.

To pass the time and prevent herself from dozing off, the woman warrior retrieved the javelins – six in total – from the cave and started to work on the metal heads, using a whetstone to grind them to a keen sharpness. From time to time, she'd pause in her labour and stare down at the darkness below, one ear cocked for anything that sounded out of the ordinary. Beyond the rattle of leaves and the whisper of the wind however, there was nothing to be heard.

When the javelin heads were honed to her satisfaction, the woman warrior put the missiles aside and mulled over the presence of the unknown *fian*. She'd been reluctant to discuss the subject with Bran, but the youth had had the right of it in terms of their hostile intent. Her own experience as *banfénnid* meant she had plenty of insight into the motivations of such groups. She knew, for example, that *fianna* rarely gathered for any reason beyond vengeance, a military opportunity, or a threat against the tribe. The key issue that intrigued her with regard to this *fian* therefore, was the identity of the tribe to which it was affiliated. Here, in the rugged isolation of the Great Wild, there were no tribal territories within four to five weeks of hard travel. The distance covered by this *fian*, and the intensity with which they continued to pursue the sole traveller, suggested some kind of feud between them. In such circumstances, it was best to stay out of their way.

Stifling a yawn, Liath Luachra stared out at the gloom and considered how best to proceed. In general, when danger reared its head out the Great Wild, her instinctive reaction was to go to ground, sink deep into the copious wrinkles of the Great Mother's mantle until the danger had passed. On this occasion however, that option wasn't open to her. Whatever destination the single traveller had in mind, he was unconsciously leading his pursuers towards Ráth Bládhma. It was certainly possible his pursuers would catch him before he reached the mountains of course, or that they'd all simply bypass the settlement without noticing it. That, however, was a risk she didn't intend to take. The settlement had to be warned of the approaching threat and readied – if necessary – to defend itself. That meant she not only had to catch up with the *fian* and their quarry, but skirt them both without being seen, to reach Ráth Bládhma before them.

All while ensuring the safety of the unblooded charges in her care.

Gloomily, she picked up a loose stick and toyed with it before abruptly tossing it aside. Over the years, Ráth Bládhma's isolated location had always been its greatest defence for it was difficult to launch an attack against a site when you didn't know where it was. Fourteen years earlier, one war-party had managed to find the settlement and although word of Ráth Bládhma's existence might subsequently have spread through the survivors, she was determined not to allow anyone else to determine its location.

She realised then that her left hand was unconsciously massaging the old wound in her left thigh, souvenir from a previous battle that had reduced her to a severe limp for almost half a year. The wound had long since healed but when she was weary or stressed, she'd noticed that it still caused her thigh to ache. A recurring 'ghost' pain, its reappearance at this moment seemed a subtle indication of her quiet distress. After almost eight years of extended peace, the prospect of fresh combat was genuinely distressing, particularly given the life of violence she'd tried so hard to leave behind.

Clicking her tongue in frustration, the Grey One turned her gaze back to the javelins, focussing her thoughts on the more practical and immediate problem of their limited inventory. Equipped for the hunt, they were less prepared for the possibility of combat than she'd have liked. True, the javelins would serve equally effectively against men as against wild animals, but the absence of a sword or a knife more suited to killing than skinning, was a concern. In her extensive experience of violence, ranged combat never remained so for long. If the *fian* learned of the Ráth Bládhma party's presence, there was little doubt in her mind that they'd attack instantly. In such circumstances, she might be able to use the javelins to keep them at bay for a time, but it was inevitable that, at some point, things would get close and personal.

Not something she wanted with two youngsters at her side.

Particularly given how well you did with Bearach.

Closing her eyes, the Grey One tried to push those memories away.

And prayed for a quick end to her watch.

***

Liath Luachra woke to an instinctive sense of danger, a disturbing conviction that something wasn't quite as it should be. Casting her blanket aside, she grasped the javelin beside her bedroll, rocking up onto her feet in one smooth, unbroken movement. Padding silently across the cave floor, the bare soles of her feet tingled at the touch of cold stone. Approaching the entrance, she dropped to a squat and took up position to one side. Listening carefully, she considered the external screen of bushes that cloaked the narrow gap, troubled by the grey light that filtered through that tangle of vegetation. After completing her watch, she'd instructed Bran to wake her at dawn. The quality of that light however, suggested it was far later than that.

The woman warrior nervously ground her molars together. Under normal circumstances, any change in the texture of light would have roused her. On this occasion however, huddled in the deepest part of the cave, the rays hadn't penetrated deep enough to do so.

Worried, she attempted to peer through the bushes but was frustrated by the confines of the tight entrance and the thickness of the foliage. Grasping one of the javelins, she exhaled deeply then squeezed carefully through, edging out from the external vegetation as quietly and unobtrusively as she could.

To her relief, the exterior of their refuge was unoccupied. The dim morning light revealed no threat along the slopes or immediately to either side, although the gloom drifting over the trees further downhill obscured everything else from sight.

There was no sign of Bran.

Although her initial instinct was to call out, the Grey One supressed that urge and maintained her silence. The youth must have had a reason for not waking her and, with a hostile force somewhere in the vicinity, she couldn't risk revealing her own position. Particularly with Rónán still sleeping inside.

As always, it was the Great Mother that revealed the truth of the situation. Examining the ground in the subdued dawn light, she found the scatter of tracks around the cavemouth and along the slopes were those made by the Ráth Bládhma party. The only prints that looked in any way out of the ordinary, were a set in Bran's distinctive tread, headed downhill in a north-easterly direction.

The Grey One suddenly felt sick to her stomach.

He's gone.

Rushing back inside the cave, two missing javelins and a waterskin confirmed her fears. Bran had left on his own accord, creeping out early without alerting her because he knew she would have stopped him.

To the aid of the lone traveller.

The Grey One cursed softly.

At the back of the cave, disturbed by the scuffle of movement, Rónán sat up from his bedroll. Rubbing the sleep from his eyes with the back of his hand, he looked around the cave.

'Where's Bran?' he asked.

***

By the time the full yellow glint of Father Sun's gaze cut through the cloud cover, the woman warrior was hurtling down the north-eastern slope. Moving at speed, she hit the flat ground, using her downward momentum to power her forward in a northerly direction. Burdened with the absolute minimum – two javelins strapped to her back, a knife scabbard secured to her left arm, and five leaf-wrapped slivers of smoked meat in the pouch of her tunic – she ran at a smooth but powerful lope, her eyes focussed on the terrain ahead with intense determination.

Earlier, when departing An Poll Mór, that determination had been sorely tested when she'd glanced back at Rónán, standing by the cave entrance to watch her depart. The sight of that forlorn figure had momentarily caused her resolve to falter but Bran's actions had left her with no option but to continue. Impulsively launching himself into the pursuit of a group far more lethal than any natural threat, the Ráth Bládhma youth had placed himself in considerable danger and she had to catch him before he was spotted. To achieve that goal, she had to travel fast, far faster than little Rónán could manage. As a result, there was no real choice but to leave the boy behind in the relative safety of An Poll Mór until she could return to retrieve him.

Assuming she did return.

A short time after leaving the base of the hill, the Grey One struck the area where they'd diverged from the intruders' path the previous evening. From that point on, it was a simple task to follow their trail, a trail which now included an additional, and more recent, set of tracks. These tracks, she noted, were widely spaced, the imprint of the toe and ball of the foot far deeper than those of the heel. Bran was moving at breakneck speed. Conscious of how swiftly the Grey One could traverse the wilderness when she had a mind to, he was clearly taking no chances she might catch him up.

Once her body had warmed up and her leg muscles loosened, the Grey One was able to increase her pace still further, eager to reduce the lead Bran had achieved. Both the Ráth Bládhma youth and the strangers had a substantial head-start on her but, fortunately, they'd left a conspicuous trail. The single traveller had made little effort to conceal his passage. Bran and the pursuing party had made none whatsoever and the clear line of heavy footprints, crushed grass, snapped twigs and branches that marked their passage meant she didn't have to waste time searching for tracks.

It was the woman warrior's intimate familiarity with the territory however that was her key advantage. Out in the Great Wild, the topography of the land tended to define one's path and steep terrain or impassable sections of forest in the trail ahead meant the intruders would be nudged inexorably down a restricted set of predictable paths. Her own knowledge of other negotiable routes meant that she could choose shorter, less obvious alternatives to reach the same destination.

As she ran, the Grey One mentally mapped out the terrain that lay ahead. A steep range of hills and impenetrable forest to the north would most likely force the *fian* in a more easterly direction but eventually, confronted by a long swathe of impassable marshland, they'd have no choice but to veer off to the south-east. Fortunately, another potential route existed that could get her there much faster: an isolated gully in the eastern ridge that she'd found and passed through several years earlier. If her luck held and she was able to locate the gully in time, she could significantly reduce the distance between herself and Bran, potentially intercepting him before he caught up with the *fian*.

Maintaining that rapid but steady pace, it didn't take the woman warrior long before she stumbled upon the area where the *fian* had spent the previous night: a glade of green fern and grass, bordered on one side by moss-covered boulders and a slow-flowing stream. The campsite was immediately identifiable due to the crushed patches of grass bearing the outlines of the men who'd been sleeping on them. Drawing to a halt, the Grey One stood, her chest heaving as she examined the ground, noting the absence of any charred wood or stones.

Fireless camp.

No wonder then that she'd seen nothing from An Poll Mór. The *fian* had stopped solely to rest and eat, spurning the luxury of a fire so that they could continue the chase at first light.

Whoever they're after, they want him badly.

14

Apart from the depressions in the grass, there was little enough to see, nevertheless Liath Luachra took the time to study each of the indentations in detail. Over the course of the morning, she'd developed a sense of the people she was following, the different sets of tracks divulging tell-tale physical characteristics that allowed her to differentiate between specific individuals. Those tell-tale traces were also reflected here in the depressions and aligned well with the mental image of the men she'd already formed.

One of the grassy hollows held several silver hairs, confirming her suspicions that one of the *fénnidi* was far older than the others. Over the course of her morning pursuit, his tracks had remained consistently to the rear of the group, and she suspected he was struggling to keep up.

Another of the hollows had a distinct print alongside it that she recognised as that from a *fénnid* who ran with an uneven gait and left tracks of variable depth. That individual had a definite limp, probably the result of an old injury.

The depression that drew her most intense scrutiny however was one that looked notably larger and broader than those around it. This she immediately associated with a set of tracks that had been far larger and heavier than the others. The size of the depression seemed to confirm that the person responsible for them was someone far bigger and, hence, more dangerous than his comrades.

The one to kill first if things don't go to plan.

She paused then, struck by the ferocity of her own reaction. For the past eight years, she'd lived in relative peace, eight years in which she'd been exposed to neither violence nor bloodshed beyond the occasional threat of wolves. Now, less than a day after encountering her first real genuine threat, she was already slipping back into the mindset of a *fénnid*, the mindset of a hardened killer.

Leaving the depressions, the Grey One followed a trail of flattened grass into the trees to a foul-smelling area that the camp's occupants had used for defecation. Amongst the turds and piss stains however, there was a more disturbing find: the carcass of a hare that was lying flat on its side, rigid in death-stiffness.

At first, the presence of the unskinned and uneaten animal confused the woman warrior. Looking closer, she saw how its hind legs had been cut at the joints, cleanly severed with a sharp-edged blade. The hare had clearly been alive at the time, for a short trail of blood revealed where it had dragged itself on its forelegs for several paces before bleeding out at the foot of an oak tree. Two sets of footprints off to the left of the tree meanwhile, indicated that a pair of men had stood watching the animal's pitiful, and probably agonized, last moments.

Tugging a green leaf from one of the nearby branches, Liath Luachra popped it between her teeth, chewing on the fibrous material as she regarded the story laid out on the ground before her. Her own experience as a *banfénnid* meant such displays of petty cruelty no longer shocked her but the dead hare was a brutal reminder of what she was dealing with. More than most, she was familiar with the timbre of *fénnid* such *fian* attracted, the violent and brutal men who offered similar levels of cruelty to anyone unlucky enough to cross their path.

The timbre of men that Bran was chasing.

Returning to the clearing, the Grey One picked up the trail with cold resolve, following it at a rapid trot into the early afternoon. Later, coming across an unusually shaped boulder that she recognised as marking the turn off to the gully trail, she cast one last look at Bran's footprints before breaking off in an easterly direction. Directly ahead, the long outline of the ridge loomed hard against the sky. Somewhere along the base of that rocky bulk lay the entrance to the gully, her best – and probably only – chance to get ahead of the Ráth Bládhma youth.

Provided she found it in time.

To her great frustration, locating the gully proved far harder than she'd anticipated. The last time she'd travelled that route – several years earlier – had been in late autumn, close to the beginning of winter. Her memory of the sparse winter terrain, therefore, was dramatically different from its current reality. The bleak foothills were now lush with vegetation, overgrown to the point where it was almost impossible to see further than a few paces in front of her.

It was far later in the afternoon therefore before she finally stumbled upon her goal – a V-shaped slash in the rock face with high cliffs looming on either side. Entering the narrow chasm, she stumbled across its treacherous, rock-strewn base as quickly as she dared, eventually emerging on the ridge's low, eastern slope.

Turning north, the woman warrior immediately started running again, breathing hard as she thundered through the forest, hoping

16

against hope that she'd made up enough distance to get between Bran and the *fian*. Those hopes were dashed however, when she intercepted their trail beyond the northern-most tip of the ridge, a patch of muddy ground where the tracks revealed that both had already passed that point.

Swallowing a curse, Liath Luachra put her head down and pushed onwards, driving herself to an even greater pace. All the prints had been relatively fresh, so neither Bran nor the *fian* could be too far ahead.

By this time, the woman warrior was feeling the strain of the extended pursuit. Sweat coated her body, and her breathing came in short, ragged gasps. Despite her weariness, she was heartened by evidence of a similar fatigue in the tracks of the *fian*, an increasing pattern of muddy patches revealing where individual runners had stumbled or tripped in their efforts to maintain the punishing pace. That revelation offered comfort but no real surprise. The *fian*, after all, had been engaged in this pursuit far longer than her.

Bran's tracks, conversely, retained a frustrating symmetry. He was young, at the peak of physical fitness and the tracks indicated he wasn't anywhere near his limit. Lacking her own lifetime's accumulation of injuries, the Grey One suspected the youth could probably continue running well into the night without flagging.

As the sky began to darken, Liath Luachra attempted to maintain her long-legged stride, but eye-watering fatigue eventually forced her to stop and rest at the treeline marking the edge of a narrow, rectangular-shaped clearing. Leaning against an oak tree, the woman warrior wheezed harshly until her head had cleared and her breathing returned to normal. Ever conscious that she was wasting time, she was about to step into the clearing when an object in the opposite treeline caught her eye and she froze in place.

Dropping to the ground like a stone, the woman warrior shuffled backwards into the shadows of the forest. Concealing herself behind the safety of a rotting tree tump, she studied the object that had drawn her eye: a wooden shaft, protruding from a tree trunk at the far side of the clearing.

A javelin.

Liath Luachra squinted, struggling to distinguish the object more clearly against the dappled background, but finally concluding that her initial instincts had been correct. It *was* a javelin. Embedded in the gnarled trunk of an old ash tree.

The woman warrior remained on her belly, the silence of the forest punctuated by her pounding heart, conscious of passing time but also fearful that the weapon might form part of some elaborate trap. Overhead, through gaps in the canopy, the visible patches of sky were growing murky. Darkness wasn't far off. When it fell, any possibility of distinguishing tracks or continuing the pursuit would be lost.

Unwilling to risk any further delay, the woman warrior worked her way south along the treeline for three hundred paces, then dashed across the open ground, hoping she was at a safe enough distance from where any ambush was most likely to be centred. Gaining the relative safety of the opposite treeline, she concealed herself in the undergrowth and waited.

A long time passed before she was satisfied that the area was clear and that it was safe to emerge from hiding. Rising to her feet, she hurried back up the length of the treeline to the oak where the javelin was embedded. Coming to a halt before it, the Grey One examined the haft, absently tapping its length with her fingers as she turned her eyes to a clear patch of ground in the forest just beyond the treeline. There, despite the fading light, the tracks could just be made out and she noted a discernible change to the pattern of the solitary traveller's tracks, the footprints much further apart, the depth of the imprints just a little bit deeper.

He's broken into a run.

Liath Luachra sucked on her lower lip as she moved forward to continue her examination of the tracks, working through the ramifications of what she was seeing. It looked as though the *fian* had finally caught up with their quarry near the clearing but, in their excitement, one of the *fénnidi* had somehow given their presence away. Spying his pursuers, the traveller had bolted with the *fian* in pursuit.

They were close.

She checked the ground again.

But not close enough.

Enraged at the single man's escape, one of the pursuers had made a javelin cast but missed, the missile striking the oak tree instead. In his haste, the caster hadn't paused to retrieve his weapon.

18

Looking back at the open ground of the clearing, the woman warrior could see how the different lines of footprints converged on that section of the treeline, like a wolf pack closing in on their prey. Turning to stare deeper into the trees, she peered into their shadowed depths, wondering if the *fian* had caught him, if Bran was safe and whether, like her, he'd be obliged to spend another night alone in the forest.

Knowing that there was nothing she could do but wait till morning, Liath Luachra swallowed her frustrations. With dawn, Father Sun's ascent would reveal the answers.

And she'd learn their fates soon enough.

Chapter Two

'I've always been of the mind,' declared Fiacail mac Codhna, 'that it shows the best of sense for a man to tackle opponents who are smaller and weaker than himself.'

Raising both hands, he grasped the protruding bars of his moustache with oiled fingers and delicately teased them back into shape, guiding his movements with the reflection from a nearby puddle. Satisfied with the result, he left his mirror image to fare for itself and, returning to the campfire, supplemented his opinion with a confirmative grunt.

'Of course,' he continued. 'From the perspective of the other person in such an altercation, it also makes the best of sense to turn one's arse and scarper when confronted by someone visibly bigger and stronger.'

Demne, the slim, fair-haired youth who was the recipient of this haughty advice, was also the sole other occupant of the cliff face hollow where they'd taken shelter from the rain. He regarded the Seiscenn Uairbhaoil man and dubiously pursed his lips. Even after six years of fosterage in Fiacail's care, the big man's general eccentricity and great love of teasing meant the youth was never entirely sure when he was being serious.

Undecided on how to respond, Demne settled on no response at all. He turned his focus to the little campfire instead, reaching down to grasp a nearby stick and using it to poke the embers while avoiding his companion's easy gaze. Over the course of the evening, their fuel stock had been exhausted, the fire had slowly dwindled and now any heat emanating from the embers was more illusionary than real. Beyond the overhanging lip of their stony refuge, sheets of torrential rain whipped by in sweeping gusts. Neither of the rocky shelter's occupants displayed any enthusiasm to venture outside to search for more wood.

Sitting back on the low boulder he was using as a seat, Demne considered the Seiscenn Uairbhaoil man across the remnants of the campfire. 'You make that claim, Fiacail, but your own actions belie your conviction. When I was a babe, you defended Ráth Bládhma against an overwhelming force of invaders. When I had seven years on me, you single-handedly rescued Bodhmhall and myself from the Brotherhood of the Bald, a group that numbered six men.'

'More like five and a half,' the big man corrected, but he acknowledged the point with a complicated flourish of his wrist.

'Years later again, when we fled Dún Baoiscne, you stood alone to oppose the Adversary's men, foiling their attempts to drag us off to Almhu.'

The big man made no response at first but from the way he rubbed his upper chest, Demne knew he was thinking back to that skirmish. The wounds he'd taken that day had been severe and, had it not been for his aunt's ministrations, he'd most likely have died. As it was, Fiacail would carry the scars to his grave.

Realising that he'd cornered himself with his own arguments, Fiacail responded with an exaggerated sigh. 'True enough,' he admitted. 'It's true I did all those things but, to be fair, I was in thrall to your aunt at that time. Romantic fool that I am, I'd have scaled a mountain slope on my hands and knees then slid bare-arsed down the other side if she'd asked.'

He paused then, as though wondering at the logic of that particular argument, before laughing out loud at his self-inflicted predicament.

'But all of that serves only to prove my point. Clearly, when burdened by the influence of passion, I can hardly be accused of showing the best of sense.'

Demne had frowned at the mention of his aunt, but he knew there was no malice to Fiacail's talk. The Seiscenn Uairbhaoil man was an individual of rare candour – some would call it bluntness – and tended to wield truth with the finesse of a blind drunkard swinging a cudgel. Fortunately, for the most part, the impact of any unintended contact tended to be softened by the warrior's gregarious natural charm.

'Has your affection for my aunt faded?' Demne asked, his curiosity genuine.

This time it was Fiacail's turn to reach down for a stick and poke at the fire. A small cloud of smoke rose from the embers, filling their little shelter with the scent of burnt pine.

'I wouldn't say my affection has faded,' he decided at last. 'Its lessening probably has more to do with the fact that your aunt isn't present. Fondness for female company and physical proximity generally tend to go hand in hand. In truth, that fatal combination has always been my greatest undoing. If Bodhmhall was here …' He raised his hands, palms outwards, allowing the gesture to speak for itself.

Demne pursed his lips in thought.

'Back at Seiscenn Uairbhaoil, I once overheard the women say that your biggest weakness was excessive *teaspaí*.' The youth paused and frowned. 'What is *teaspaí*, Fiacail?'

'An affliction,' the warrior answered without missing a beat. 'It's a common enough malady but it affects some individuals far more than others. Like a silent cold, it masks its symptoms. It starts off harmlessly with a warm flush, a rising sensation of wellbeing and …'

He paused momentarily, his eyes taking on a faraway look. Abruptly, he tossed his stick aside and fixed his gaze on Demne once more.

'And afterwards, it leaves you breathless, lagging and less enamoured with your surroundings and company.'

With that, the Seiscenn Uairbhaoil man grunted and kicked irritably at a nearby pebble, sending it bouncing across the flat rock floor of the hollow, to disappear out into the torrential rain.

'That particular affliction has debilitated me greatly over the years. Were it not for *teaspaí*, I would be a respected leader and a figure of great reputation. My exploits would lie jealously on the lips of all men and, when my name was raised, songs of my victories would ring about the campfires.'

He grew quiet then and loosed a half-hearted shrug from his left shoulder.

'Such is the yoke I bear.'

Demne stared, his eyes wide. 'My sympathy, Fiacail. I didn't know.'

'That's no matter, *a bhuachaill*. It's a curse I prefer to bear in silence. It's not one with which I'd care to burden others.'

'You're very brave, Fiacail.'

To his surprise, Fiacail's eyes glinted, and he gave a belly-deep chuckle. 'Yes, Demne. Yes, I suppose I am.'

Rising to his feet, the big man stood looking out at the darkening gloom beyond the cliff where the rain was finally showing signs of respite. 'Come,' he said. 'Let's make our beds. Tomorrow we'll rise early, strike for the coast and my sister's home at Trá Mór. Until then, we can settle for a sound night's sleep. And ... if I'm lucky, sweet dreams of your aunt.'

***

Demne also dreamed of his aunt that night but this came as no great surprise. Since the day his mother had dragged him from Ráth Bládhma, he'd dreamt of the settlement on a regular basis, reliving happier times of talk and *fidchell* with Bodhmhall or hunting the western hills with Liath Luachra.

Over the years in the estuarine territories of Seiscenn Uairbhaoil, his yearning for his childhood home had intensified those dreams, infusing the green pastures and steep ridges of Glenn Ceoch with an emotional poignancy that resonated within him long after he'd woken up. Although the residue of those night-time fancies sometimes extended to his waking hours, he was sufficiently pragmatic to recognise the rosy-hued influence of nostalgia for what it was. There'd been plenty of hard times at Ráth Bládhma. Plenty of violent times as well.

The following morning, the rustle of wind through the surrounding trees roused Demne from his rambling on the Bládhma mountains. Sitting up, he looked about, confused by the misalignment of his dark surroundings with the sun-drenched slopes of his dreams and it took a moment for the present to slip back into place. The previous night's downpour had mercifully ceased but beyond their rocky shelter the forest pulsated with an earthy moistness and a scent of wet trees and foliage laced the air.

Dawn, when it came, was little more than a grey smear in the eastern skyline but it provided enough light to reveal Fiacail's empty bedroll on the far side of the now-extinguished fire. Pushing his own blanket aside, the youth got to his feet and stretched, stiff muscles creaking like tree limbs in a harsh breeze. Using the palms of his hands to wipe grit from his eyes, he reached down to his backpack, rummaging through it until he'd located a leather scabbard. Withdrawing a short metal sword, he stood up straight and flexed the weapon experimentally in his right hand.

Stepping out onto the damp patch of grass beyond the overhang, he chose a flat section of ground, adjusted his position and commenced a series of sequential exercises: sharp downward cuts, carefully controlled lunges and short curving sweeps of the sword to test his control of the weapon's weight and the strength of his wrist. Finally, satisfied, he transferred the weapon to this left hand and repeated the exercise once more.

The pattern of movements Demne followed was one he'd developed himself, mostly adapted from the drills and motions he'd learned under Liath Luachra's tuition but also including a number of moves and thrusts picked up from sparring with Fiacail. The Seiscenn Uairbhaoil man and the woman warrior had very different fighting styles, very different approaches to combat, but both offered plenty to learn from. Liath Luachra, although tall for her gender, was more slender than most of her male opponents, hence her preference to come from the side or from the rear. Avoiding frontal confrontation where possible, when she was left with no choice she depended greatly on the advantage of her natural agility and suppleness in combat.

Fiacail, by contrast, used his greater bulk to maximum effect, combining the momentum of his fleet footedness with the unique fighting style of his combined axe pair.

By the time he'd completed the second pattern, the youth was sweating heavily but he forced himself to complete a third. Although breathing hard, he'd just commenced a fourth when the crackle of forest litter from the northern trees announced the Seiscenn Uairbhaoil man's return.

Fiacail entered the narrow patch of clearing just as the youth was completing the pattern's final movements. Observing the youth in mid-activity, the warrior stood quietly to one side and waited, watching with interest until the pattern was complete and Demne had resheathed the sword.

'Every morning,' he declared loudly. 'Every morning since leaving Seiscenn Uairbhaoil you've exercised with sword or sling. Sometimes with both.'

Uncertain as to whether he was being admonished, the youth's brow creased in irritation. 'I thought it'd please you to see me practice.'

'Of course, it pleases me. In truth, when we first departed Seiscenn Uairbhaoil, I'd believed it a fancy on your part. Your continued commitment to honing your fighting skills is admirable but, at the same time, I'd question its frequency and fervour. Is it truly necessary to practice every single morning? After all, a man should also have his time abed.'

'You know there are those who wish me harm, Fiacail. These past few years in Seiscenn Uairbhaoil have kept me safe but that good fortune can't last forever. One day, my opponents will find me and I'll need to be prepared, to have fighting skills that surpass any opponent who presents himself. For that, I must practice.'

Fiacail scratched thoughtfully at his stubbled chin.

'A commendable goal but a man could wear himself out with all that early-morning huff and puff.'

Demne sighed. 'You're hardly in a position to scold. I see you venture out to converse with Father Sun every morning before the break of dawn. Even on days when cloud chokes the sky.'

Fiacail shrugged. 'We all have our roles. Yours is to listen to my endless advice and repeated stories. Mine is to coax Father Sun above the horizon every morning.'

The youth shook his head in agitation, the warrior's eccentricities still managing to perplex him, even after all these years.

'And what happens when you're no longer here?' he asked, a tangible trace of irritation on his breath. 'Do you truly believe Father Sun will remain sulking below the horizon?'

'It's certainly likely,' Fiacail answered gravely. 'But we shouldn't let that happen.' He chewed on a knuckle with fierce attention, maintaining an uncharacteristic hush until his face split wide in a toothy grin.

'I suppose I should find a replacement, a suitable acolyte willing to take on that burden. Perhaps someone already well accustomed to regular early rising.'

With a wink at the confounded youth, he chuckled and moved to pack for their departure.

***

Towards noon of the following day, the two travellers broke free of the forest, emerging onto a high clifftop that offered them their first true sight of the sea. Dazed by the unexpected brightness of open sky, they stood struggling to absorb the sheer scale of the view and the incomprehensible body of water that stretched to the horizon.

Off to their left, a pair of seagulls floated effortlessly on the seaward draughts, their keening cries sharp but lonesome against the emptiness of the sky. Far below, waves smashed against the base of the cliffs, venting clouds of spray upward. Even on that high ledge, the salty tang to the air was bracing, a startling contrast to the musty scents and smells of the forest to which they'd become so accustomed.

Demne swallowed as he stared out at the sea. After endless days of the forest's tightly constricted views, he felt unprepared and exposed before such a sweeping outlook. Turning his head to the north, he saw the rugged coastline continue, disappearing around a promontory several hundred paces or so from where they were standing. To the south however, the land appeared to gradually flatten out, dropping behind a wall of forest to a distant beach and another headland far in the distance.

Fiacail broke the silence then, pointing out a flat shape off the coast to the north, a low island with a slight hillock at one end topped by steeply angled trees.

'I recognise that island.'

He pursed his lips in thought before turning his gaze to the south.

'Trá Mór won't be far now.'

Demne grunted, his conviction stunted by the fact that Fiacail had already uttered those exact words on at least three previous occasions over the course of the early afternoon.

Following the cliffs, the travellers continued south, veering in and out of the forest, never entirely losing sight of the sea. After a time, the ground dropped sharply, and they descended a series of gradual slopes until the terrain levelled out completely. Emerging from a grove of ash trees, the pair found themselves overlooking the stretch of beach they'd spotted from the escarpment, situated at a point approximately mid-way between the high cliffs they'd come from and the more southerly headland. A substantial mass, the latter's lower sections were coated with forest and bushes, a wave of green that rolled up from its base to halt abruptly approximately two thirds of the way to the summit.

Tugging thoughtfully at his moustache, Fiacail gazed down the stretch of grey-brown sand then turned his focus to a slight smudge near the base of the headland where a thin thread of smoke snaked up from the foreshore.

'That's my sister's holding,' he announced with sudden conviction. 'And that'll be her fire. She burns seaweed for ash to nourish the fields. She even trades some with Seiscenn Uairbhaoil from time to time.'

With a fresh surge of enthusiasm, the warrior started down to the beach, Demne following closely at his rear. Hitting that stretch of grainy sand, he led them south, his whole being exuding a heightened sense of excitement.

As he marched briskly alongside the Seiscenn Uairbhaoil man, Demne's eyes were drawn to the water. The sea seemed a lot calmer along this part of the coast, its earlier energy dissipated as it rolled sluggish, grey waves onto the foreshore. To his surprise, he felt an odd sense of exhilaration at pounding across the gritty sand, traversing a surface unsullied by marks or any other footprints apart from the ones they were leaving in their wake.

Drawing closer to the southern headland, the detail of its long mass became more distinct, particularly where the easternmost bulk extended doggedly out to the sea, stoically enduring the surge and froth of dark, green waves smashing against its sheer rock cliffs. Further inland, up from the strand, a narrow track wove its way uphill past a cluster of low, thatched buildings with a small patchwork of green fields to their rear. Several figures could just be made out working those fields, or carrying wicker backpacks up and down the track.

Down on the foreshore, the source of the smoke column soon became apparent: a blazing bonfire fed by a slim female figure with bright, copper hair. Clad in a *léine* and a long leather apron, the woman had two wicker baskets, and was alternatively feeding the fire with pieces of wood from one and large screeds of seaweed from the other.

Prompted by some unconscious instinct, the woman looked up and glanced in the travellers' direction, stiffening perceptibly when she spotted them. Fortunately, she seemed to recognise them, or Fiacail at least, for her posture loosened and, wiping her hands on her *léine,* she advanced excitedly towards them.

'I see you, my sister Íte,' roared Fiacail.

'I see you, ugly brother,' the woman shouted back.

Roaring with laughter, they rushed forward to embrace each other fiercely, holding onto one another closely for a very long time. Finally, releasing his sister, Fiacail took a step back as though to examine her more carefully. 'Look at you,' he declared. 'The years slide from you like rain on angled stone. You're still the steadfast blossom of the East Coast.'

The red-haired woman snorted in amusement at such blatant flattery. 'You've changed,' she countered.

'Of course, I have. I'm older. Perhaps I look wiser?'

Íte's lips twisted dubiously as she considered the possibility. 'You look leaner. Are you wiser too?'

'Probably not,' he admitted.

With a surprisingly deep chuckle, Íte turned her gaze to Demne who'd hung back several paces, watching the reunion in silence. 'And you, Demne. You've changed far more than my worthless brother. Look at you! You're a grown man. *Fáilte romhat ar ais go Trá Mór.* Welcome back to Trá Mór.

'*'maith agat,* a Íte.'

Demne came forward and stiffly returned her warm embrace. Many years had passed and although he had fond memories of the time he'd spent at Trá Mór when he was younger, he was also acutely conscious of the debt he owed her. When Bodhmhall, Liath Luachra and Fiacail had escorted him to *Clann Baoiscne* territory many years earlier, Fiacail had sought – and obtained – her consent to pass him off as one of her children. The deception, although minor, had been critical to explaining his sudden appearance at Seiscenn Uairbhaoil. Posing as Fiacail's fostered nephew had not only ensured his immediate acceptance within the community but diverted a whole range of awkward and unwanted questions. With Íte supporting that deception by confirming his false identity to anyone who passed through Trá Mór and asked, any remaining suspicions were effectively assuaged.

Approaching the youth. the red-haired woman hugged him then stood back and reached up to ruffle his hair. Ignoring his discomfort at the unbridled display of affection, she turned her attention to two children who'd just arrived down from the cluster of buildings and who now stood regarding the visitors with open curiosity. The bright, copper-coloured hair and freckled features confirmed them as Íte's offspring, but Demne had already recognised them from his last visit to Trá Mór. The girl, Catan, was the eldest of the two and had fifteen years on her. She was regarding him with quiet suspicion, coolly running one hand through her unruly curls. Her brother Gormán meanwhile, three years her junior, was gazing at the newcomer with a broad smile and an expression that was far less guarded.

'Catan. Gormán. This is Demne, your … cousin.' Íte gestured towards the *Clann Baoiscne* youth. 'You may not recall but he stayed here with us some years ago. Back when you were all much younger.'

Gormán looked at Demne blankly, his mother's prompting clearly having little impact on his recall. The girl however, pursed her lips in thought.

'I remember him. He came with Fiacail and the two tall women.' She paused and considered the youth with fresh interest. 'He cried a lot when they left.'

Demne's jaw tightened at that. He *had* cried, he recalled with a twinge of embarrassment. He'd bawled like an infant as he'd watched his two guardians walking stiffly away, intuitively comprehending in that single, brutal instant, that they weren't coming back.

He turned his head and glanced back up the northern stretch of sand and surf, momentarily seeing their dark silhouettes against the paleness of the horizon as they walked away from Trá Mór, refusing to acknowledge his plaintive cries.

The youth swallowed, struggling to contain an unexpected welling of emotion. During his extended time in Trá Mór, he'd suffered from terrible loneliness. Fortunately, that sensation had faded over time as a result of Fiacail and Íte's kindness, but he knew that memory of abandonment had marked him. It had been the first time in his short life that he'd felt truly alone.

And you forgot. Or, rather, intentionally dismissed it from your memory.

'Yes. Er … Well, Demne was far younger then.' The red-haired woman diplomatically moved the conversation forwards. 'Now that he's returned to us, we have the privilege of offering him our best hospitality, of welcoming him back to our hearth.'

She wiped her hands down the front of her apron to remove the last greasy residue of seaweed from her hands.

'Tonight, we'll treat our guests to a feast. I'll have the main course prepared but a hare or two would make a fine addition. Catan and Gormán, that responsibility rests with you. Perhaps Demne can accompany you while your uncle and I catch up on old times. Would that please you, Demne?'

It was an effort for the *Clann Baoiscne* youth to conceal his irritation at being dispatched with the other children but he nodded politely.

'Of course, Íte.'

'*Tá go maith.*' Good. Nodding in satisfaction, she turned back to Catan, apparently viewed as the more responsible of her two children. 'Make sure to check the snares on the northern slopes but make no delay. There'll be plenty of other tasks to complete before the night is out. *Brostaígí oraibh, anois.* Hurry now. Be back before dusk.'

With one sharp look to each child to emphasis her expectations, she turned and took Fiacail's arm, then escorted him away towards the path leading up to the small cluster of buildings. Demne watched the two adults go, leaving him alone with his two … cousins. Transferring his attention to the siblings, he realised with a start that both were staring at him.

An uncomfortable silence spooled out into the space between them. Finally, complying with her mother's instruction, Catan dutifully approached, although Demne sensed no real enthusiasm to her actions. 'Welcome, cousin,' she said, somewhat grudgingly. 'Although you're not really our cousin, are you?'

'No.'

With a shrug Catan deflected the response. The confirmation made little difference.

'Are you Fiacail's son?' asked Gormán.

Demne's forehead creased as he turned his gaze to the younger sibling, unsure as to whether he was being facetious or not. The boy's eyes however, revealed no obvious evidence of guile.

'No,' he answered sharply, putting any rumour of that possibility firmly to rest.

'Oh.' Gormán's expression momentarily slipped, then his face brightened and he beamed at his visitor with even greater fervour. 'Do you want to see the Shit Cliffs?'

Taken aback by the abrupt, and bizarre, change in topic, Demne stared at him.

'He means the *Aillte na Amhasáin* – the Gannet Cliffs,' Catan clarified. 'The headland has a colony of *amhasáin* – gannets – that's been there since the time of the Ancient Ones. So many generations of birds have lived there, the rocks are white, thick with layers of hardened bird shit.'

Demne glanced back up to where Fiacail and Íte had started up the path towards the wooden buildings and kicked resentfully at the sand. 'Why not. There's no other draw on my time'.

Catan's eyes widened slightly at the bitter edge to his voice. His rancour had clearly overshot Gormán's notice however, for the boy was already scampering towards a different path visible through the trees at the base of the ridge. 'Come on!' he shouted over his shoulder. 'It's this way!'

Demne threw a bewildered glance at his sister, but Catan simply shook her head, offering up a weary sigh before she started towards the path as well.

Exhaling heavily, Demne resignedly proceeded in their wake.

Following the younger boy's lead, they took a circuitous route that meandered uphill through the headland's lower forest to emerge abruptly at a point two or three hundred paces below the summit. From there, the slope was almost entirely barren rock, bare and exposed apart from the occasional bush or scrap of grass that had somehow managed to grasp a tenuous purchase.

Completing a steep and strenuous climb, they crested the summit to find themselves on a broad plateau coated in fern and rough grass and spotted with sporadic stands of stunted trees. A well-trodden path stretched east towards the tip of the headland.

After progressing along this path for several hundred paces or so, Demne realised the headland was far broader than he'd imagined and didn't project directly out into the sea but curled in a rugged, splintered arc towards the south. As the bulk of the arcing promontory slid into view, Demne spotted the cliffs: jagged vertical slabs of black rock, stained with vast patches of white bird shit, just as Catan had described. Partially obscuring the cliff face was a flapping, shrieking cloud of movement, the source of that avian guano: sleek, white gannets, short, comical puffins, forked-tailed terns and blue-grey fulmars. Even at that distance, the volume of their chaotic chatter was loud and grating, soundly oddly similar to the harsh sound of an angry crowd.

As they continued closer to the curved tip of the headland, Demne found himself growing increasingly nervous, unnerved as much by the birds' raucous clamour as by the precipitous drop now drawing inexorably closer on either side of the narrowing path. After the marshy flats of Seiscenn Uairbhaoil, such dizzying heights were unfamiliar and unnerving. Exposed on this open headland, the horizon spread wildly to every side and the sky swarmed with gannets, sweeping, screeching, and whooshing about, alighting precariously on sheer cliff ledges or plunging into the sea.

Far below, waves pounded against the base of the cliffs, their hollow boom a sullen, low-pitched rumble very much at odds with the relentless, high-pitched cries of the birds.

And this is a calm day!

In front of them, Gormán came to an abrupt halt and, looking back at Demne, flung his hand out in a grandiose manner in the direction of the white cliffs.

'Aillte na Amhasián!' he declared proudly.

Strolling nonchalantly forward, Catan made a point of ignoring her younger brother as she paused to consider the distant cliffs. Then, with a sniff of disdain, she abruptly veered off towards a section of one of the nearer precipices, now little more than five paces to their right. Here she paused, gesturing for Demne to approach.

'This is where we climb down to gather eggs and *gúga*,' she informed him. 'It's too late in the season now but during the spring months ...' She closed her eyes, licking her lips in apparent rapture at the memory of the taste. 'Mmmmm.'

Demne glanced nervously at the cliff edge, the perilous fall dropping sharply out of sight, the undulating waves stretching off into the distance. It was a struggle to imagine anyone voluntarily walking along the edge of such a precipice, not to mind clambering down the sheer cliff face to gather eggs.

Easing carefully forwards the edge, the youth was just about to peer over when a gannet hurtled up from below, whipping past less than an arm's length from his face and screeching raucously as it swept him by. Stumbling back in alarm, Demne tripped over a stone and landed heavily on his arse.

Furious and embarrassed, he clambered hurriedly back onto his feet, attempting to disguise his disorientation with an exaggerated grunt of disgust. The other children saw through it straight away.

'You don't like heights,' accused Catan.

'I don't like falling off them!' Demne countered hotly.

'Your knees are trembling.'

Demne snorted but in truth, his knees did feel watery. He resisted the temptation to look down, knowing they'd interpret it as yet another sign of weakness.

'Did you shit yourself?' asked Gormán. 'There are dock leaves over here you can use to clean up.'

'I did *not* shit myself,' answered Demne through gritted teeth.

'If this drop doesn't make you shit yourself,' Gormán continued, apparently oblivious to anything Demne said, 'wait till you see Inne Danu – Danu's Gut. That'll truly brown your arse.'

Apparently considering his point satisfactorily made, Gormán sniffed and regarded Demne innocently, completely insensible to the hostility of the gaze being offered in return.

Realising that any attempt to visually browbeat the boy into submission was a waste of time, Demne grunted in annoyance. Turning his eyes to Catan, he was surprised to discover that she too was glowering at her younger brother.

'Mama says we're to avoid Inne Danu. It's dangerous there and the Great Mother's hunger is never sated.'

Gormán snorted, screwing his face up in that scornful manner only a younger sibling could pull off. 'I go there all the time.'

Catan scowled in response, twisting her freckled nose up in the air of superior disdain only an older sibling could pull off.

'Very well, then. We'll see if you'll truly embrace the lips of the Great Mother's open yaws.' With a haughty *hruumph*, she turned on her heel and started purposefully back along the path in the direction they'd just come from.

Gormán huffed, doing his best to convey the impression he was undaunted by his sister's challenge. Nevertheless, as it became clear his sister wasn't going to come back, he frowned and nervously hurried after her.

Demne, forgotten, stared after the two departing children. With a shake of his head, he too started forward and, once again, proceeded in their wake.

Chapter Three

Dawn spilled over the valley of Glenn Ceoch with a pallid light that softened the contours of its rugged ridges. Standing on Ráth Bládhma's solid eastern ramparts, Bodhmhall ua Baoiscne considered that view with eyes half-smudged from sleep.

And a smouldering sense of unease.

The *bandraoi* had suffered a rude awakening, roused by dreams of contorted shapes that twisted in the darkness around her. Coated in sweat, she'd woken with a start, reaching fearfully for Liath Luachra only to find a hollow space on the sleeping platform beside her. Too shaken to return to sleep, she'd dragged herself from the warmth of her furs to stand on the reed-strewn roundhouse floor. Retrieving a green *léine*, she'd dressed quickly in the dull gleam from the embers of the fire, cinching the garment about her waist with a wide leather belt.

Wiping a yawn to one side of her mouth, she'd pushed the heavy door of the roundhouse aside and stepped through, emerging into the *lis* – that circular open space at the settlement's centre. Bathed in the grey, pre-dawn gloom, the *lis* was quiet and still, the only sign of movement above the barricaded gateway where Ferchar – the red-haired sentinel – kept watch. Hearing the creak of wood as she mounted the ladder to the ramparts, he spun tersely about, spear levelled at waist height. Recognising her, he immediately relaxed, nodded in acknowledgement and returned to his scrutiny of the pasture beyond the *ráth*. Dawn, that period when visibility was most blurred, was generally considered the most effective time for a hostile attack. Ironically, for that same reason, it was also the period when guards tended to be at their most alert.

From the height of the palisades, Bodhmhall ran her eyes down the length of Glenn Ceoch, her view shifting east to west through the early morning haze. Contemplating that terrain, she found comfort in the familiar contours: the high, forested ridges to north and south, the broad stretch of pasture dotted with grazing cattle. It had been more than sixteen years since she'd first led her little group of settlers to this valley and despite great sacrifices, years of toil and bloodshed, there was much to be proud of. Surviving the first harsh winters, they'd also survived periods of extreme hunger, of sickness and, even one terrifying assault from unknown – up to that point – enemies.

Over the subsequent years of peace, the settlement had thrived, succeeding far beyond Bodhmhall's original expectations.

Absorbing survivors from the settlements of Ráth Dearg and Coill Mór, Ráth Bládhma's growing numbers had been bolstered further by several births. The *ráth's* population now stood at seventeen men, women and children, a number that stretched the tiny settlement's ability to house them. In response to the over-crowding, Aodhán and his woman Morag had already moved out to create a new home at the eastern end of the valley. There, enclosed by high cliffs and shielded from the west by the presence of the *ráth*, they'd built a small dwelling of wood and sod where they lived with their two children. More recently, Ferchar and Cumann – now pregnant – had expressed interest in doing the same.

The community's pig and dairy herds had also thrived in the years following the repulsion of the Adversary's forces and Ráth Bládhma was now in the enviable position of producing dairy and meat in excess of its needs. Combined with the produce from Bodhmhall's expanded *lubgort* – vegetable garden – its inhabitants ate well, not only in terms of quantity but in terms of choice and diversity as well.

Driven by a need to venture beyond the fortifications, Bodhmhall had Ferchar unlatch the gateway once the sky had brightened. Passing through the stone passage, she emerged to clear the encircling ditch via a narrow stone causeway. As she strode out onto the ankle-high pasture, beads of dew glistened coldly and chilled her bare feet.

Sensing some element of *An Tíolacadh* influencing her mood, the *bandraoi* allowed her intuition to guide her, surprised to find it leading her to the southern treeline where the community's burial ground was located. Set in a small clearing just inside the trees, this was the site where some of Ráth Bládhma's previous inhabitants had been laid to rest. The little burial ground also contained several people from the Ráth Dearg and Coill Mór settlements, men and women who'd died repelling a common enemy during the 'Great Invasion'.

Glancing briefly at the line of grass-covered graves, Bodhmhall acquiescently yielded to the instinctive urge that drove her past the cemetery, then further east along the treeline to where a low mound was located. Guided by a definite sense of 'pertinence', she nimbly scrambled up the side of the mound to attain its low summit, relieved to find it free of the dew coating the rest of the valley's open pasture.

Lowering herself onto the grass, she made herself comfortable and waited.

An appealing aura of calm surrounded the isolated mound and the *bandraoi* felt a muted sense of peace overtake her. Watching Father Sun drag his glowing bulk above the eastern cliffs, she felt the soft caress of a breeze against her face while a subtle, oddly sonorous, drone emanated from the crickets in the grass around her. Twisting around, she glanced back towards the forest at her rear. Shafts of silver light from the rising sun were now slanting through the upper foliage, illuminating the forest's complex indigo and greens with an unusually detailed clarity.

Although the sensitised state of her nerves was a clear indication, it was that heightened sense of perception that confirmed *An tíolacadh's* imminent approach. Increasingly anxious now that she knew what was coming, the *bandraoi* shuffled backwards into the shadow thrown down by the trees so that she couldn't be observed from the settlement. Stretching flat on the grass, she closed her eyes, and readied herself

The *Gift* surged in like a sudden squall, striking her with a force that would have knocked her off her feet if she'd been standing. Panic-stricken, she barely had time to pull her thoughts together before the visions exploded in her head.

The images came in rapid sequence, a rush of kaleidoscopic scenes from a multitude of different angles, that were not only too fast to absorb but impossible to grasp. Swooping in like a flock of screeching seagulls, each image filled a space in her head, increasing in frequency and force until her mind could take no more. Overwhelmed, the *bandraoi* was powerless to stop them and feared her mind would snap.

In the end, it was the reaction of her body that saved her. Gagging and wheezing, it responded to the heightened stress by vomiting up the previous night's meal. Fortunately, that simple physical reaction was enough to break the flow and, with the connection severed, the stream of impressions blinked out and disappeared. As suddenly as they'd appeared, the images were gone.

Bodhmhall rolled onto her side, her head still reeling, mentally bloated and half-blind from the residue of chaotic images. Frothy bile bubbled about her lips. Numb and barely conscious, she clutched fistfuls of grass to anchor herself to the earth, terrified at the possibility of being whisked back into that mental maelstrom.

It took a little while but, finally, her head cleared and her awareness began to return. When her ragged breathing steadied, the *bandraoi* sat up, numbly wiping the tendrils of spit from her mouth as she took note of her pounding heart, her sweat-drenched clothing, and the spray of vomit down the front of her *léine*. Stunned and shaken, she attempted to stand but her legs were trembling and refused to support her.

Conceding defeat, Bodhmhall remained where she was and focussed instead on trying to work out what had happened. As usual she had no idea how long the experience had lasted. Such violent expressions of *An tíolacadh* were infrequent and this one had struck with a severity she hadn't experienced since her first childhood exposure to the rigours of the *imbas forosnai* ritual, in the dark caves of the *draoi*, Dub Tíre.

Dazed and fearful, she used her sleeve to wipe the sweat from her forehead. The ferocity of the visions had shaken her and although she knew they had to be important, she struggled to work out how she might even start deciphering them. On previous occasions when *An tíolacadh* was triggered, she'd always had some degree of control and, hence, some understanding of what she was seeing. This time however, the *Gift* had surged through her like a swollen river that had burst its banks. As a result, her recall was choked by the sheer volume of mental debris she'd been forced to adsorb, most of it passing so quickly she had no clear memory of it.

Naturally, the image she retained most clearly was the first she'd absorbed: a strange depiction of her two dead brothers – Cumhal and Crimall – poised to enter the treeline of a dark section of forest. Just as they were about to step forward into the trees, Crimall had paused to look over his shoulder and stare at her. The impact of her brother's gaze had sent a frisson down her spine but, even now, despite the complex emotions the sight triggered, she had no idea what it meant.

Another firm recollection was the image of a fair-haired youth striding purposefully through the woods, a pair of lethal-looking javelins slung over his shoulder. The familiar features left little doubt as to his identity.

Demne!

Her nephew was alive! And grown. Almost a man. Closing her eyes, Bodhmhall felt her heart beat faster once more.

The third image she could recall was far less endearing: the fearsome visage of a monster. Vaguely human in aspect, the facial features had appeared unnaturally blotched and waxy, and she wasn't sure whether this was how the subject looked in reality, or the result of some empathetic distortion caused by the *Gift*.

Thin slits had occupied the space where the eyes should have been. There'd been no nose to speak of, just a section of flat tissue with two small holes. Drawing that image up fresh in her mind, the *bandraoi* also drew up an unmistakeable sensation of rage entangled within it. Whatever this thing, this individual, was, it bore an unadulterated hatred towards her or those she held dear.

The final vision. once she'd realised what she was seeing, was the one that caused the *bandraoi* the most distress and it took all of her self-control not to jettison it from her mind. Moving the image about in her head, she struggled to grasp its contours and draw more sense from it but, despite her efforts, the image just blurred and fell apart under her probing.

Bodhmhall tensed, her fingers closed into fists. Her *Gift* had shown her an image of a figure sprawled face down on the floor of some shadowed, stone passage, a dark pool of blood spreading out across the grey flags beneath it. From the short-cropped hair and the red leather battle-harness, there'd been no mistaking who it was.

Liath Luachra.

With a sinking sensation, Bodhmhall realised that she'd seen this same vision once before, years earlier while travelling the route to Dún Baoiscne with Fiacail mac Codhna. On that occasion, *An tíolacadh* had been triggered as a result of imbibing *uisce beatha* and her recollection was hazy, not only because of the alcohol, but because of the other confusing desires her *Gift* had stirred up.

Fiacail.

She groaned. By attempting to suppress the memory of what had happened that night, she'd also, involuntarily, suppressed her memory of the image. Now, dislodged by the latest expression of her *Gift*, it bobbed like unwanted flotsam in the back of her mind.

But Liath Luachra …

It was difficult to fight the hollow despair that threatened to devour her. Breathing deeply, she finally managed to push it to a place where she could control it, reassuring herself with the knowledge that the image could mean anything. Or nothing. Everything she'd seen could presage the present or the future, but such occurrences could just as well reflect the past and have no further relevance.

That's it. That's all there is.

Unclenching her stomach muscles, the *bandraoi* exhaled heavily, resisting the nervous urge to scratch at her palms.

That *was* it. Four disparate scenes, no obvious pattern, no obvious connection between them.

Driven by a new sense of urgency, the *bandraoi* pushed herself to her feet once again and this time she succeeded in remaining upright. She spat a curse under her breath as she stumbled unsteadily down the side of the mound. As always with *An tíolacadh,* everything remained open to interpretation. People called it a *Gift* but over the years, she'd increasingly recognised it for the burden and the curse it truly was.

With tentative steps, she tottered back in the direction of the *ráth* and, in the time it took her to cross the grassy pasture and follow the curve of the ditch around to the gateway, she succeeded in regaining her composure. Crossing the causeway, she glanced up at the stone rampart above the gateway, surprised to see that Ferchar had been relieved by the warrior woman, Gnathad. A slim woman with more than thirty years on her, she regarded Bodhmhall without acknowledgement, although a muted facial reaction revealed her surprise at the *bandraoi's* dishevelled appearance.

Averting her eyes, Bodhmhall entered the stone passage, swiftly passing through to emerge into the *lis.* In the time she'd been absent, the settlement had roused and now that open space was busy with the habitual morning bustle of a working community. The central fire pit was ablaze. Lí-Bán and Cumann were serving a breakfast of porridge from the metal cauldron dangling above the flames. Several children were sitting together, happily eating the result of the women's labour. In the lean-to off to the left of the fire, a place where firewood was stored to dry, the eccentric warrior Tóla was gleefully chopping a number of logs into smaller pieces to feed the blaze.

Fortunately, the two people Bodhmhall was hoping to find – Aodhán and Morag – were also present. Talking quietly together on a rough wooden bench by the fire, they were watching as their daughter ate with the other children, a community ritual they still participated in, despite having moved out of the *ráth.*

The *bandraoi* marched swiftly towards them and, catching the movement, both looked up, the conversation dying on their lips when they saw her haggard expression.

'Aodhán. Morag. I'd have words with you both.'

'Is it about *An tiolacadh*?' asked Aodhán.

Surprised, Morag glanced sideways at her man, but Bodhmhall knew he'd recognised the haggard and haunted expression that always remained on her face after a manifestation of her *Gift*. That, or the trail of vomit down the front of her *léine*.

She confirmed his question with a sharp dip of her head.

The young couple glanced at one another, their own expressions grave. Bodhmhall could understand their reticence. Revelations shared through her *Gift* rarely signalled events of a fortuitous nature.

Returning towards the roundhouse she shared with Liath Luachra, she heard Aodhán and Morag rise to follow. Entering the wicker-walled building, Bodhmhall moved to a high bench that was lined with wildflowers and prepared herself a herbal drink with hot water retrieved from a clay jug in the embers of the fire. Her stomach was still queasy from the violent retching and needed something to settle it and she found it helpful having something to occupy her trembling hands. The ritual of preparing the drink also allowed her a few moments grace to assemble her thoughts and prepare herself while the young couple entered and settled onto two of the three stools beside the stone-kerbed fire pit.

Pouring the liquid into a wooden goblet, she turned, pulled up a third stool and shifted it around the fire so that she could sit facing them both. Taking a deep breath, she came straight to the point.

'Fresh danger descends upon us.'

Both of them stared at her. 'From where?' asked Aodhán. 'From who?'

'I'm not certain. As usual *An tiolacadh* was unclear although the threat seems linked to my nephew.'

'Demne?' Morag looked at her in surprise. 'I'd understood Demne was in hiding, that you'd placed him in some secret refuge far from here, for his safekeeping.'

Bodhmhall nodded, appreciating the young woman's bewilderment. The last time Morag had seen the boy would have been more than seven years earlier, the day they'd departed the settlement for Dún Baoiscne with his mother Muirne and an escort of *Lamraighe* warriors.

'He was. And I did. Nevertheless, *An tiolacadh* seems to be telling me that he's returning to Glenn Ceoch.'

Bodhmhall frowned. The latter sentence had been complete supposition on her part but even as she'd spoken the words, she realised that she believed them.

Lifting the goblet, she took a sip from her brew. Made in haste, the herbs hadn't had sufficient time to steep and the result was unappealingly bitter. An appropriate taste then to match the traumatic memories of that failed expedition and her subsequent decision to place her nephew in fosterage. She'd raised Demne from the day he was born and had loved the child as her own. Exiling him, albeit for all the right reasons, had cut her far deeper than she could have imagined.

She took the goblet in both hands, conscious that her hands were trembling and fearing she'd drop it. It was something of a surprise to find the pure ache of that decision still lingering so close beneath the surface: just as keen, just as sharp.

'Is he safe?' asked Aodhán.

'For now,' said Bodhmhall but she didn't elaborate further. Only four people had known of Demne's location: herself, Liath Luachra, Fiacail and his sister Íte. It had been something of a risk placing him at Seiscenn Uairbhaoil, territory precariously close to her father's stronghold of Dún Baoiscne. Nevertheless, with The Adversary's identity and murderous intentions revealed, it was obvious the boy was no longer safe at Ráth Bládhma. They'd had few viable options available and although placing the boy in Fiacail's care had been a gamble, it had been a calculated one and one she'd hoped her enemies wouldn't expect. Recalling the easiness in her nephew's face from the vision, she realised she'd observed nothing to suggest they'd seen through that deception.

Aodhán shifted uneasily on his stool, unsure what to make of this new development.

'Did you see anything else?'

'I saw the face of an enemy.'

'Tadg mac Nuadat?'

Bodhmhall shook her head. 'No. It was …' She hesitated. 'Someone I didn't recognise. A figure of uniquely gruesome aspect.

Not the kind of face I'd forget too easily.' She pursed her lips briefly. 'Mind you, that doesn't mean Tadg has no hand in another action against us. We know well enough of his liking for others to do his bloodwork.'

She shivered briefly as she recalled the melted features from her vision, the vitriol and rage oozing from within them. 'Whoever this particular enemy is, his inner flame blazes with malice for the people of Ráth Bládhma.'

'Was there nothing else?' Aodhán persisted. 'No indication of the numbers he leads or the tribe to whom he affiliates? It would help to counter the threat if we had a better understanding of our opponents.'

Bodhmhall's grip tightened on her goblet. All the images in her visions would certainly have some common connection but it was difficult to decipher what those might be. The image of her brothers made little sense and she couldn't explain its relevance. As for the image of Liath Luachra …

'Nothing else I can share with you for now. If the Great Mother wills it, further knowing will come my way but the *Gift's* not something I can influence.'

The *bandraoi* stood up abruptly, reached over to place the goblet on a nearby herb shelf and grabbed a wet rag which she used to scrape some of the dried vomit from her *léine*.

'Liath Luachra and the boys were due back from the hunt days ago. While we wait on their return, I suggest we look to our defences. We can start by herding the cattle in closer, bringing the best breeders inside at night. The others can be driven to the eastern pens.'

Aodhán nodded. 'Easily done. I'll have the main herd driven east this morning but it'll take a day or two to round up the stragglers. The internal stockade could also use some repair to hold the breeding cattle but I'll set to it myself once I've replaced the javelin rack atop the gateway. We've been keeping that inside the huts to protect the metal heads from the weather but they'll be little use there if we're attacked.'

'*Go maith.*' Good. Bodhmhall nodded her satisfaction. Already overwhelmed by the number of tasks piling up as a result of this new threat, it was a relief to have such competent people to help, people she could count on, particularly as she had little head for battle matters.

Because you could always leave that to Liath Luachra.

She glanced sideways towards the wooden stand that held Liath Luachra's battered leather battle harness then roughly shook that thought away.

'We should also avoid any movement beyond the valley. Tell the others not to venture beyond the valley's western treeline. There's no point in creating trails that would draw the enemy in on us. Meanwhile, lets also cease all fires in the *lis* firepit. It creates too much smoke and the column it produces can be seen from afar. This morning's breakfast will be the last time we use it for a while. From now on, any food should be prepared in the smaller roundhouse pits where the roofs can diffuse the smoke. It'll be an inconvenience of course, but a small and necessary one.'

She paused then to regard them both with new intensity.

'The pattern I'm sensing behind this new threat feel similar to the events leading up to the raid by Tadg mac Nuadat's forces. There'll be a cramping and crowding but you may wish to consider returning within the *ráth* for a time. If the invaders reach Glenn Ceoch we won't be able to protect you outside the embankment. Lí Bán has some space to share. I'm sure she'd be happy to do so if you ask. If not, this dwelling is also open to you.'

Aodhán turned his gaze to Morag. The dark-haired woman's own expression was grave as she considered the *bandraoi*. 'Thank you, Bodhmhall. I'll speak to Lí Bán and start preparations this afternoon.'

Aodhán nodded his agreement, visibly pleased at his woman's decision. Sitting back on his stool, he flexed his long fingers as he chewed his lip in thought.

'I'll set a scout at the outskirts to the valley's entrance. There are plenty of hidey holes among the trees that offer a view over the western approach. During the light of day, at least. It won't give us much time to prepare but even a little forewarning is better than none.'

'Who will you place there?'

'Tóla. To be relieved by Gnathad.'

Noting the disapproval on Bodhmhall's face, the young man stubbornly pushed his case. 'Tóla may have his strange ways but he's no fool when it comes to forest fighting. I trust his judgement and he's more than proven his abilities. As for Gnathad, it's true she's unblooded but she can stand watch as well as anyone. Having her available to replace Tóla means I can keep Cónán and Ferchar close to the settlement. Those two are our strongest fighters and it'd be my preference to have them at hand to defend the *ráth* should it come to that. If Liath Luachra prefers an alternative use of our forces on her return, then it's certainly her right to do so.'

Bodhmhall breathed deeply. In the Grey One's absence, Aodhán held responsibility for the settlement's defence and for the safety of its people. By questioning his decisions, she realised, she was effectively undermining his authority.

'Very well,' she conceded. 'That's your judgement to make. For now, we'll let the others enjoy their last meal in peace before we share our poor news. There'll be plenty enough time for despair once we've told them what we know.'

Aodhán and Morag got to their feet and she accompanied them to the doorway, watching as they departed and returned to their seat on the wooden bench. Sitting there, they held each other's hand as they watched their daughter chatting happily with her friends, conscious no doubt that they'd soon be obliged to destroy her sense of peace and that of everyone else in the settlement.

Making her way towards the gateway, Bodhmhall scaled the ladder to the ramparts and pressed eagerly against the wooden palisades as she looked towards the west.

Come back to me, Grey One. Come back safe.

'Bodhmhall?'

The *bandraoi* turned her head to find Gnathad standing close by. Returning from a circuit of the rampart, she seemed surprised to find Bodhmhall standing at her post.

'Gnathad.'

'Were you seeking me out?'

Bodhmhall shook her head, unwilling to discuss her concerns just yet. 'No. I just had a need on me to look to the west.'

Her response didn't seem to satisfy the *banfénnid*, however, for her jaw tightened into a frown. 'What is it, Bodhmhall? Was it *An tíolacadh*? What have you seen?'

'What makes you think I've seen anything?'

'You had a trail of vomit down the front of your *léine* when you entered the *ráth* earlier. Unless Lí Ban's porridge was off, that's usually a sign your Gift revealed something to you.'

Bodhmhall pursed her lips in thought, weighing up the pros and cons in sharing what she knew. In the end however, she grudgingly decided on the truth. Gnathad would learn of the situation soon enough in any case.

'Yes, it was *An tíolacadh*,' she confirmed. 'I've seen a possible danger to the settlement.'

The woman warrior exhaled heavily as though her fears had been proven true. 'And to the children? To Bran and Rónán?'

Although irked by the other woman's persistence, Bodhmhall had to acknowledge that there was no element of selfishness to the question. Every action the *banfénnid* took, every decision she needed to make made, nearly always predicated to the safety and wellbeing of her daughters and her adopted son, Bran.

'The *Gift* showed me nothing of Bran or Rónán. Nothing of any of the Ráth Bládhma children.'

Gnathad took that on board with a soft exclamation of relief.

'And what of the Grey One?'

Bodhmhall inhaled deeply to control her mounting anger. She could understand Gnathad's concern for her children but the woman had a interrogative bluntness about her that she found off-putting at the best of times.

'I have nothing to tell you relating to Liath Luachra.'

The *banfénnid* regarded her closely, opened her mouth to speak but then hesitated. The *bandraoi's* unconcealed coolness was a clear indicator she'd overstepped the mark. 'Should we raise a defence?' she asked at last. 'I can start to organise things.'

Bodhmhall shook her head. 'I've already discussed such matters with Aodhán and as com- '

'But ...'

Bodhmhall paused, the interruption catching her by surprise.

'Yes?'

Gnathad quickly shook her head. 'It was nothing. Please continue.'

The *bandraoi* eyed her closely, curious as to what she'd intended to say but then dismissed it with a shrug. 'As combat leader in Liath Luachra's absence, Aodhán will speak to you further on the tasks you'll be assigned. Meanwhile ...' She moved to the side to bypass the warrior woman and grasped the wooden ladder leading down from the ramparts to the *lis*. 'I should stop distracting you and let you get back to your post.'

45

'Bodhmhall.'

The *bandraoi* paused, one foot on the top rung of the ladder. Gnathad looked flustered, almost embarrassed.

'I regret the sharpness of my tone, Bodhmhall. I'm very grateful for everything you've done for my children and I, for accepting us into your community and offering us safety and support for so many years.'

Bodhmhall nodded, acknowledging the other woman's words. 'Then let us work together, to ensure many further years of safety,' she suggested.

Chapter Four

That night, Liath Luachra slept in a nest of dead leaves trapped in the narrow nook between two buttresses of a gigantic oak. Like the tree, the buttresses were far bigger than most others in the surrounding forest, the solid woody bulk of them offering excellent concealment and shelter from the rising breeze. Curled in that bed of forest litter, she stared up at the boughs splayed out directly above her, struck by how they seemed to arch down, curving as though poised to gather the earth in a passionate embrace.

Closing her eyes, the warrior woman burrowed deeper into the woody debris, scraping layers of desiccated leaves over herself to keep the cold at bay. Satisfied with her efforts, she pulled a sliver of dried meat from her tunic pocket, chewing on it perfunctorily as she tried to unravel her thoughts and let her body relax.

Despite her fatigue, slumber was slow in coming. No matter how much she tried, her mind remained active, invariably returning to thoughts of Bran. The Ráth Bládhma youth, she imagined, would be sleeping somewhere out in the darkness of the forest ahead. That was, of course, if he hadn't already caught up with the *fian*, a prospect that made her shiver even more than the cold evening breeze.

With a grunt, the Grey One rolled onto her side, now dreading the prospect of dawn and what it might reveal.

Struggling to sleep, she lay listening as the wind grew stronger, rattling the leaves of the forest canopy. Barely conscious of that wispy clamour, the woman warrior tried to comfort herself with her knowledge of the youth's competence. Bran had accompanied her through the Great Wild on many occasions over the years and she'd taught him much of what she knew of woodcraft and forest survival. She had no fears with regards to his ability to survive in the wilderness. Whether those same abilities would help him survive an encounter with a *fian* of hardened warriors however … Well, that was something she very much doubted. Skilled and competent the youth might be, but he was unblooded and had no direct experience of dealing with truly violent men.

Liath Luachra ground her teeth in agitation. Her own history as a guardian of children was not one to be proud of. Fourteen years earlier, with another Ráth Bládhma youth in her care – she'd failed that responsibility miserably. To find herself back in such a similar situation felt like reliving those circumstances all over again.

Squeezing her eyelids tight, she focussed on the sound of the rustling leaves, pressed her face against the coarseness of the trunk to drive the thoughts away.

And prayed that Bran still breathed safely.

***

Rising with the first glimmer of light, Liath Luachra got to her feet and took to the trail without delay. By the time Father's Sun gleam was brightening patches of the forest floor, she'd already covered a fair stretch of ground and felt cautiously confident that she'd reduced the distance between herself and Bran.

It was sometime around mid-morning when she came across the site where the lone traveller had passed the night, and the discovery prompted a certain measure of stark amusement. Like her, the traveller had slept in the shelter of two oak buttresses. His prints suggested, that, like her, he had risen before dawn, possibly even a little earlier. The feeble pre-dawn light may have been too dim to track by, but it was certainly bright enough to flee by.

More curious than the behaviour of the sole traveller, however, was the behaviour of the *fian,* who'd also stopped to examine his resting place. Their tracks indicated that the *fian* warriors had gathered around the buttresses to stare down at the flattened nest of leaves. What they'd been looking at, or what might have been going through their minds, the Grey One couldn't even begin to imagine. Intrigued, she might have considered the issue further, if she hadn't noticed a separate set of distinctive footprints off to one side of the oak.

Bran, it seemed, had stopped to investigate as well, drawn no doubt by the roughly trodden earth where the *fénnidi* had congregated. His own footprints appeared slightly more recent than those of the *fian* but, in truth, all the tracks looked relatively fresh.

Looking down at that trampled earth, Liath Luachra bit her lip in apprehension. Since waking, she'd been burdened with a growing conviction that the pursuit would come to a natural conclusion – one way or another – over the course of the day. No pursuit could continue indefinitely, particularly one carried out with such sustained intensity. Eventually, a point would be reached where the lone traveller either succeeded in losing his pursuers once and for all, or made a critical error that allowed them to run him to ground.

Unsettled by that prospect, the woman warrior set off once again, her jaw tight with renewed determination. This time she held nothing back. Pounding through the shadowed undergrowth, she adjusted her pace furiously in response to the fickle undulations of the terrain, her eyes focussed predominantly on the tracks but regularly glancing up to consider the ground ahead. Even at that breakneck pace, she noticed how all the footprints were now spaced decidedly further apart than when she'd first started following them. If the *fian* was setting a hard pace, it seemed their quarry was driving himself without mercy.

By mid-day, winded and close to exhaustion, the first queasy tendrils of despair began to weigh her down. By then, she'd expected to have caught up with Bran and, although she was inexorably reducing the lead of the sole traveller and his pursuers, the Ráth Bládhma youth was successfully maintaining a distance between them that her growing fatigue prevented her from reducing.

Fortunately, despite that fatigue, her body retained sufficient untrammelled instinct to react automatically when an indistinct streak of red flashed through the trees ahead. Throwing herself onto the ground, the woman warrior swiftly rolled into the cover of the nearest trees. Shrinking into the shadows, she lay on her belly, trembling and alert, praying that she hadn't been seen. Finally, reassured by the lack of cries or any other sign of activity, she edged forward. Rising to her hands and knees, she crawled through the undergrowth until she hit an unexpected treeline and found herself overlooking a narrow inlet that was fed by a wide lake several hundred paces to the south. Maintaining a regular width of ten paces or so, the inlet effectively carved that section of the forest in two.

Gnawing nervously at the inside of her left cheek, Liath Luachra thoughtfully scanned the treeline at the far side of that waterway and quickly located the source of the red flash – a brightly coloured patch sewn into the otherwise muted, grey cloak of a bearded warrior. Situated on the opposite bank of the inlet, about twenty paces south of her own position, he seemed absorbed in the task of picking at his teeth with a splinter of wood and displayed no inkling of her presence. Standing out in the open as he was, she had the luxury of being able to study him freely without fear of being seen in return.

Massively tall and physically compact, the *fénnid* looked sturdy as an oak trunk. Two muscular shoulders spilled from the armless leather tunic that enveloped a strapping upper body. Both, like the skin on his forehead, were adorned with garish designs that gave him a particularly fearsome and intimidating appearance.

Liath Luachra recognised him immediately from the heavy footprints she'd been following over the previous days. It was the big man. The same one who'd left such an impressive dent in the vegetation at the *fian's* first campsite.

Settling in for a long wait, the woman warrior made herself comfortable. After a time, wearying of his dental probing, the warrior tossed his makeshift toothpick aside and took a seat on the bank, gathering a small pile of pebbles, then flipping them aimlessly, one by one, into the water. Visibly bored, his continued presence suggested he'd been stationed there to guard the shallow waterway, yet his relaxed composure exhibited a complete lack of concern at the prospect of any threat in the wilderness. Given the warband he was travelling with, that was probably a safe enough assumption.

Finally, tiring of this activity as well, the warrior got to his feet and started to stroll slowly along the bank, in the direction of the lake. Scrutinising his movement, the Grey One frowned as she noted how lightly he carried himself. Despite his obvious bulk, the man looked a formidable opponent. His size gave him a deceptively ponderous appearance, but she could tell he'd move lethally fast when he needed to.

The warrior hawked then stopped to turn his head and spit a gob of white phlegm into the water. Pausing to study the results of that tubular discharge, he stared at the waterway's dark surface for a moment, before spitting once again, Unimpressed by the result, he turned and continued on his way. As he neared that section of the bank directly opposite her own position, the Grey One unconsciously shrank into the shadows and lay very still. Pressed into the earth, peering through the undergrowth, she watched as he walked by, her eyes following his sedate trajectory until she noticed a plume of smoke rising from the trees beyond him, far closer to the lake.

They've captured him! They've captured the solitary traveller!

She caught herself for a moment, unsure whether she could trust that intuitive deduction but the more she thought about it, the more convinced she became that she'd had the right of it. There was no other rational reason for the *fian* to have abandoned their pursuit and settled in with the luxury of a fire.

Liath Luachra anxiously rubbed her nose. Such a development had both positive and negative connotations. If the *fian* had captured their quarry, their mission was accomplished and there was no reason for them to continue towards Bládhma. At the same time, if she'd succeeded in catching up with the *fian*, that meant Bran must have overtaken them as well.

An icy frisson tickled the woman warrior's spine, and she fought to suppress a growing sense of disquiet. Over the years she'd hunted with Bran, she'd always laboured the importance of staying close to the shadows, of avoiding trouble wherever and whenever it raised its head. Surely then, the youth would have known better than to try and approach them.

Liath Luachra scrutinized the forest on either side of the inlet, this time with a far greater sense of urgency. If the youth was nearby however, he'd hidden himself well for she couldn't detect any trace of him.

Settling back on her haunches, she grasped a nearby twig and rolled it fretfully between her fingers, wondering if he might have moved north to skirt the inlet and the warrior guard, bypassing the waterway in order to return from a different angle and get a closer look at their camp.

You're going to have to get over there too.

With a scowl, she tossed the twig aside.

Once again, she scrutinised her surroundings. Once again, she saw nothing.

Agitated now, the Grey One watched impatiently as the warrior reached that section of the bank nearer the lake, where the trees grew more profuse and impenetrable. Turning brusquely on one heel, he started back the way he'd come, retracing his steps along the bank.

Waiting until he'd bypassed her hiding place and continued further north, the woman warrior edged carefully out of the bushes, retreated to the treeline, and plunged deeper into the forest. Satisfied that she was beyond the warrior's line of sight, she turned south, working her way through the greasy undergrowth in the direction of the lake.

Eventually, she emerged from the trees and onto a grainy strand where the inlet widened, her side of the bank curving dramatically to the east as it connected with the lake. A few steps further on and the lake loomed fully into view, a vast spread of sombre green water that completely opened up to the sky.

Hugging the shadows of the treeline edging onto that strand, Liath Luachra considered the view in silence. It was remarkably beautiful. The dark water perfectly mirrored the gloomy sky above it, the smooth surface rippling sporadically in isolated patches where flurries of wind brushed in from the west. Several hundred paces away, at the centre of the lake, a pair of forested islands looked as though they were floating on a broad plain of featureless, black stone. Five smaller islets also ran across the now broad mouth of the inlet but, muddy and devoid of vegetation apart from a few reeds and tufts of marsh grass, they looked more like pimples protruding from the face of an unblooded youth.

At the far side of the lake, a strange hummock loomed above the shoreline. More a large mound than a hill, its lower slopes were oddly bare of vegetation, its upper section and summit capped with some kind of withered, white-coloured, grass.

An Mullán Bán.

The Grey One grunted softly. She knew where she was. An Mullán Bán – the White Hillock. A place of the Ancient Ones that Bodhmhall had once told her about but which she'd never actually visited herself. According to the *bandraoi*, the site had once been sacred to the *Clann Baoiscne*. Over the intervening period, when the margins of their tribal territories had retreated from this area however, the reasons behind its sacred nature had long been forgotten.

To the west of the lake, a pair of white ducks suddenly took flight, wings flapping along the glassy surface until they took to the air in a blur of white against the shadow of the forest. Climbing skywards, they swooped around to the south before disappearing over the trees.

When they were gone, a hush settled over the lake and the surrounding shores. Liath Luachra exhaled slowly. In that languid calm it was hard to believe this place had ever been touched by human eyes, even harder to believe five brutal warriors, who'd kill her without compunction, dallied just across the inlet from her current position.

That thought and the column of smoke visible above the trees began to erode the muted sense of calm. A hoot of maniacal laughter from across the inlet ate it away completely.

Squatting in the shadows, the woman warrior was still trying to work out her next move, when her eyes fell on a heavy bough bobbing in the water little more fifteen paces offshore. A ragged white scar at its thicker end indicated it had snapped from the upper section of a tree at the shoreline before toppling into the water. Now, it floated, the heavy vegetation of its extended branches catching the breeze and causing it to drift gently eastward.

As she stared at the bough, a sudden thought struck the woman warrior. Almost immediately, she rose to her feet, stripped out of her tunic and leggings, and concealed them – with her javelins – beneath one of the nearby bushes. Securing the knife-belt tightly around her waist, she slid down to the lake at a crouch and quietly eased into the water.

The chill, startling touch of that murky liquid rose goosebumps on her skin, but she ignored the shock of it as she pushed off from the bank and swam quietly out to the bough, diving under its leafy bulk to surface on the other side. Grabbing hold of a broken branch, the Grey One brushed the water from her eyes and slid down the bough's length where the foliage was dense enough to conceal her presence. Grasping a second, ideally placed stump, she started kicking, using her feet to push the woody flotsam towards the islets, keeping its movement slow and natural and creating no disturbance on the water's placid surface.

It seemed to take an age for the *fian* campsite on the shore to come into view but once she'd drifted past the third link in the islet chain, she finally caught a glimpse of their fire. Flickering yellow and orange, the flames looked to be located thirty paces or so, in from the water's edge and it created a bright backdrop to the raucous silhouettes of the *fénnidi*, laughing loudly now as they celebrated their success. Hearing the hoarse guffaws float out across the water towards her, the Grey One pressed closer to the sodden wood, lowering her head until the chin was beneath the surface.

As the woman warrior drifted east, further evidence of the *fian's* success came into view at a solitary oak close to the water's edge where a mane with a shaggy head of wild, grey hair had been bound. After a moment, it seemed to her that the captive was unconscious, for although his hands were trussed above his head, his body hung limp and his head was slumped forwards onto his upper chest.

Peering through the branches the Grey One chewed silently on her lower lip, ignoring the cold tingle of the water against her skin as the bough continued to drift. After a moment or two, a second figure came into view, this one bound by the wrists just a few paces along the same branch from the first.

She recognised him instantly.

Bran!

The woman warrior's heart lurched, and she clenched the wooden stumps, clamping her mouth shut to prevent herself from crying out. Suppressing the pounding throb of panic in her chest, she forced herself to focus on kicking silently, driving the bough slowly but surely east, past the clearing and the *fian* campsite.

Once she'd judged that she'd travelled far enough not to be easily seen, the Grey One abandoned the bough and dived, swimming underwater towards the nearest islet and rounding it to surface quietly on its southern side. Pulling herself around the damp mound, she quietly drew in a lungful of air, keeping the islet's muddy bulk between herself and the *fian* encampment.

She repeated the same process to reach the final islet, which was less than ten paces away, relieved to find that she was now almost completely out of sight from the *fian* campsite. Unwilling to take any chances, she continued to swim further west. Finally, veering in towards the shore, she struck it at a point several hundred paces from where she estimated the campsite to be.

Dragging herself up onto a grainy strip of sand between the water and the trees, Liath Luachra crawled forward into the heavy forest undergrowth and lay still, water dripping from her skin as she took a moment to catch her breath. Once her heartbeat had settled, she started forward again, crawling silently through the damp bush, her presence little more than a damp, grey smear within the shadow of the forest floor.

By the time she made it to the edge of the *fian* encampment, the warriors' earlier celebrations around the fire looked to have already drawn to a close. Although it was still bright, the *fénnidi* were clearly exhausted for two of them had already retired, wrapping themselves in thick cloaks within the shadows of the overhanging trees. Two others meanwhile, were sitting at the fire, chatting calmly in quiet voices, their backs turned to her.

Setting into a thick clump of fern, the Grey One continued to watch them, grudgingly impressed by the practical choice of the site they'd chosen to set camp. Bordered by the inlet and the lake, the forest effectively concealed the fact they were situated on a section of a small peninsula, making their campsite extremely difficult to approach.

Unless, of course, you came in from the lake.

Much of the ground close to the southern end of the clearing was free of trees, particularly where it ran up against the lake – the sole exception being the large oak to which the captives were tethered. The area where the *fian* had chosen to set their campfire and lay out their bedding meanwhile, was located at the northern end of the clearing, situated under the protective canopy of the trees in case the weather turned to rain overnight.

As Liath Luachra was considering potential approaches to the individual *fénnidi*, she saw the big warrior return, his guard duty concluded or, perhaps, simply dispensed with. He didn't look the type that people would attempt to argue with. Lumbering out of the eastern bushes like a bad-tempered giant, he didn't deign to make conversation with the pair of men by the fire but grunted loudly, scratched his arse and lay down near the other two snoring warriors. Within a few moments, he too was snoring softly, producing a high-pitched nasal whistle that underscored, and oddly complimented, the basal tones of his comrades.

Situated mid-way between the lake edge and the campfire, the woman warrior decided to shift closer to the lake in order to get a better view of the tree where Bran was held prisoner. Crawling southwards along the inner treeline with almost painful slowness, she finally edged into a shaded hollow between two trees that allowed her a clear view of the distant oak.

What she saw made her heart grow cold. Despite the shadow thrown down the branches, there was enough light to see that the youth had been badly beaten for his face was bruised, his lips swollen, and one eye puffed up and shut. With his wrists tied to the branch overhead, Bran's short stature meant he was forced to teeter on the tips of his toes to ease the strain on his arms created by the downward weight of his own body. By now, she imagined, the burn on his arm and shoulder muscles would be excruciating.

Gnawing at the inside of her cheek, the Grey One considered her options. Any attempt to free the youth in daylight was doomed to failure. The oak's isolated position, on a patch of open ground in full view of the campfire, meant there was no chance of reaching Bran unseen. Spiriting him away in such conditions, with nothing more than a single knife to defend them, seemed an impossible task.

Trembling with frustration, the woman warrior gritted her teeth. Once again, there was little she could do but wait until nightfall and attempt a rescue under the cover of darkness. If luck was with her, it'd be a moonless night, there wouldn't be a guard and ...

She paused, struck by the sheer number of different variables on which such a plan depended.

It's a shit plan.

The woman warrior frowned. It was a shit plan. Unfortunately, as things stood, it was also the only plan she had.

***

Father sun was starting to sink when the two *fénnid* sitting by the fire rose to their feet. Instead of retiring to their beds however, they casually made their way over towards the oak tree where the two prisoners still dangled helplessly.

Concealed beneath a thorn bush at the edge of the area where the other *fénnidi* were sleeping, Liath Luachra watched the pair leave with mounting exasperation. Having painstakingly crawled back to that position to get a better view of the men she was up against; it was infuriating to see them now stroll away in the opposite direction.

Despite the battering he'd taken, Bran regarded his captors' approach with a cool, dry hatred. His evident hostility did little to impress the two men for, as they drew up alongside him, the taller one, a scar-faced individual with a bushy moustache, scratched at his stubbled chin with apparent indifference. Then, without any warning, he stepped forward and punched Bran hard in the stomach.

Even at that distance, the Grey One winced at the audible expulsion of air, swallowing the snarl of anger curdling in the back of her throat.

Wheezing for breath and unable to keep his balance, Bran swung defencelessly while the two men looked on, neither displaying the slightest hint of emotion. The second *fénnid,* a short, stickly-thin figure with a weasel-like face, took a seat on a nearby tree stump and watched, his left knee jigging excitedly as though in involuntary anticipation of what was to come. With a rising sense of dread, the Grey One recalled the hare she'd seen back at the *fian's* previous camp, its legs hacked off for the amusement of its tormentors.

The taller man edged closer to his captive, pressed his face into Bran's and growled something inaudible but, unmistakably, a question. Struggling to draw air into his lungs, Bran was incapable of answering.

Taking a step back, the warrior scratched the side of his face in irritation, chewed briefly on one tip of his moustache, then repeated the question a second time. This time, although still inaudible, there was a detectable air of menace to his voice.

Once again, Bran was too winded to respond.

The warrior exhaled heavily. Glancing back over his shoulder towards his companion, he shrugged and gave a broad grin that revealed a mouthful of missing teeth. Turning back to Bran, he leaned forward to place one hand on either side of the youth's hips, grasped the waistline of his leggings and yanked them down about his ankles.

The skinny *fénnid* gave a hoot of manic laughter, slapping his knees in amusement at the expression of horror on the youth's face as his genitals were exposed to the air.

'*Craiceann a ghearradh,*' he cackled. '*Feoil an ghiorria a bhaint don cnámha.*' Flesh to cut. Meat of the hare to pull from the bones.

Bounding off the stump with disturbing enthusiasm, the shorter *fénnid* scurried forward to join his comrade. Placing one hand on Bran's right shoulder, he swung the Ráth Bládhma youth fiercely around. Unable to prevent himself from being propelled in such a manner, Bran's body spun on the short rope that fastened him to the branch, the twisting cord coiling tighter and tighter until it could coil no more. The youth cried out in pain as the bindings constricted even more firmly about his wrists. Gasping, helpless, and completely terrified, he released a wail that, exacerbated by his shortness of breath, came out as a great, gasping sob.

Both *fénnid* paused to consider their prisoner with surprise. After a short discussion, the smaller one snorted and, muttering under his breath, headed back to reclaim his seat. He sat on the stump, with his arms folded, leaning backwards with the air of someone anticipating an evening of pleasant entertainment.

The taller *fénnid* continued to regard the Ráth Bládhma youth in silence. Finally, appearing to come to some kind of decision, he reached down to the boot on his right foot and carefully withdrew an object that had been concealed within a hidden inner sheath. As he raised it to the light, it glinted evilly through the gloom. It was a knife: a sharp, short-bladed boning knife.

The forest suddenly seemed devastatingly quiet. Seeing the weapon in his captor's hand, Bran's face paled and he gaped from the *fénnid* to the knife and back with pleading eyes. If there was any mercy to the man however, he hid it well.

Coming in close, he lifted the blade, placed the point under the youth's chin and slowly began to raise it. Desperate to avoid the edge of the blade, Bran was obliged to stretch his head back, followed relentlessly by the knife until his neck was fully exposed and he couldn't force it any further.

With a laugh, the *fénnid* abruptly pulled the blade away. As the youth's neck muscles involuntarily relaxed and his head began to drop however, he gave a deft flick of his wrist and sliced a shallow cut across his captive's left cheek.

Bran gave an involuntary yelp, which caused both men to laugh yet, somehow, that mocking rebuke seemed to shore up the youth's resolve. With the knife now removed from his face, he was able to turn his head and spit directly into the *fénnid's* eye.

Taken by surprise, the warrior stumbled backwards, grunted in anger, and raised one hand to wipe the spittle from his face. Looking at his saliva-strewn palm, he lowered it, wiping it wordlessly on his tunic as he advanced on the youth once more.

This time, he caught Bran by the throat and squeezed it violently, crushing the larynx with his left hand. While the youth choked and gurgled, the *fénnid* placed the flat of the blade beneath his genitals and used it to lift them in an ominous manner. 'Have you a mind to dance?' he asked in a low, guttural rasp.

Just as the *fénnid* made to raise the blade higher however, he stiffened and froze in place, his full attention focussed on a different knife that had appeared silently from his rear and which now pressed firm and cold against his throat.

'Cast down your weapon.'

The whisper in the *fénnid's* ear was harsh and chill, and completely unnerving. Although clearly shaken by this unexpected intervention, he knew better than to try his luck. Reluctantly, he complied and there was a soft thud as his weapon hit the grass.

'Turn yourself about.'

Although it was a challenge to circle around with the blade biting into his neck, the *fénnid* did as he was told, inching carefully around with careful steps, conscious that a single nick could send his life's blood spilling onto the forest floor.

As he turned, the Grey One moved with him, her own knife blade locked tight beneath his jaw, noting how he feverishly attempted to peer back from the corner of his eye, desperate to identify his mysterious assailant.

These attempts ceased as his eyes fell on the body of his companion, stretched flat on the ground beside the stump where he'd been seated. The smaller *fénnid's* lacerated throat still oozed blood that pooled on the darkened grass beneath him.

Liath Luachra sensed the *fénnid's* glance towards the shadows beyond the fire where his three other comrades lay, calculating his chances of alerting them before her blade took him out.

'They can't help you,' she informed him bluntly. Having moved directly behind him, clamping him between the pressure of her body and the knife, she was able to hold her left hand up briefly, displaying the thick film of scarlet that enveloped her wrist and dripped freely from her fingers.

She'd come at the sleeping men in an act of desperation, prompted by the *fénnidi's* interrogation. Crawling silently out of the shadows, she'd taken them one by one. She'd killed the big man – the most dangerous man – first, drawing the cold steel across his jugular with her right hand while she clamped her left over his mouth. Terrified that his enormous bulk might be too powerful to hold down, she'd taken no chances and lay across his chest, pressing the full weight of her body against him, even as his blood spurted up across her face and neck.

Her luck had held, and she'd succeeded in dispatching him without rousing the others. Exhausted from the pursuit, the two other *fénnidi* had slept on without stirring, and she'd moved to them, dealing with each in a similar manner, equally quiet, equally deadly. All three men had passed, unaware of their own demise, rousing briefly at the draw of cold steel against their windpipes, then fading to the Black Lands before full consciousness could grasp its meaning.

As her captive stared towards the shadows by the fire, Liath Luachra felt his body tense even further. It was too far and too dark to make out the blood pool around the corpses, but he must have sensed the truth to her words for his earlier bravado had completely dissipated. 'Stay your hand!' he exclaimed urgently. 'I know you.'

Liath Luachra snorted.

'Killer of children, torturer of beasts. You've all the knowing of a worm beneath the sod.'

'I know you,' he insisted, that strange guttural rasp growing audibly stronger under the duress. 'I've seen that tattoo on your cheek before. You're the twisted branch who once ran with *Na Cinéaltaí*.'

He went silent for a moment, swallowing delicately, belatedly realising it probably hadn't been the smartest move to risk antagonising her and cause further pressure on the blade. Although he must have known there was no help coming from that quarter, his eyes flickered back to the space beyond the fire.

'As one who was *fénnid*, you must know the poor judgment in crossing *Clann Morna*. We're famed for our long memories, the long grievance we retain for insult and injury.'

Liath Luachra relaxed her knife-hand a fraction as she considered this coolly. 'You're *Clann Morna*? You're a long way from the west. Why do you traipse these lands?'

Encouraged by the tentative reprieve, the *fénnid* slowly, and very carefully, raised his left hand to gesture towards the grey-haired captive still hanging from the oak just off to his left.

'That one's linked to a long-held blood feud. As with all such feuds, *Clann Morna* ventures where it deems fit. Similar retribution will follow you if I'm to pass by your hand. Release me to settle my tribal score and *Clann Morna's* gratitude will be yours. Spill my blood, and from this day forth, you'll have no rest.'

'Just *your* blood?' The Grey One didn't try to disguise the cynical edge to her words. 'And what of your comrades? Those whose fluids already sweeten the grass?'

The warrior looked as though he was about to shrug but, recalling the blade at his throat, he caught himself in time. 'Vassals. Lower men of no great importance.'

Liath Luachra considered that for a moment.

'And your captive? What great injury did he commit against *Clann Morna* to have a full *fian* dispatched across the country for vengeance?'

Feeling a little more confident now, the *fénnid* attempted a grin. Although Liath Luachra couldn't see it, she could tell from the tightening muscle beneath the skin on his face, that he was baring his mouthful of rotting teeth.

'I don't know.'

'You don't know?' The Grey One's voice was heavy with scepticism. 'How could you not know?'

'Because I wasn't told. The tribal elders instructed me to bring the fugitive back to *Clann Morna* territory or slay him before he reached the Bládhma mountains. Either outcome would have satisfied the requirements of retribution. More than that, I had no need to know.'

Liath Luachra, impassive, mulled that over. Finally, keeping the blade firm against the *fénnid's* throat, she shifted around to face him directly.

'You should have stayed west, Morna man.'

The *fénnid* blinked and a frantic dread flared in his eyes but by then the Grey One had already sliced his jugular. Releasing him, she swiftly shifted back to avoid the spray of blood.

The warrior stared at her with a mixture of incomprehension and disbelief. Belatedly noting the warm stream of blood from his throat, he numbly raised both hands, clumsily trying to stem the flow.

But, by then, he was already a dead man.

Even as his hands clutched ineffectually at the ragged wound, his eyes began to glaze. Staring fearfully at the warrior woman, for a moment it looked as though he had some vital communication to convey. Instead of speaking however, he tottered over to one side and lost his balance.

Collapsing onto the ground, he lay in the spreading puddle of his own blood. His legs were still kicking feebly when Liath Luachra stepped around him and moved forward to the tree where Bran was still bound, staring at the fallen *fénnid* in horror. As she reached up, raising the knife to saw through the ropes that held him, the traumatised Ráth Bládhma youth started to cry with relief.

With one final slice knife, the rope parted. Too weak to remain upright, Bran fell to his knees, shuddering with emotion, barely able to breathe. The Grey One crouched beside him and made to reach out but the youth flinched and twisted away.

He's scared of me.

The unexpected rejection was like a slap to the face, the rebuff all the more hurtful for its candour.

Stepping away as he continued to cower, the Grey One realised the youth's reaction probably wasn't in response to the spatter staining her face and chest alone, but the brutal display of violence he'd just observed. In all his years at Ráth Bládhma, Bran had never once observed the Grey One on a genuine war footing, never seen her with the death lust in her eyes or blood on her hands, never seen the base levels of brutality to which she'd sink to protect herself and those she held dear. A foundational plank of his childhood had forever been changed.

Lacking the words to comfort him, the woman warrior decided to let him be and moved away to approach the second prisoner. Dangling from the taut single chord that secured his wrists to the branch above, the grey-haired man was still unconscious, his face sagging forward on his chest. Sidling in alongside him, the Grey One grabbed a handful of greasy, grey hair, and yanked his head up to get a better look at him.

It wasn't a face she recognised. Lined with deep wrinkles, the sagging stranger had a small nose, high cheekbone, surprisingly large lips, and a ragged silver beard that matched his hair. Despite the man's obvious fitness, she guessed that he had fifty years or more on him. No wonder then that, despite his efforts, the *fian's* much younger *fénnidi* had managed to run him down.

Like Bran, his craggy features showed signs of a severe beating. The absence of knife marks however, suggested the *fian* hadn't got around to torturing him, presumably because he'd passed out.

Letting the old man's head drop back on his chest, the woman warrior slipped around to his rear, raising her knife to saw through the rope. When the final threads severed and snapped apart, the captive collapsed to the ground, without a single stir out of him. Crouching beside the prone figure, Liath Luachra placed an ear against his chest, surprised to detect a strong, regular heartbeat.

He'll live.

Glancing over at Bran, Liath Luachra saw that he'd got to his feet and pulled his leggings back up, but, ashamed or fearful, he continued to avoid her eyes. Leaving him be, she returned to the fire to begin the arduous task of dragging the dead *fénnidi* close to the oak tree where their two companions lay. Manoeuvring the bodies into a macabre pile, she heaved the first of them down to the water's edge and rolled it into the lake. Following it into the water, she waded out to waist depth and pushed the corpse offshore.

With their *Clann Baoiscne* tribal background, Bodhmhall and Demne had inherited a long-held tribal enmity with *Clann Morna* but she could do without the complications of such a blood feud. The last *fénnid's* threats of tribal retribution hadn't particularly impressed her but disposing of the *Clann Morna* men's bodies where they'd never be found would make it difficult to associate her with their demise.

By the time she'd consigned the dead to the lake and returned to the oak tree, Bran had moved to sit by the freshly stoked campfire, wrapped in a cloak he'd purloined from one of the dead men. His face was crestfallen when he looked up at her approach.

'Grey One, I regret.'

He bowed his head in apology and remorse but the Grey One made no answer. She knew the contrition was heartfelt, that the youth genuinely regretted the foolishness of his actions, the trouble he'd caused and the danger in which he'd placed them. She acknowledged and accepted that regret but when it came down to it, regret didn't dry the bloodstains, regret didn't fill the lungs of dead men and make them breathe again.

Knowing the physical impact of shock and trauma had yet to truly hit him, she tossed the distraught youth another cloak and added some more wood to the fire. By the time she'd finished building up the flames to produce a comfortable heat, Bran had passed out on the ground close alongside it and was lying there, dead to the world.

Making sure the youth wasn't too close to the ashes, Liath Luachra left him and returned to the lake, moving some distance downstream from where she'd dumped the bodies of the *Clann Morna* warriors. Paddling into the shallows, she crouched to wash the clotted blood from her hair and body, scrubbing her skin by moonlight until her knuckles were raw. Afterwards, although tempted to return to the western side of the inlet to retrieve her weapon and clothing, her fatigue convinced her to sit at the water's edge, wrapped in another of the dead men's cloaks.

Breathing deeply, she massaged her lower legs to relieve the ache brought on from two days of running, conscious that, in the morning, she'd have to start running again, back to An Poll Mór to fetch Rónán. There, once she'd retrieved the boy, there'd be the long route home to contend with, another three days of hard travel to the safety of Gleann Ceoch and the sanctuary of Ráth Bládhma.

A safety she no longer felt so assured of.

The woman warrior tugged the cloak a little closer about her bare shoulders, the worn material already soaked in patches from the moisture on her body. Exhaling heavily, she closed her eyes. She had hoped her battling days were behind her, that the peace of these last eight years would continue undiminished.

Now she knew better.

In hindsight, she now realised that peace had been little more than a temporary respite. Already her instincts warned her that the wind had shifted, rolling in now from the west where *Clann Morna* were mustered, sharpening their blades, and turning their eyes east to the hills and valleys of Bládhma.

She cast a resentful glance at the insensible, grey-haired man and wondered what she should do with him. In her experience, the arrival of strangers to Bládhma never boded well. Akin to the gathering of ravens, such events always seemed to foreshadow treacherous times, bloodshed and changes that never augured well for those who lived there.

She pondered that dilemma for a time. Her immediate instinct was to slit the old man's throat, thereby preventing his taint from reaching Ráth Bládhma. If he had some genuine connection to Bodhmhall or any other member of the settlement however, they were hardly likely to appreciate such zealousness.

She exhaled heavily.

No. She had no choice but to hold her hand. For the moment at least. Or until she'd learned more of the old man's intentions and his reason for travelling this region.

Unfortunately, given the old man's almost comatose state, it looked like that would have to wait until she returned from An Poll Mór. This, of course, posed a fresh dilemma. Given the time it would take to retrieve Rónán and make her return, she'd have to take some precautions. When she left in the morning, she'd leave the grey-haired man bound and gagged, watched over by Bran and the threat of a blade to the guts if he attempted an escape.

And, this time, she knew she could trust Bran to do as he was told

With that decision made, the Grey One could relax a little. Settling back against the trunk of a nearby tree, she turned her head sideways to watch the play of the moon's reflection on the surface of the lake. For a time, she watched dark clouds roll across the darkened sky, watched the lazy flutter of a passing owl. Eventually, lying back on the grassy bank, she eased herself into the night, submerging her thoughts in the whisper of the wind, the flutter of leaves in the breeze, the scuffle of small animals in the nearby foliage.

And slept.

Chapter Five

Retracing their steps along the cliff-top path they'd followed to the gannet cliffs, Demne, Catan and Gormán soon reached the turn-off where the track dipped and began the steep descent to An Trá Mór. Ignoring that downward route however, Catan stomped imperiously ahead, moving straight pass the intersection and advancing to where the widening base of the headland connected with the mainland. Neither of her companions dared question her decision as she strode across the rocky ground, red curls bouncing wildly in response to the uneven terrain.

Trailing several paces behind, Demne realised the girl was headed for a distant hillock that looked to be at least several hundred paces inland. As they trudged towards that grassy mound, the youth considered it with increasing curiosity, struck both by the uncommon uniformity of its slopes and the flat, plateau-like summit.

At the base of the mound, some of the mystery behind the strangeness of the hillock's shape was explained when Demne saw it to be formed from rock rather than from earth, an assumption influenced by the thin layer of rugged grass and scrub that coated its surface and disguised its true composition. Clearly accustomed to this peculiarity, Catan and Gormán didn't pause but immediately started up a path that slanted at an angle towards the summit. Intrigued, Demne followed, trailing them up the steep slope until they reached the top of the path. There, as his guides came to an abrupt halt, he moved in alongside them and bit off an exclamation of surprise. The interior of the mound was hollow, the centre a wide shaft that dropped straight down from a rocky ledge encircling the upper rim. Twenty paces or so, directly below, a pool of black water glimmered, limp and dark in the shadows.

Poised on the lip of that perilous drop, Demne experienced a sudden shortness of breath for he now understood what Gormán had been talking about. Although nowhere near as precipitous as the cliffs at the gannet colony, the tunnel-like effect created by the circular shadows of the mound's internal circumference meant the drop looked far more precarious than it probably was.

Nonetheless, it was still a long way down.

Swallowing the sudden lump that had formed in his throat, Demne considered his surroundings. The narrow ledge on which the three of them were standing was the highest part of the crater. On the opposite side of the central shaft however, a wide stretch of that same ledge looked to have fallen away and pulled a large section of the shaft edge with it. The resulting fissure in the otherwise vertical cliff face split several paces lower than the ledge. There, someone had cut steps into the rock and created the beginnings of a steep, and very narrow, track that descended to a large pile of boulders and rubble at the edge of the pool: the remnants of that ancient landslide.

Sheltered from the wind by the high walls encircling it, the pool was flat and very still. Because of the lack of light against its surface, it was also completely black.

Demne licked his lips carefully and edged back a little, the height and the stark drop combining to make his head spin. 'Why is it named Inne Danu?' he asked Catan quietly, feigning a level of calm he didn't feel.

'This is where the Great Mother accepts offerings from the land, the people and animals who fall in and drown. Once she's digested them, she spits them out.'

As she spoke, the red-haired girl studied him closely, curious to see if her words triggered any suggestion of fear or trepidation. Demne's genuine curiosity however meant his expression remained neutral.

'Where does she spit them out?'

'There's a passage at the base of the pool that connects to the sea.' She pointed to the distant track leading down to the collapsed section of the cliff face. 'Several years ago, one of our sheep slipped in. We used that path on the far side to get down to the water, but the sheep had already sunk and disappeared before we could retrieve it. The next day, it washed up on the Trá Mór.'

Catan paused and gave a nervous wince.

'Mama told me that a woman fell in and drowned some years before I was born. Her body washed up on Trá Mór too.'

The three of them looked down at the pool in silence. As he considered that dark, viscous looking surface, Demne took note of the eerie hush. The lack of trees meant the usual background swish and crackle of leaves was absent and, despite their exposed height, the wind was decidedly still. 'Was this a sacred site?' he asked. 'A site of the Ancient Ones?'

'Yes,' the two siblings replied simultaneously. They glanced at each other in annoyance. Gormán opened his mouth to speak but his sister got in first, interrupting him with an angry hiss. Scowling, he closed his mouth again.

Satisfied that she'd put him in his place, Catan offered the smug, self-satisfied smirk of an elder sibling. 'They say,' she began, then stopped to cough gently and clear her throat. 'They say that the Ancient Ones had a site here but that it fell into disrepair long ago.' She pointed across at the broken ledge and the fissure where the section of cliff had fallen away.

'My father said there used to be a *gallán* – a standing stone – over there in his grandfather's day but the cliff crumbled away and it tumbled into the water.'

All three peered briefly down at the placid waters. For just a moment, Demne imagined he could see the dark shape of the fallen monument beneath the surface but immediately discounted such a possibility. Had any trace of the *gallán* remained after all this time, the people of Trá Mór would certainly know of its location. What he'd seen, if he'd seen anything, was the play of clouds reflected on the water's surface.

Sighing softly, the youth continued to stare down at the dark pool. Black and flat, it had an oddly hypnotic appeal to it, a soothing quality that spoke to something deep inside him. Shifting his weight, he accidentally dislodged a stone on the ledge, causing it to tumble over the edge. Leaning forward, he watched it drop until it had faded from sight but then thought to see a single liquid pulse throb briefly on the surface of the pool and tiny wrinkles ripple out towards the surrounding walls.

'Move back,' Catan warned him. 'You're too close.'

Annoyed at the girl's high-handedness, Demne glowered at her. 'Rest your breath. The ledge is solid.' He stamped provocatively on the flat stone surface. 'See,' he said.

And it gave way beneath him.

Demne lurched desperately to one side, scrambling to try and grasp a handhold, but his weight and the downward momentum worked against him, snatching him away before he could get a grip. He felt himself spin backwards and, in that moment, it was as though

68

his perception of the physical world was completely overwhelmed. There was a series of rushing impressions: a girl's scream, the whistle of air in his ear, the black circle of the pool rushing up to fill his view from all the wrong angles.

Bizarrely, he felt no impact when he hit the pool. From his numbed perspective, that connection was little more than a jolt, a warm embrace and once it happened, time and sense reduced to shadow. Somehow, some part of him was vaguely aware that he was in the water, but that no longer seemed important. His eyes were full of shades and a long, rectangular passage was beckoning him deeper, stretching down to some dim light in the distance. Sliding forwards into that tunnel, he sensed walls to either side, strange wedges comprised of shadow so thick they could have been solid.

Apart from the shadows and the distant light, there was nothing. No sound, no odour. Floating in those surreal surroundings, he had no true sense of physical context and, even at a visual level, everything seemed odd and indistinct. That distant glow was the tunnel's sole illumination.

Shapes flickered at the edge of his vision. Closing on that eerie glow, he watched it take the form of a wide doorway and, a moment later, he was drifting through it.

He emerged, standing, into a strange clearing encircled by trees with smooth black trunks crowned by smoky green foliage. Coated with an odd, dull-white grass, the clearing had a small spring that bubbled at its centre.

A dark-haired girl in a blue gown was kneeling beside the spring, filling a clay pitcher with the silver-like liquid that gurgled from it. Her task completed, she stood up with care, bearing the weight of the container against her chest as she eased cautiously around. Making to take a step forward, she abruptly froze in place. Although taken by the girl's unexpected beauty, Demne was startled to realise that she was staring through the hazy air in his direction.

She can see me!

Visibly alarmed by his presence, the girl edged warily towards the left side of the clearing, where a doorway – a structure the youth hadn't even noticed until that very moment – shimmered dully in the shadows thrown down by the trees. Tense and poised to flee, the girl continued to edge towards her goal, moving in a manner that maintained as great a distance between them as possible.

Opening his mouth to call out in reassurance, Demne was disturbed to find that no sound emerged from his lips. Without thinking, he stepped forward and, with that simple movement, spooked the strange girl and sent her running. Despite the pitcher in her hands, she bound forward with the litheness of a deer and bolted for the doorway. Galvanized by her sudden flight, Demne lunged onward, intending to intercept her.

The dark-haired girl moved remarkably swiftly, however. By the time he'd closed in on her, she was already at the doorway and, seeing him bear down on her, she reacted instinctively, casting the contents of the pitcher in his face.

Drenched and blinded by the wave of silver liquid, Demne staggered to a blundering halt. Taking advantage of his plight, the girl slid beyond his reach. Slipping through the darkened doorway, she disappeared and a heavy metal door slammed in his face.

Demne, however, was too preoccupied for any thought of pursuit. The water from the pitcher turned out to be of greater volume than made sense and, even as he struggled to wipe it out of his eyes and mouth, he felt it clogging up his nose, burning his nostrils with an unexpected salty sensation. Desperately trying to swallow, he found the liquid filling up his throat, preventing him from breathing.

I'm drowning!

With that realisation, all physical sensation abruptly returned to his body, absorbing him in a giddy surge of debilitating discomfort. Everything was black. He couldn't see. He was engulfed by water so cold it froze him to the core. His throat and nostrils tingled from the press of freezing liquid. His entire right side was numb above the hip. He couldn't feel his right arm.

Panic-stricken, he kicked out desperately and was rewarded by the sensation of movement although he couldn't tell in which direction. Completely disorientated, he could equally well have been diving deeper as ascending.

Through good fortune rather than design, Demne broke surface and, and although still choking, his mind retained enough function to work out where he was: floating in the black pool, less than three or four paces from the rocky debris where the cliff face had collapsed.

Slapping the water desperately with his left hand, he managed to paddle towards solid ground but with his lungs still choked up, he was struggling to breathe and the edges of his vision began to blur. Just as his sight began to fade, his hand slapped against a solid surface, and he dragged himself onto the mercifully flat incline. There, lying half-in, half-out of the water, he retched, coughed and wheezed the freezing liquid from his lungs.

The cold air seared his throat as he coughed violently and threw up some more water, but he managed to suck in another mouthful. Slowly but surely, repeating that process, he inhaled more and more air for every throatful of water expelled. Finally, breathing easier despite the burning sensation in his lungs and chest, he lay flat on the rubble, incapable of doing any more. With darkness nibbling the edges of his vision, he gave into the pain, the shock and the exhaustion.

Demne wasn't sure how long he lay unconscious but the first sensation he became aware of was pain.

And cold.

His body ached but, ingrained within that pain, a bone-deep chill cut through to his core.

Doing his best to ignore the aches, his shivering limbs and his chattering teeth, the youth tried to push himself upright. Despite the excruciating distractions, he became aware of the unyielding cold surface beneath his belly.

Rock.

That simple recognition was oddly reassuring

He succeeded in rolling over and, lying on his back, creaked open one weary eye. Far above, the blurred outline of a clouded sky was a bright, clear circle against the backdrop of the encircling cliffs. Much less clear were two fuzzy silhouettes hovering directly above him and it was only as his eyes adjusted and his focus steadied, that he recognised them for Catan and Gormán.

Both Trá Mór children were staring down at him. The girl's eyes were wide, her mouth slightly open as she considered him with an expression of undisguised horror and dismay. Beside her, Gormán's face also bore a troubled expression, but his disquiet seemed to be derived more from curiosity than genuine concern. Leaning forward, the boy held out something that was soft and green, but too close for Demne's beleaguered, unfocussed eyes to get a grip on.

'Do you want these dock leaves now?' asked Gormán.

71

The evening meal at Trá Mór was a subdued affair for the youngsters given the perilous events at Inne Danu. Catan and Gormán kept their eyes low and ate quietly, mortified at having let a visitor to their home come to harm, yet clearly grateful that he hadn't revealed as much to their mother.

Demne, conscious that the fault was mostly of his own making, also kept his eyes to the ground, chewing silently as he did his best to avoid drawing the attention of the adults. His right side still ached from where he assumed his body had hit the water and it took some effort to disguise that discomfort whenever he shifted position. Although he suspected he'd be carrying bruises there for some time to come, he was also acutely aware of his own good fortune. If Catan's tales were to be believed, he was probably one of the rare few who'd fallen into that dark pool and survived.

Fortunately, preoccupied with the business of feasting and the howling good humour, the adults – Fiacail, Íte and eight other men and women from An Trá Mór – took little notice of the youngsters' subdued manner. Eventually, realising they'd got away with it, the youngsters relaxed and allowed themselves to enjoy the evening's festivities.

After the first course – dried strips of dulse – the main dish of the evening was manhandled into the building in a great wooden bowl, by two strong Trá Mór men. Filled to the brim, it held mussels and periwinkles harvested from the headland tidal pools, steamed in seawater and mixed with fresh cream to a succulent texture. As the bowl was loaded onto the central table, it was supplemented with pitchers of water and fresh milk, slabs of griddlebread and morsels of *grainneóg* – hedgehog – served up on wooden platters. Helping himself to the contents of the bowl, Demne spooned a portion into his mouth and sighed, closing his eyes in bliss as the shellfish melted on the tip of his tongue.

Darkness had taken a firm grip over the headland by the time everyone had eaten their fill. With the dishes put aside to be dealt with in the morning and the other guests departed, Íte bolted the longhouse door from the inside and bedding was arranged for the guests. Demne was assigned to a reed mattress at the southern gable which he shared with Gormán and Catan. Fiacail, the guest of honour, was provided the luxury of his own mattress against the western wall. Despite its obvious comfort, the Seiscenn Uairbhaoil man evidently felt no draw to it for he remained by the fire with his sister, talking and sipping from a leather waterskin that smelled strongly of *uisce beatha.*

It wasn't long before the two Trá Mór children were snoring softly. For Demne however, sleep proved elusive, his mind railing with chilling recollections of his near-death tumble and the extraordinary vision in the depths of the black pool. It was the latter that dominated his thoughts, and he twisted his memory of the young woman from the clearing this way and that, struggling to find an alignment that fully fit his recollection of her face.

Eventually, frustrated, he admonished himself for focussing on such fancies. The girl had been a delusion, an attractive but chimeric fancy brought on by the closeness of death. Dwelling on such a fancy not only suggested a morbid fascination with it, but risked drawing ill fortune upon himself to boot.

To distract himself from such sinister topics, Demne turned his attention to the conversation taking place by the fire where, believing the youngsters asleep, Fiacail and his sister were speaking softly, their muffled voices clearly audible in the confines of the building. Loosened by *uisce beatha,* they were also speaking with surprising candour and the youth listened with interest. There was far more to be learned from adults when they didn't know they could be overheard.

'Will you have another?' he heard Íte ask.

'A bird does not fly on a single wing.'

There was a gurgling sound as she poured liquid into a bowl.

'How long will you remain with us, brother?'

'Two nights. No more. We have a hard trail to the Bládhma mountains.'

'Truly?' There was a hint of amusement in the Trá Mór woman's voice. 'You're back to chasing the skirts of Bodhmhall Ua Baoiscne?'

Fiacail's response was a disgruntled clearing of his throat. 'There are matters of some urgency that drive us to Ráth Bládhma.'

'Of course, of course! Although ...' She coughed delicately. 'I must confess, the firm flanks of *An Cailleach Dubh* have never struck me as a matter of great urgency. But then, I'm but a simple woman.

What would I know? Men have fought each other often enough for far less reason than a firm pair of breasts and rounded hips.'

There was a loud slurping sound as Fiacail emptied his bowl, followed shortly after by a delicate burp.

'It'd hardly be my way to refuse an offer of Bodhmhall's breasts and hips. Sadly, that's not the reason for my visit. Recent happenings to the north mean I've an obligation to return Demne to the safety of his kin. It's been six years, after all. It should surely be safe enough to return by now. Besides, Demne's an *óglach* now, grown to a point where there's little more I can teach him. Soon enough he'll face the trial to manhood and it's best he does so with his kin at Ráth Bládhma.'

'And what of his immediate kin? What of his mother Muirne Múncháem?'

'Muirne?' Fiacail sounded surprised by the question. 'The last tidings I had of Muirne Múncháem were that she'd found refuge somewhere in the Great Wild with Gleor of *Na Lamraighe*.'

'I can't imagine a shack in the forest would satisfy the Flower of Almhu.'

Íte's scepticism was endorsed by Fiacail's deep-rooted chuckle. 'I understand that after their escape from Tadg mac Nuadat's forces, Gleor's own son was dispatched to locate them but ...' Fiacail paused as though trying to dredge up some ancient memory. 'That titbit dates from several years back. I've heard no mention of her since. In truth, I believe Muirne ...'

The Seiscenn Uairbhaoil man paused abruptly. Íte, despite the effects of the *uisce beatha*, picked up on that hesitancy immediately.

'Words tangle your tongue, brother. What is it you're struggling not to say?'

An uncomfortable silence extended within the darkened dwelling. Trapped in a position facing the wall, Demne was unable to see the two siblings. Although he burned with eagerness to turn and see the expressions on their faces, he didn't dare move lest he alert them to the fact he was still awake.

'Demne's not the child you met when I first brought him here six years ago.'

'I have eyes, brother. I can see the young man he's become. I can also see the gold in his hair. He no longer uses the dye his aunts left to conceal his origins?'

'No. Since leaving Seiscenn Uairbhaoil, he refuses to use it. But those are all external changes, sister. There are deeper changes you cannot see. These past two years have seen him grow brash and reckless. Defiant of hierarchy, insolent of convention.'

There was another silence then Íte's laughter tinkled through the shadows. 'Then the dye of the flower has stained the pestle.' She chuckled again, more softly this time. When it became clear her brother did not intend to share in her good humour, that too faded. 'I'm teasing you, brother. You never used to be so moody. Tell me what you mean.'

An extended silence followed, punctuated by a heavy sigh.

'I've known Demne since he was a babe.'

There was an uncharacteristic gravity to Fiacail's voice that made Demne listen even more intently.

'A wrinkled bag of skin gnawing on Muirne's nipple before he was passed to Bodhmhall for rearing. As a child he was always self-contained.' The warrior grew quiet, as though searching for words in the darkness around him. On his bed, intrigued, Demne strained to hear, desperate to understand Fiacail's comments and how they related to himself.

'It's my belief that Muirne's selfish political machinations have left their mark on Demne. Certainly, their consequences have done so. And that's to say nothing of his two grandfathers. Over the years since Tréanmór attempted to manipulate the boy, and Tadg mac Nuadat attempted to slay him, Demne's heart has hardened.'

'If that's true,' said Íte carefully, 'those are serious tidings.'

'Sadly, it is true.' Fiacail coughed, cleared his throat and spat, presumably into the fire for the hiss was audible across the room. 'I agreed to foster Demne to keep him from harm but also to spare him the troubles of his early years. At Seiscenn Uairbhaoil, I'd expected him to form friendships and live a life like other boys his age. Unfortunately, I neglected to make allowance for his upbringing.'

'What do you mean?'

'Is it not obvious? With Bodhmhall, Demne was raised by one of the sharpest minds in the land. From the moment he could grasp a stick, he was also trained in combat by Liath Luachra, a creature of such solitary violence, I still struggle to comprehend her after all this time. These two women were Demne's guardians for ten years and more. Over his time at Ráth Bládhma, he took their influence as his own. As a result, he resembles no other youth his age.'

His sister mused on that for a moment. 'There's probably some truth to that,' she decided at last. 'Demne's always been uncommonly grave for his years. He's also a very insightful young man but I'd hardly consider either aspect a matter for concern.'

'You say that, for you've not seen what I've seen. Bodhmhall's influence gave Demne an innate shrewdness, but Liath Luachra's influence means he's solitary by nature and lethally fierce when provoked. Such individual characteristics do not sit well in an unfamiliar tribal setting.'

Fiacail grunted unhappily.

'In hindsight of course, it's no surprise the Seiscenn Uairbhaoil youths excluded him, shunned him as they'd shun an *éclann*.'

'Oh.' Íte's surprise was evident. 'Was there an incident?'

'You could say that. While I was away on the hunt, some of the older boys attempted to bully Demne in my absence. Most still bear the scars of that ill-advised endeavour.'

Fiacail paused to slurp on his drink. On the far side of the room, Demne's mind reeled, struggling to absorb opinions the Seiscenn Uairbhaoil warrior had never revealed to him, struggling to align them with lines of consequence he didn't fully understand.

'Since then,' Fiacail continued, 'I've watched Demne grow cold. At heart, he's a youth of good character, but exclusion from kin and community, have left their stain and help feed an internal fury that drives him to excel and surpass the abilities of his contemporaries.'

'Have you not advised him down a different path?'

'Of course, I have! When I learned of Demne's routing of the Seiscenn Uairbhaoil youths, I encouraged him to try his hand at *iománaíocht* – hurling. I felt certain his athletic prowess would allow him to blossom there and hoped that working within a team might temper his aggression. And to be fair, it did. At first. Unfortunately, his unbridled competitiveness meant he was soon surpassing his contemporaries on the field. A little later, he was surpassing the older boys as well. Humiliated by his easy victories, they expressed their resentment through violence and, soon enough, most of those ended up nursing injuries as well. Needless to say, Demne was excluded from those games too.'

There was a scrape of wood on stone as Fiacail shifted around on his stool.

'The unfortunate truth is I'm a warrior, not a father nor a rearer of children. I know nothing of raising boys. I can feed Demne if he's hungry, I can tend him if he's hurt. I can teach him of hunting and battle, but I lack any notion of teaching him how to live or grow into the man he should be.'

Once again, the warrior grew quiet. Demne listened carefully but it was some time before either of the adults spoke again. When a voice finally broke that heavy silence, it was Íte's: soft, hesitant, and laden with concern.

'I understand your vexation brother, but I suspect it's misplaced. Bodhmhall and Liath Luachra are rare individuals, but you can be sure they also raised Demne with gentleness and affection. I imagine he still struggles with the pain of being ripped from his childhood home but that wasn't their doing. Or yours. Your duty was to keep him safe while he was still a child and, in that objective, you've been successful. No-one could ask more of you. Demne's an intelligent young man and, at an age where he'll seek to carve his own path. If he has the wisdom and intellect you credit him with, he'll recognise the affection you bear him for what it is, just as he'll recognise all you've done for him.'

That drew a low chuckle from the *Ua Baoiscne* warrior.

'And would you soften the edge of a man's vexation with another *uisce beatha*?'

'I would, but it'll be the last. We've had no fresh supply received at Trá Mór since Sárán was taken and ...' Her voice trailed off, leaving her words unfinished.

Clearing her throat, she attempted to rekindle the conversation but there was a forced lightness to her tone as she attempted to drive the conversation down a different route.

'Let us speak of other subjects. Tell me of your route to Ráth Bládhma.'

'Well ...' Fiacail hesitated, before quickly deciding to align with her lead. 'It was my intent to cut inland from Trá Mór, find a path to the south-west until the Bládhma mountains slid into view. It's not a trail I've travelled before so any counsel you'd care to offer would be welcomed.'

'Then my first counsel is to tarry a while. It's been too long since my children have spent time with their uncle. Why not put yourself at your ease and share the bounty of Trá Mór. We can eat good food, grow fat as we look out at the eastern sea. You can tell me tales of Seiscenn Uairbhaoil and I ...'

Suddenly, the Trá Mór woman choked again. This time she was unable to continue.

'What is it, sister? Do you still grieve for Sárán?'

After a protracted silence, Íte released a tight, pent-up sigh. 'No. I still grieve for Sárán from time to time of course, but the years have helped soften that particular ache. It's your intention to travel west that disturbs me.'

Fiacail grunted softly. 'Why does that disturb you?'

'For no reason I can put a finger on. And yet, my instincts quailed when you mentioned the route you wished to follow.' She paused. 'I had a similar sensation when Sárán was late returning from the hunt.'

Fiacail made no answer but Demne could tell he was thinking of how wretchedly precise his sister's instincts had proven on that occasion. Slain by 'The Brotherhood', an eccentric band of strange, but very lethal individuals, Íte's man had also ended up in their dinner stew.

There was a gurgle of liquid being swallowed.

'I regret what happened to Sárán but I don't think th-'

The Seiscenn Uairbhaoil man abruptly ceased talking and although he couldn't see it, Demne somehow knew that Íte had reached out to silence him. When she spoke again, her voice was soft but it had a firm crispness to it.

'There's more to my unease than instinct, Fiacail. Every year, on the cusp of summer, my cousin Balse and her man travel here from their home beyond the western mountains. They've come to visit Trá Mór and gather sea ash for their soil every year without fail, for the last fifteen years. This year we've seen and heard nothing of them but silence.'

'There could be any number of reasons for your cousin's absence. They may have had the fevers, their cattle or land may have needed tending. They ...' He let his voice trail off, his point made.

'True. That is true. And my concerns would be softened by such thinking if my heart didn't convince me otherwise. Something gnaws at the edge of my thoughts, Fiacail. There's danger to the west and my instincts tell me it's a danger best avoided.'

'Danger or not, west is where Ráth Bládhma lies and that's our destination.'

Íte exhaled heavily, audibly struggling to keep her calm. 'If it's truly your intention to follow the setting sun then humour me in one respect.'

'Yes?'

'Give consideration to a more southerly route. Follow the coast south for three days before cutting inland to the west.'

Captivated by that conversation, Demne lay still as a stone, his breath tight in his lower chest. Although he couldn't see the Seiscenn Uairbhaoil warrior, he could almost imagine him considering her appeal, frowning and scratching the stubble on his chin as he thought the matter through.

'Well, sister. In truth, it was the prospect of a more southerly route that brought us here in the first place. On previous travels to Ráth Bládhma, I'd usually cross the northern Cualu ridge direct from Seiscenn Uairbhaoil. Nowadays, that route cuts too close to Tadg's stronghold at Cnoc Alúine for my liking. Dún Baoiscne also lies within striking distance and to make matters worse, Conaire and the *Uí Cuaich* have recently extended their reach south as well.'

'The "recent happenings to the north", you referred to earlier?'

'Yes. Under Conaire's leadership, the *Uí Cuaich* are pressing further into *Clann Baoiscne* territory. Of late, there's been talk of a northern incursion all the way south to Seiscenn Uairbhaoil. For that reason, your counsel aligns closely with my own thinking.'

'Then follow the coast south past the lower flanks of Cualu,' urged Íte. 'You'll find lower ground there that girdles its southernmost rise and provides a path west across Mag Life – the Plain of the Liffey. Stay a straight course and the Bládhma mountains will eventually loom into view. It's a longer route, rugged and rarely travelled but it'll keep you from your enemies' sight and Demne from their grasping hands.'

Fiacail sighed. 'There's plenty of sense in your counsel but the *uisce beatha* clouds my mind. I will sleep on the matter tonight and make my decision in the morning.'

As the adults got to their feet and moved about, Demne could feel his own fatigue now threatening to overwhelm him, and he tugged his blanket close about his neck. Listening to Fiacail and Íte retire to their own beds, he struggled to resist the drowsy comfort, trying his best to remember what he'd heard and learned, fearful that he'd forget everything over the course of the evening's slumber.

Ironically, having struggled to sleep for so long, he now found himself struggling to resist it, but by then his fatigue was an inexorable force that simply wouldn't be refused. As his mind began to cloud, his last real conscious thought was the indubitable conviction that his world had changed for ever.

***

The following morning, to please his sister, Fiacail agreed to accept the hospitality of An Trá Mór and delay their departure. Over the subsequent five days, he spent a lot of time with his sister and her children, while Demne kept his distance and watched on politely. On the afternoon of the fifth day however, the warrior approached and instructed him to prepare for an early start the following morning. Their time at An Trá Mór, it seemed, was drawing to a close and they were taking up their journey once again.

Concerned by her cousin Belse's continued absence, Íte remained unconvinced by Fiacail's assurances that travelling west would be safe. Nevertheless, knowing her brother as she did, she also knew there was no swaying him once his mind was made up. When Fiacail and Demne rose at dawn therefore, she was already up and waiting for them, a package of smoked fish and tubers prepared for their journey.

It was an emotional farewell between Fiacail and his half-sister, both conscious that it might well be years before they saw each other again. The *Ua Baoiscne* warrior also spent some time making his farewells to his niece and nephew, embracing the sleepy Catan with affection and ruffling Gormán's hair. 'Put some meat on those bones,' he told the boy. 'I want you ready for *fiannas* – warband activity – the next time I see you.'

When the travellers finally departed and started south along the coast, Íte and her children accompanied them to the summit of the headland. There they remained, waiting patiently as Fiacail and Demne descended to the beach on the far side, and waved tirelessly until they were just too far away to be seen. Staring back at the dim landmass to their rear, Demne felt an odd softness in his stomach and was struck by a sudden urge to weep. Blinking the tears away, he turned and hurried after Fiacail.

Taking his sister's advice, the Seiscenn Uairbhaoil man led them directly south, following the coastline for the remainder of the day. For the most part, their route was an undemanding one, consisting predominantly of forested flatland, broken by occasional stretches of grey-sanded beach, although there were occasional inlets and silted estuaries that took time and effort to negotiate. On that first night after leaving An Trá Mór, they camped in the shelter of sand dunes lying forty paces inland from the water's edge. Although it was too dark and overcast to see the sea, Demne could hear its waves roll methodically onto the distant beach. He slept soundly, lulled by the regularity of its ceaseless rhythm.

The following morning, they rose at first light to breakfast on roasted tubers before continuing the trek south. This time the going proved slightly more challenging, the coastline becoming far more rugged and unyielding, with fewer stretches of open ground or beaches. After a day of hard walking, the high bulk of the Cualu could finally be seen to wane a little, offering the promise of a more substantial drop the following day and access to an alternative route west.

Spending another night on the coast, their sleep soothed by the surge of distant waves, the travellers rose early and continued their journey. Again, the coastline route proved physically challenging but by mid-afternoon, the heights of Almhu had dropped substantially and the southernmost terrain opened out to free access to the west.

Starting inland, the travellers were initially propelled by a strong sea-breeze to their rear. As they penetrated deeper into the forest however, this quickly dissipated and, finally, disappeared altogether.

Over the course of the late afternoon, a heavy rain descended, pelting through the forest canopy to leave them sodden and increasingly dispirited. Their ill humour deteriorated further when the terrain changed and they found themselves skirting swampland, sinking ankle-deep in black water or squelching through soggy earth at the edge of the mire. Where possible, they stuck to areas where the vegetation was most dense and the earth somewhat firmer, avoiding the worst of the puddles and layers of crusted slime, hastening their steps to make solid ground before it grew dark.

Night was just starting to fall when they finally reached the edge of the marsh and, tottering from fatigue, they collapsed in the shelter of a nearby elder grove that was choked with fern. Too tired to make a fire, they ate some of the smoked fish, wrapped themselves in their blankets and rolled over in the fern to sleep.

The early air was chill when they emerged from their fern nests a little after sunrise. By the time they'd breakfasted on a meal of porridge however, the sun had crested the mountains, now visible far to the east, and the sky had cleared. With the prospect of more pleasant weather, they broke camp in a far better mood than when they'd first arrived.

Over the next few days, as the travellers maintained their westerly trajectory, Demne noticed a marked change in Fiacail's behaviour. Within *Ua Baoiscne* territory, land he was for the most part familiar with, the warrior had strolled with ease and confidence. Here however, within the deeper entrails of the Great Wild, he displayed far greater wariness, pausing regularly to study the terrain and adjusting their route to avoid open ground and other areas that might leave them exposed.

Six days after leaving the coast, the Cualu mountains were little more than a sooty outline against the sky, virtually indistinguishable within the bruised smudges of cloud. By then however, the forest had grown increasingly dense, offering scant opportunity to see any great distance in any direction. Over the next few days therefore, they trudged westward using the position of the sun to guide their steps, diverging from that direction uniquely when obliged to skirt steep hills or tangled groves of impenetrable forest. Occasionally, they'd hit a clearing or waterway and pause to rest where slivers of sunlight offered a pleasant respite from the gloom of the surrounding undergrowth.

It was early afternoon on the fifteenth day after leaving the coast that they encountered their first sign of human activity since leaving Trá Mór, a spread of cultivated fields in a low valley that they'd probably have missed if they hadn't been traversing a high ridgeline at the time. Looking down on that jumbled patchwork of fields, Fiacail scratched at his stubbled chin, visibly curious at the presence of a farm so deep in the wilderness. Intrigued, and attracted by the possibility of trading for supplies or learning more detail on the terrain ahead, the warrior suggested an abrupt change of course. Without waiting for a response, he started downhill.

Demne frowned briefly as he watched the warrior proceed into the valley. Finally, with a grunt of resignation, he adjusted the straps of his backpack and followed.

At the base of the ridge, the travellers struck the fields they'd spotted from above, several small, cultivated sections of barley and other crops, hemmed in by low, forest-covered hills to the north and south. Skirting the fields' northern perimeter, a well-worn track stretched west for several hundred paces before curving sharply to the north and disappearing into the trees. Concealed within a shadowed stand of oaks at the edge of the easternmost field, Fiacail studied the distant bend for a time, before turning his gaze to the field directly before them. He clucked his tongue softly. 'Does that not strike you as odd?'

Surprised by the question, Demne looked at him blankly but then turned to consider the expanse of golden stalks with greater attention. Noting nothing out of the ordinary, he shook his head.

'It's just barley.'

Fiacail said nothing but he reached out to tug a handful of grains from the heads of the nearest stalks. They came off easily and as the warrior rolled them between his fingers, Demne saw how the upper grains were firm and golden, the lower grains green and oozing a white, cheese-like fluid when Fiacail squeezed them.

'This crop's at perfect ripeness.'

Tossing the grains away, Fiacail wiped his fingers on the hem of his *léine* and surveyed the surrounding fields once more.

'The sun is full, the weather's calm and yet there's not a single person out to gather the harvest. That strikes me as an odd manner to farm your land.'

Now that he understood the root of his companion's disquiet, Demne also understood the truth behind it. The situation *was* odd. Back at Seiscenn Uairbhaoil, no-one would ever ignore such prospects for harvest. Susceptible to the whims of the weather, wildlife, and other factors, the crops were usually gathered in at the first viable opportunity.

Glancing sideways at Fiacail, he saw the big man drop to one knee, divest himself of his backpack and remove one of the javelins slotted into its rear loops. Following his example, Demne hurriedly unloaded his own backpack, pulled one of the javelins free and quickly looped a leather *suaineamh* – throwing strap – around a slot in the haft. Wrapping the leather strap twice about the javelin's point of balance, he held the remainder loosely in his hand with two fingers.

With weapons at the ready, the Seiscenn Uairbhaoil pair replaced their backpacks and started cautiously across the field in the direction of the track. Quickly traversing the open ground, they reached the refuge of the trees on the opposite side. There, keeping to the treeline, they moved at a crouch, following the muddy trail, prepared to bolt at the first sign of trouble.

Reaching the point where the trail curved into the western forest, the travellers continued along its twisted contours, weaving through the trees for several hundred paces until it deposited them at the edge of a wide clearing. Here, the pair edged further off the track, settling into the shadows of a particularly dense cluster of oaks from where they could study the clearing in relative safety.

Squatting behind a tree trunk that was five or six times his own girth, Demne chewed nervously at his lower lip, gripping his javelin so tightly the knuckles of his right hand shone white through the gloom of the under-canopy. The clearing contained two burned-out buildings. Beyond them, a further fifty or sixty paces up a narrow track at the far side of the clearing, two animal pens and a third building, which looked to be intact, were visible.

Little remained of the nearest structure beyond a charred skeleton of blackened posts – the internal supports – and a blistered northern gable where the fire looked to have snuffed out of its own accord. The second structure was even more badly damaged with little more than a singed stone chimney surrounded by layers of charred rubble. Miraculously, a single corner roof support and a patch of roof attached to its upper section were also untouched, standing upright at a slight angle to the chimney. Despite all the destruction, there were no bodies, no obvious signs of violence.

Demne glanced uncertainly at his older companion, but Fiacail remained silent, preoccupied with his scrutiny of the farm buildings. Rising to his feet, the youth was just about to step into the clearing when the flat of Fiacail's javelin head slapped him hard across the shoulder.

'*Crom síos, a amadán!*' Get down, you idiot!

84

Startled by the warrior's furious whisper, Demne immediately did as he was told, seething in humiliation as he squatted in the shadows, unsure whether his anger was directed at Fiacail or at himself. Avoiding the warrior's eye, he cast another frustrated glance over the open ground for any evidence of danger.

'*Ansin!*' Fiacail muttered suddenly. There!

He pointed to a section of ground to the left of the burnt-out structures. Following the warrior's extended finger, Demne quickly spotted a trampled patch of earth, strewn with footprints and several stains of unusual darkness. The youth swallowed then, fear catching in his throat as he realised the true extent of his own recklessness and the danger he'd almost put them in. Mortified, he breathed in deeply, his earlier anger dissipated, replaced by an overwhelming sense of shame. The Seiscenn Uairbhaoil man had cause to be furious. Stepping out in the open, in the middle of unknown and potentially hostile, territory …

The travellers remained in the shadows for a long time, studying the scene before them until Fiacail was satisfied it was safe enough to stand. He cast a glance down at the youth who remained crouched in the bushes, displaying an intense determination to remain where he was, in direct contrast to his earlier enthusiasm. Fiacail raised one hand to tap his nose.

'No smell of smoke. Whatever happened here took pace more than a day ago at least. Possibly, two days.'

Still too embarrassed by his earlier gaffe, Demne said nothing, relieved that his reddening checks couldn't be observed easily in the shadows.

Fiacail stepped forward into the clearing and advanced towards the nearest structure, javelin resting lightly along his extended arm, ready to be snapped back and cast at a moment's notice. Stepping into the burnt remains, he started poking desultorily through the ashes with his foot.

Overcoming his discomfort, Demne forced himself to get up and move out to join him. He, too, started searching the ruins, unearthing a few melted tools, a warped metal pot and several other blackened items that were too damaged to identify. When it became evident that there was nothing of interest or practical use to be found, he left the ruin and crossed the flat ground to examine the muddy patch Fiacail had pointed out earlier.

It was only as he looked down at that churned-up piece of earth that Demne understood the sheer scale of the activity that had occurred in the clearing. There was an extraordinary number of tracks but the sheer diversity of their markings and haphazardness of their patterns meant it was impossible to estimate how many pairs of feet had been involved.

Appearing at his side, Fiacail regarded the ground quietly and poked on of the stains with the head of his javelin. The sticky substance left a faint ruddy stain on the metal point.

'That's bloodwork, all right.'

Turning his head, the warrior spat into the ruins.

'Let's see if we can salvage some supplies from that last building. Then we can leave this place behind. We've affairs of our own to attend to. We don't need to be caught up in whatever happened here.'

Although the age and the general wearing of the tracks indicated that whoever had made them had long departed, the two travellers kept their weapons to hand as they followed the trail towards the third building. When they were within thirty paces of the structure however, a sudden breeze bore the unmistakeable stench of decaying meat towards them. Demne felt the bile rise in his stomach.

There's been death here!

They found the source of the stench in the pens just south of the building: the rotting carcasses of over ten slaughtered cows and goats. All of the animals looked to have been cruelly hacked and bore open wounds or gashes that were riddled with buzzing flies and other insects. Approaching the wooden enclosures, Demne leaned against one of the support posts and stared silently at the carnage within, the hoofprints and blood trails revealing the gruesome detail of what had taken place. Trapped within the pens, the animals had been chased and slaughtered, most of them struck or slashed several times until a death blow had put an end to their suffering.

Demne shook his head in disbelief. The animals had endured a needlessly cruel and painful death. More disturbing however, was the fact that none of them had been butchered. They'd been slaughtered, not for food but for sport.

Beside him, Fiacail mac Codhna also considered the bloody sight, his nose crinkling at the stench of rotting meat. Exhaling heavily, he took a fresh grip on his javelin. 'Let's scavenge what we can and go,' he told the youth. 'This place reeks and I'd put it behind us.'

Continuing towards the third building, a rudely constructed structure that looked to be used more for storage than habitation, they found the occupants of the little farm, or rather what was left of them. Two men had been nailed to the wall, facing away from the path and concealed from view of the two travellers until they'd almost reached the entrance. Spread-eagled against the rough, timber surface, both bodies had numerous gashes that matched the irregular notches in the wood surrounding them. It took Demne a moment to work out what had caused them and he suddenly felt sick to his stomach.

The raiders used them as targets for javelin practice.

They found a third male – little more than a boy – a few paces out from the wall. Decapitated, the headless corpse was lying in the dust, the head impaled on a pole and placed so that it faced the two men on the wall. Demne suspected that the wide eyes and mouth had provided great amusement for the raiders although, in his opinion, the head's overall expression reflected one of surprise rather than horror.

Once again, Fiacail said nothing but Demne saw his fists clench and unclench repeatedly. Whistling through his teeth with implausible nonchalance, the warrior approached the building's single door and smashed it inwards with a kick.

They found the bodies of the women inside, dumped like detritus in one corner. The absence of clothing and the wounds left little doubt as to their fate prior to their throats being cut. Staring down at those sprawled, discarded corpses, overcome by the concentrated stench of blood, Demne staggered against the doorway and spewed the contents of his stomach onto the ground. He was still bent over, strands of greasy saliva dripping from his lips, when the Seiscenn Uairbhaoil man approached from behind. Placing one hand on the youth's shoulder, he gently urged him outside, closing the door behind them both with a dark expression on his face.

'It seems my sister's instincts had the right of it,' he said a last. 'I recognised one of those women.' He shook his head sadly. 'It looks like Belse and her family won't be visiting Trá Mór again.'

Moving around to the corner of the building, the warrior stared towards the head impaled on its solitary post. 'This is no raid,' he decided aloud. 'This isn't some random *díbhearg*. It's the carnage of a *fian* intentionally laying waste to the countryside.' He paused. 'This is war.'

Demne's stomach had settled and, standing upright, he wiped his lips with the sleeve of his tunic. By then, Fiacail had returned and was headed back towards the clearing and the trail they'd arrived from. '*Ar aghaidh linn*,' he spat. 'Let's go. Let's leave this slaughter in our wake.'

It was only when they were halfway up the ridgeline slope that Demne realised they hadn't even thought to search for supplies.

Chapter Six

Following her discussion with Gnathad, Bodhmhall decided to alert the wider settlement of the threat against them directly after the shared breakfast. The timing was opportune given that the greater part of *Muinntir Bládhma* – The People of Bládhma – would be gathered in one place at the same time. More importantly, she felt it best they heard the news from her directly rather than later, piecemeal, through other sources.

When she stood to deliver the bad news, it was received with about as much enthusiasm as could be expected. To their credit however, the people listened without interruption, their years at Ráth Bládhma giving them enough faith in the validity of her visions to hear her out. Afterwards, while the children played off to the side with oblivious cheer, the adults regarded her in silence, the reactions on their faces varying from outright fear, to anger, to white-faced despair.

There were many questions of course, questions the *bandraoi* did her best to answer, although her limited ability to decipher what the *Gift* had shown her meant there was little further clarification she could add. All she could really do was try and reassure them that, although the warning of the threat was real, that same threat might never actually eventuate. She also made a point of reminding them that the settlement had survived similar threats in the past and that, although they'd not come through unscathed, they had – as a group – survived. Until they heard otherwise, or the danger was known to have passed, she suggested they focus on shoring up their defences and addressing any vulnerabilities.

That evening, to follow through on those suggestions, Bodhmhall hosted a gathering in her roundhouse with the settlement's warriors: Aodhán, his brother Conán and Ferchar. While the discussions took place, Gnathad, the least experienced of the *ráth's* defenders, was assigned the responsibility of guarding the valley's eastern approach, a role that she accepted with obvious resentment. Tóla, a veteran of the settlement's previous battles, had more than earned the right to attend but, eccentric as ever, he ignored the invitation when it came. Instead, he remained on watch at the ramparts above the bolted gateway and, accustomed to his odd ways, the others started without him.

Having fulfilled her host responsibilities with a fire in the firepit and hot herbal drinks for those present, Bodhmhall took the lead and initiated the discussions, a duty which in the Grey One's absence fell jointly to herself and Aodhán. The initial conversation focussed on improving the sturdiness of the *ráth,* the repairs needed for those sections of the pilings that had fallen into disrepair, and other security arrangements on top of those already agreed to with Aodhán. Over the course of those discussions, a number of suggestions were proposed, different options assessed and, where possible, a final decision made.

Other potential defensive measures were then considered, measures that included the possible stockpiling of food and water in case of a siege and concealing the settlement's cattle herd in the valley's easternmost reaches on a more permanent basis. Cónán suggested dispatching scouts to patrol beyond the valley's western entrance to watch for any sign of danger while also keeping an eye out for Liath Luachra and the boys. That proposal was the subject of some discussion but, in the end, the group decided against it, conscious that their limited defence force meant the warriors would be more effective at the site of their strongest defence – the *ráth.*

It was growing late and those present were showing signs of weariness when the gathering finally came to its natural close. As Bodhmhall bade the warriors a good night, Conán and Ferchar were quick to depart but she noted how Aodhán tarried, clearly wishing to speak with her alone.

'What is it, Aodhán?' she asked once the others had left.

The warrior responded with a slight grimace, an expression he subsequently tried to temper with a smile. Although he clearly had something on his mind, he seemed to be struggling to articulate it for he responded with small talk instead.

'You have a burdened air about you, Bodhmhall.'

'Well, I have good reason for that. Several good reasons, in fact.' She eyed him more closely, observing the stiffness of his stance. 'What troubles you, Aodhán. What is it you wish to ask of me?'

The warrior seemed to hesitate, shuffling awkwardly on his stool. 'Has there been further manifestations of the *Gift?* Any learnings of Liath Luachra and the boys' whereabouts?'

Bodhmhall shook her head. 'No.' She leaned back on her own stool with a tired shrug. 'I suppose the one thing I've come to learn over these many years, is that there's little purpose to worrying about Liath Luachra. She is who she is. She does as she does. Despite some misgivings in that regard, I'd not have her change. As for the boys, if Liath Luachra can't keep them safe, then no one can.'

Aodhán clucked his tongue in gentle agitation, unconvinced by the *bandraoi's* expression of faith.

'Now is a time I'd truly call on the Grey One's skills. The breadth of my own combat experience wouldn't even fill her shadow.'

'You underrate yourself, son of Cairbre. I saw your fierce battling on the ramparts during the Great Invasion. You've also fended off several threats to Ráth Bládhma since then.'

The lean man looked up at that and offered her a sad smile. 'Wolves and half-starved raiders. Hardly threats on the scale Liath Luachra had to deal to during the Great Invasion.'

'Maybe not in scale, but repulsed threats all the same. And don't forget. Liath Luachra may well have helped save the settlement, but it was Fiacail mac Codhna who led our defence at that time. It was he who laid out the plan of resistance, who bolstered our spirits, and who antagonised our opponents to the point where they made poor errors in judgement.'

Aodhán grew quiet but she suspected he wasn't really hearing her arguments. That suspicion was proven correct when he redirected the conversation in another direction entirely.

'Bodhmhall, you may not recall, but … several years ago, when you feared for your nephew's safety, you made mention of a ritual that offered insight into things that couldn't otherwise be known. I believe it was called the *imbas forosnai* ritual.'

The *bandraoi* regarded the warrior in surprise, understanding now that this was the question he'd been building up to.

'Yes. I vaguely recall that conversation. We were striving for a means to conceal Demne from the Adversary's grasp and identify the enemy's intentions. Someone else suggested the *imbas forosnai* ritual. I recommended a different approach. The ritual was never used.'

'Of course, but could it be used as a means to locate Liath Luachra?'

Bodhmhall felt a fatigued stiffness seep through her spine. 'I suspect you don't understand what you're asking, Aodhán.'

The warrior held her stare and for a moment she thought he might argue the point even further. In the end however, he simply sighed and dropped his head. 'I suppose not,' he conceded. 'The prospect of another Great Invasion chills my heart now I have a woman and child to protect.'

He exhaled heavily.

'I have a far greater understanding for what my father must have had to confront all those years ago. With three boys of his own, it can't have been easy. And he was an old man by then.'

With that reflection, the warrior wearily shook his head.

'I'm grasping at straws, Bodhmhall. Without Liath Luachra's war experience, I fear our ability to successfully defend the settlement. It was an unfounded hope that prompted me to ask. I know you've made no mention of the ritual since that last conversation.'

'No. No, I haven't.'

Bodhmhall got up from her stool and gathered the drinking bowls, stacking them onto the nearby tabletop. 'Tell me ... What do you think you know of *imbas forosnai*?'

'Little enough,' Aodhán admitted. 'Only what I overheard from my parents or from Dub Tíre when we lived back at Dún Baoisnce. At the time, it held my attention for what I heard seemed to suggest the ritual was a powerful one, one that resulted in glimpses of the future for the purpose of divination. My assumption was that it works a little like your *Gift* but allows a greater level of ... control.'

'And that's the sum of your knowledge?'

'It is. My father had told me a little of how the ritual proceeded, but he'd never seen it himself. He could only describe it through what others had told him.'

'And what did he say?'

'He said that whoever was undertaking the ritual – the seer – began by eating a meal of red flesh. He also said that person then spent several days fasting in complete darkness, numbing the physical senses to ease the connection to the Otherworld so that secret knowledge could be drawn from the ancestors.'

Bodhmhall frowned at that, a reaction that didn't pass unobserved by the warrior.

'What is it, Bodhmhall? Have I said something to offend you?'

She shook her head and smiled. 'Hardly. No. In this case, I merely find myself ... disappointed.'

'Disappointed?'

'There's no disappointment with you,' the *bandraoi* was quick to assure him. She hesitated then, taking a moment to think through her response.

'You'll find a trait in some people, Aodhán. They have a … yearning. A yearning that's beyond themselves. In their efforts to address that yearning, they seek out what they see as hidden powers or secret knowledge – *imbas* – of our ancestors. In some cases, they end up spending their lives in the search for imagined powers and knowledge rather than addressing the issue with the resources and knowledge they already have to hand.'

The warrior regarded her carefully, clearly intrigued.

'You're saying there's no such knowledge, no such power to be had from the ancestors?'

'Well, there's knowledge of course … but not all knowledge is relevant or useful. People generally gather the knowledge they need to survive and thrive. If knowledge doesn't fulfil either of those goals, it has limited use or value except, perhaps, as entertainment. As for power …' She chuckled softly. 'Well, there's little enough of that.'

Aodhán seemed to mull on that for a moment, rubbing his long fingers together as he thought through what she'd said.

'But *Na Draoithe* tell us that such power exists,' he countered, at last. 'They use it to guide us, to intercede with the ancestors for our benefit.'

Bodhmhall gave a cryptic smile at that.

'And have you ever seen a *draoi* use such power?'

'Of course. Dub Tíre used it often enough when carrying out rituals to interpret the omens or during *imbolc* to ensure a successful harvest.'

'So, you actually mean you saw him performing rituals.'

Aodhán nodded. 'Well … Yes. He performed the rituals to gain the knowledge he needed to ensure the effect.'

'And you never saw a direct effect from that supposed power.'

The warrior opened his mouth as though to respond, but then frowned and closed it again. 'Well,' he began, a moment later. 'Not directly. The effect would have been much later and Dub Tíre was always …'

His voice trailed off and he regarded her uncomfortably.

'I ask,' the *bandraoi* continued. 'Because *Na Draoithe* have a preference for ritual over effect. They create complex ceremonies using steps ascribed with a contrived sacredness or significance that purports to achieve an end effect. Unfortunately, those effects are rarely achieved and *Na Draoithe* always have some vague excuse as to why that is.'

Sensing the young man's discomfort, Bodhmhall reached over and placed a hand on his arm.

'If I threw a rock into the air and then created a ritual to stop it falling ...' She held his eyes intently. 'Do you think I'd be able to prevent it from hitting the ground?'

'Well ... I, er ...'

'Of course, I wouldn't,' she exclaimed, both disappointed and annoyed by his hesitancy. 'It makes no matter what rituals or manufactured ceremonies we invent or use. None hold any interest for Father Sun or the Great Mother, or indeed for any of our ancestors. Rituals and other sacred platitudes serve the realm of human interest for they imbue a degree of legitimacy and authority to influence those fickle enough to believe what they're told.'

Conscious that she was becoming overly agitated, Bodhmhall pulled back a little and took a deep breath.

'When it comes to *Na Draoithe*, Aodhán, my advice is to question who benefits from the performance of rituals. You should *never* believe what a druid wants to tell you.'

The *Clann Baoisnce* woman drew back and sat upright on her stool, her hands folded meekly in her lap. Aodhán remained silent, clearly struggling with the challenging concepts the *bandraoi* had just flung at him. Observing his disquiet, Bodhmhall felt a momentary twinge of conscience, conscious that she'd probably just forced him to question some of the fundamental beliefs he'd always adhered to. It was almost a relief when he threw that challenge right back on her.

'And what of you then, Bodhmhall? You're a *draoi* and part of the Druidic Order and my father, a learned man, told me that you'd successfully communicated with the ancestors. As for your *Gift*, I've seen its impact with my own eyes and have direct experience of your powers during the Great Invasion.'

'Sadly, your father was mistaken, Aodhán. With the exception of Liath Luachra, I've spoken to no-one of my experiences. Such beliefs are based on hearsay or where people have come to their own conclusions from the limited views of what they think they've seen.'

She stopped for a moment, reaching down to stoke the fire before she continued.

'As for the *Gift*, even now, after all these years, I'm no closer to understanding what it is. I make use of the practical benefits it offers where I can but, honestly, if I had the means, I'd as soon shed its effect than live with it any longer.'

As Aodhán's eyes widened, the *bandraoi* felt her shoulders sag.

'But enough of this, Aodhán. A weariness rests upon these shoulders and I have a need to sleep. Besides, this is not a topic I'd ever choose to speak of. Suffice it to say, that if I had an otherworldly ritual for locating Liath Luachra, I'd have used it a long time ago, certainly well before now. Attempting to use any kind of ritual for such a goal would just be a waste of time, an act of complete desperation.'

Aodhán sighed and gloomily shook his head.

'Sadly, Bodhmhall, such acts may be necessary. For these are, indeed, desperate times.'

Despite her earlier claim of a need to sleep, when the warrior departed the roundhouse, Bodhmhall busied herself with domestic chores instead: adding wood to the fire, reorganising her herb stocks on the nearby shelf, putting dishes aside for the following morning. By the time she'd finished, the freshly stoked flames were radiating a comforting warmth, the cosy atmosphere further emphasised by the steady patter of rain against the roundhouse roof.

Settling onto a mat beside the fire, the *bandraoi* stretched, the movement producing an audible *crunch* from the knotted muscles in her shoulder blades. Bodhmhall grimaced. A side-effect of the *Gift's* manifestation that morning, she suspected the muscles had knotted even further as a result of her conversation with Aodhán.

It had been a mistake to reveal her frustration with druidic rituals, of course. In hindsight, it would have been far smarter to have simply denied any knowledge of the topic and kept her opinions to herself. Those opinions had formed over many years of considered contemplation and introspection so it was unrealistic – and probably unfair – to expect others to have achieved such levels of reflection. As it was, Aodhán was probably still reeling from her assault on some of his more fundamental beliefs.

And yet, in truth, she didn't feel any true sense of regret. The lies of the druids had always infuriated her, and there'd been a surprising satisfaction to venting her exasperation, albeit to someone she trusted. Nonetheless, she'd probably have to apologise to Aodhán the following morning. Discussing druidic politics and explaining concepts like the *Gift* was difficult at the best of times, particularly to someone with no meaningful understanding of the topics. In her case, such a task was even further complicated given the emotional hooks the subject had in her own personal history.

Conscious that she was far too agitated to sleep, the *Clann Baoisnce* woman decided to make use of the opportunity and reconsider the images she'd been smothered with during that morning's manifestation of the *Gift*. At the time, overwhelmed by a storm of kaleidoscopic imagery, she'd had little chance to make much sense of what she was seeing. Mentally battered and preoccupied with subsequent responsibilities of warning *Muinntir Bládhma*, she'd had no real opportunity to pause and consider them in more detail until now.

Closing her eyes, Bodhmhall breathed evenly through her nostrils, working to quieten her mind. Emptying that space behind her temple, she steadily slowed her breathing, restoring her focus until she could reconstruct the images accurately in her head. Slowly, tentatively, they emerged from shadowed crannies, fully defined and almost completely reformed.

She started with the first vision, for that was still the clearest, presumably because she'd had more time to consider it before her mind had become inundated. Drawing that still representation into focus, she considered the odd depiction of her brothers – Cumhal and Crimall – at the treeline of a dark section of forest. With both men deceased for several years, the image seemed an oddly poignant conduit for any associated message, and one fraught with emotional encumbrances she'd have to work hard to sidestep.

Studying the image closely, she could see the fair-haired Cumhal stepping forward into the trees, one foot already dipped into the shadow of the treeline. Because his back was turned towards her, she couldn't make out his face and although she tried to shift the image around to observe him from a different angle, it stubbornly refused to comply. In the resulting flush of her frustration, the memory abruptly blinked out and disappeared.

Cursing under her breath, Bodhmhall forced herself to calm.

Concentrate.

She drew the image up again, moving it around in her head, tasting it, focussing in on its opaque detail.

Cumhal and Crimall at the edge of the forest.

The grass and the forest canopy are lush and verdant. Between the deeper tree trunks, the shadows are black and eerily impenetrable.

Both men are advancing into the trees. From his stance, Cumhal looks to have committed fully to the movement for his body's arched forward, poised to take all his weight on his right foot.

Crimall, however, seems to have paused. He's standing straight. Although he appears to be preparing to join his brother, he's also looking back over his shoulder.

Staring in her direction.

Bodhmhall swallowed, chilled by the disturbing representation of her brother's face. Inhaling deeply, she worked to suppress any emotional response. From experience, she knew the *Gift* tended to express its messages in abstract, even symbolic, terms. Despite the temptation therefore, the vision couldn't be interpreted as an accurate representation of events in the future or even from the past.

At the edge of the forest. Does that represent … A passing?

The *bandraoi* returned her attention to her eldest brother. Cumhal was stepping into the forest, had already partially done so. She felt her lower jaw muscles tighten. She couldn't be certain her interpretation was correct but, instinctively, she sensed she'd had the right of it.

If death … Does this mean Cumhal was accepting of his fate?

It was possible.

But then, why was Crimall looking back? Unlike his brother, her younger sibling was paused at the treeline, presumably some kind of depiction that signified the boundary separating this life and the Other life. Was Crimall resisting his fate? Did his death involve some troubling measure of injustice? Or was it simply a reluctance related to some unfinished business, a regret, or a simple desire to right some wrong?

The *bandraoi* groaned unhappily. Without further context, the potential interpretations seemed endless and, having not seen Crimall since leaving the *Clann Baoisnce* fortress – some seventeen years earlier – she had no insight into his thinking between that time and his death, that could help her.

Bodhmhall could feel the mounting urge to scratch at her palms, a nervous trait from childhood that had taken years to overcome, but which now seemed to have returned as strong as ever. On her last venture to Dún Baoiscne, her childhood comrade Becal had provided an account of her brothers' death during the Cnucha ambush – as far as he'd been able to witness at the time. The outcome of that massacre had been devastating on both a personal and tribal level. The passing of her brothers had left a hole in her heart but, from a tribal perspective, the loss of Cumhal – *tánaiste* and future *rí* of *Clann Baoisnce* – had also left the future leadership of the tribe in chaos.

I still miss you, Cumhal. Even after all these years.

Bodhmhall winced then, a slight tremor of guilt prompted by the realisation that she'd been focussed uniquely on her older sibling.

Forgive me, brother.

She had to acknowledge the truth that although her relationship with her younger brother had been forged on genuine fondness, their bond hadn't been as deep or as strong as that she shared with Cumhal. There'd been no reproachable reason for that. All three siblings had simply been very different people. She and Cumhal had shared a similar sense of humour and an affection for intellectual puns, but Cumhal had always been far more obedient and deferential to their father than she'd ever managed. Crimall, for his part, had been attracted more to physical rather than cerebral activities, deriving far greater enjoyment from pursuits such as hunting or feasting with like-minded men while gently contemptuous of her own intellectual considerations.

Despite their differences however, both her brothers had shared a similar fate, slaughtered at Cnucha by long-time tribal enemies, *Clann Morna*. There, in the bloodstained forest, their bodies had lain with the pride of the next *Clann Baoiscne* generation, mauled and mutilated as a reminder of *Clann Morna* dominance.

Enough!

Bodhmhall's eyes snapped open, the image of her brothers receding as she struggled to catch her breath and straighten up from the hunched position into which she'd unconsciously settled. Breathing deeply, she massaged her temple for several moments in an effort to recover her earlier equilibrium and consider her next steps. The thought of discontinuing her examination of the image was upsetting, but she knew she had to accept the reality. It was impossible to make sense of the vision without further context, equally impossible to separate her emotions from the message it contained.

For a long time, the *Clann Baoiscne* woman sat quietly by the fire, gazing deep into the flicker of flames, barely conscious of the sound of rain beating against the roof, the swirl of a strengthening wind through a small gap in the doorway. Finally, she felt prepared to consider a second vision.

That of the 'Angry Man'.

Recalling the strength of emotional malevolence embedded in that particular image, Bodhmhall braced herself, suppressing her own emotions as she prepared to filter the worst of it. Even then, as she pulled the image to the fore, she was struck by the sheer strength of malice, the visual expression of the individual more than sufficient to convey the pure sense of undiluted malevolence.

Repressing her repugnance, the *bandraoi* examined the individual's twisted expression with all the detachment she could muster, looking past the scarred features for any element that looked familiar, or offered some clue as to what this representation meant for her.

But there was nothing.

Bodhmhall exhaled slowly, pushed the image away and let it drift off into darkness. Her initial impressions had been valid then. She'd sensed no meaningful connection with the individual in the image, no inkling of any connection between them. Whoever he was, and whatever he raged against, he was a stranger to her.

But what grievance does he hold?

She paused to mull on that. Perhaps the man's venom wasn't directed against her but against someone close to her.

That thought was accompanied by an almost immediate sense of affirmation and, instinctively, she realised she'd got the right of it. That was it! The man's vehemence was vindictive, but it wasn't personal. It wasn't directed at her but at someone who meant a lot to her. Liath Luachra or …

She paused, a sudden fear constricting her throat.

Demne.

She fought the urge to scratch at her palms.

Could this individual have some link to 'The Adversary'?

She forced herself to think that through calmly. It was certainly possible. Tadg mac Nuadat might well be staying his hand for now, but she had no doubt he had a longer game in mind. He continued to send underlings out searching the land for Demne and she suspected he had shadows keeping watch on the settlement – and on her – to see what he could learn of his grandson's whereabouts.

Or the link could be to the traitor.

As always when her thoughts turned to this topic, Bodhmhall experienced a slight clenching of her stomach muscles. The thought of the malevolent shadow who'd provided Tadg mac Nuadat with the means to ambush them on their visit to Dún Baoisnce and send *An Fear Dubh* to prey on her dreams, still troubled her deeply. After all these years however, despite immense rumination and racking of her brains, she remained no closer to identifying that traitor.

Some years earlier, suspecting one of her father's three advisors, she'd set a trap for them that had never been triggered, thus confirming the traitor was someone much closer. The possibility that individual could be a member of *Muinntir Bládhma*, or someone else associated with the settlement, still depressed her deeply and occasionally kept her up at nights.

Outside, the wind had strengthened further and now its low howl echoed beyond the doorway. Within the roundhouse, the temperature had also dropped perceptibly. Tossing another piece of wood on the fire, Bodhmhall ua Baoiscne closed her eyes once again and turned her attention to the third image now forming in her mind.

Demne.

The image from that morning was just as she recalled: a fair-haired youth striding through the forest, a determined set to his features. Young and fit, he looked healthy and handsome, just as his father looked at that age. Despite her best efforts, Bodhmhall felt her heart beat a little faster. Her nephew was almost a man.

The forest growth is thick, the tree trunks closely crowded. Individual shafts of sunlight poke through the upper canopy however, so the surroundings are bright and clear.

Demne has a determined set to his features. His eyes smoulder and his lips are thin and tight. He stalks purposefully through the woods. The metal heads of the javelins slung over his shoulder glisten each time they enter a shaft of light.

The *Clann Baoisnce* woman considered that for a moment. Her nephew seemed angry, almost in a rage. But, without context, the possible source behind that anger remained a mystery. All she could tell for sure was that he seemed to have set himself on a definite course of action and looked determined to see it through.

Is it anger that draws him to Ráth Bládhma? Is that anger directed at someone in the settlement?

The *bandraoi* considered those possibilities in silence. It was hard to imagine her nephew with a great anger on him, but she had to accept that it was possible given the years since she'd last seen him. A lot could have happened over that time and their final separation must surely have wounded him.

Just as it had almost broken her.

With a frown, she pushed such thoughts aside, turning her attention back to the image and probing gently at the additional detail it contained.

To the youth's rear, through the distant trees, a shallow clearing can just be made out. There appears to be a figure standing in that clearing, a shadowed profile staring directly in her nephew's direction.

Bodhmhall chewed thoughtfully on her lower lip.

And who are you then?

The dark silhouette was too far away, too indistinct to make out clearly but, strangely, it exuded an air of unexpected familiarity – as though she was acquainted with the individual, even if she didn't quite recognise him

And it was definitely a *him*. That much at least, she was sure of. The silhouette looked far too strapping, far too powerfully built, to be female.

Fiacail?

Again, it was possible, but ... it just didn't fit the depiction she'd have expected for the Seiscenn Uairbhaoil man. Fiacail mac Codhna had appeared in two previous manifestations of the *Gift*. On both of those occasions, his depiction in the associated images had accurately reflected his true personality: colourful, boisterous, and extremely visible.

She mused on that thought for a while.

If the figure wasn't Fiacail, then it was potentially a portrayal of one of Demne's enemies: *Clann Morna* or his grandfather Tadg mac Nuadat. Again however, that possibility didn't feel quite right to her. The silhouette didn't emanate the innate sense of menace she'd have associated with either of those parties.

With a sigh, the *bandraoi* opened her eyes, the after-image in her head flickering once before disappearing completely.

She exhaled heavily. She'd achieved little enough from her efforts but, emotionally and physically, she felt completely spent.

But there's one last image to consider.

A figure in a red battle-harness sprawled on the floor of a stone passage. A dark pool of blood spreading out across the grey flags beneath.

The image flared, insistent if unwanted, in her head. With a wince, the *bandraoi* furiously drove it back into the shadowed recesses from which it had emerged. At that exact moment, the wail of the squalling wind outside increased in volume to a sustained moan.

As the low-pitched sound wavered and then ceased, the *Clann Baoisnce* woman grunted and gently rubbed her eyes with the palms of her hands.

It was late. She was tired.

And there were some things even she didn't have the strength to confront.

Chapter Seven

From An Mullán Bán, it took Liath Luachra three days of hard running to reach the foot of the hillside where An Poll Mór was located. Scrambling painfully up that slope in the shadows of the afternoon, she spotted Rónán from a distance, staring down at her from a position just outside the cave. It soon became apparent he was doing his best not to cry, but as the warrior woman crested the summit, he flung himself at her, latched to her midriff like a limpet and wept. Disconcerted by the strength of his reaction, all she could do was offer mumbled reassurances, patting him awkwardly on the back as she struggled to catch her breath.

Later that evening, in the shelter of the cave, the Grey One quietly ate her fill of smoked meat while the boy talked non-stop, desperate for company after so many days on his own. When she laid her blankets out, she said nothing when he shifted his own bedding directly alongside hers, sensing his fear that she'd up and leave again during the night. Too tired to comfort him, the woman warrior lay down. As she drifted off, she could still feel the weight of his gaze on her back.

The woman warrior slept well beyond daybreak the following morning, rousing to find the boy absent, his bedding packed away, his backpack full and ready to travel. Conscious that her body was crying out for rest, she levered herself off the bedding with care, her leg muscles stiff from several days of running, hips creaking at the dreaded prospect of further physical effort.

Leaving the blankets, she tottered cautiously outside, joining Rónán at the tiny fire where they shared the breakfast of bacon and mushrooms he'd prepared. For one of the few times in her life, the woman warrior took time to savour the flavours of the food, relaxing in the early sunlight as she recovered her strength and listened patiently to the boy's excited prattle.

In the end, it was early afternoon before Liath Luachra felt up to leaving the shelter for the long journey back to An Mullán Bán. Starting downhill, she set a pace that was little more than an amble, conscious that although the trip would take longer, she'd reach their destination better rested and physically recovered. As a result, they didn't cover much ground over the remainder of the afternoon, and when they camped before sundown, the weathered hollows of the hill slopes they'd left behind were still clearly in view.

The following day proceeded at a similar pace, albeit with a far earlier start. Leg muscles tingling, the Grey One led an easy step, guided by the trampled earth of the *Clann Morna fian* and her own prints, still fresh from the previous day. The morning's progress was slow but uneventful, the sole impediment a brief rain shower that blew in from the west and drove them further into the forest for shelter. Although the dark cloud passed swiftly and they returned to the trail, Liath Luachra stood for a time on a patch of open ground, grinding her teeth anxiously as she sniffed the moist air. Her instincts told her that bad weather was on the way. When it was going to arrive, she couldn't tell for sure, but it was even further incentive to get back to An Mullán Bán.

That night the travellers camped in a meadow overlooking a narrow gorge with a fast-flowing stream at its base. The sides of the gorge were steep, fractured granite, however a quick search revealed an accessible route down to the water and a pool suitable for tickling trout. Between them, they successfully caught three of the fish, gutting and cleaning them on the hard rock before returning to the campsite to cook them over the fire.

The following morning's breakfast consisted of cold scraps of the previous night's fish washed down with river water. When they were done, the travellers packed and broke camp to start the long ascent to a hilly outcrop where the trail dipped sharply to a broad valley on the other side. As the Grey One recalled, an east-flowing river followed the run of that valley, eventually draining into the lake at An Mullán Bán, a distance that would still take two to three days to cover at their current pace.

Approaching the crest of the hill, Liath Luachra was about to step out of the treeline when she froze, grabbed a startled Rónán by his shoulder and propelled him into the deep undergrowth beneath a nearby rowan tree. Dropping to a crouch, she took position in the shadows alongside that same trunk and peered out through the trees at the valley below.

Broad, and flat, the valley ran east for as far as the eye could see, carpeted by a green layer of almost impenetrable forest, intermittently broken by rugged hilltops or glimmering slivers of the river. Bordered to either side by precipitous hill ranges, it was by far the easiest and most direct route to An Mullán Bán. A pity then that it looked to be obstructed, with two different smoke columns that snaked up into the air between the travellers and their destination.

Liath Luachra stared hard at the distant smoke. The presence of yet more strangers in this isolated area could hardly be a coincidence, particularly as the fires creating those columns looked intentionally placed, almost a quarter of the way down the valley, equidistant from each other and the hill ranges to either side.

Clann Morna. It must be another Clann Morna fian.

The woman warrior felt her jaw clench in an involuntary grimace. That prospect was one that came accompanied by a bunch of unpleasant ramifications, but it was also the only one that made sense. More concerning, however, was that although the *fénnid* she'd interrogated had openly admitted the importance of capturing their quarry, this new display of *Clann Morna* commitment suggested that goal had an importance far beyond even his reckoning.

Liath Luachra used her knuckles to knead the twinging muscles in her thigh as she attempted to make sense of the scene before her. The position of the fires, and the late arrival of this secondary grouping – it hadn't been present when she'd passed just a few days earlier – suggested it was a reserve force. Apparently, convinced the first *fian* had everything in hand, they'd taken on a far more passive role, remaining in the background as a precaution in case the stranger somehow bypassed his pursuers and attempted to double back.

The Grey One rubbed her jaw at that. That could well work in her and Rónán's favour. With the focus of the *Clann Morna* warriors directed towards the east, they wouldn't be expecting anyone to come from the west. She and Rónán could potentially slip through without being seen.

She bit her lip nervously.

Unfortunately, the risk of detection remained. And if they were spotted, flight wasn't a worthwhile option given her current physical condition.

'Is it the *díbhearg?*'

Liath Luachra started in surprise at the disembodied whisper from the shadows. Absorbed in her study of the distant columns, she'd temporarily forgotten about Rónán. Clearing her throat, she nodded slowly.

'Oh! Do they bar the path back to Ráth Bládhma?'

'They do.'

There was a momentary silence.

'What should we do, Grey One?'

Although Rónán was doing his best to be brave, he couldn't prevent the slight quaver in his voice. Liath Luachra pondered his question for a moment before making her final decision.

'We'll skirt around them. If we tread warily, it should be easily done. They can bring all the men they want but they'll never be able to scrutinise such great swaths of ground, particularly in this rough country. The forest grows thick in that valley and there's plenty of hidden nooks and gullies we can use to bypass them. Besides …' She scratched absently at her nose. 'They don't really know what they should be looking for.'

Rónán looked at her in surprise. 'What should they be looking for?'

'Us,' she said.

***

For the remainder of the early afternoon, Liath Luachra used her knowledge of the terrain on the valley floor to devise a route that might get them past the two smoke columns and through the *Clann Morna* lines. Finally, satisfied that she'd chosen the best she could, she tapped Rónán on the shoulder and started down the steep slope, doing her best to ignore the cold weight in her chest.

On the densely forested valley floor, the task of following the theoretical path she'd mapped out from the western heights proved even more difficult than the Grey One had anticipated. Nevertheless, working from the natural features she remembered and guided by the smoke columns, she was able to keep them roughly aligned with the route in her head. Although at one point, that path brought them precariously close to the easternmost smoke column, as the woman warrior had predicted, the dense forest and vegetation impeded any effective scrutiny, and they managed to slip by without being seen.

By mid-afternoon, although they'd successfully bypassed the smoke columns, the Grey One insisted on putting further ground between them. Easing through the forest for another eight hundred paces, she called a halt only when they reached a cluster of rowan trees choked by some particularly dense undergrowth.

There, in spite of Rónán's objections, she had the boy crawl into the scrub and hide while she started back to the nearest smoke column. The dramatic escalation of *Clann Morna* activity so close to Bládhma had changed the situation considerably in that flight was now no longer the key objective. Now, it was just as important to get a better understanding of the reasons behind the tribe's presence in the area, and whether they posed any threat to Ráth Bládhma. Unfortunately, the only practical means of identifying those reasons – and it was a limited means at that – was to get a look at the individuals making up the force present. If she recognised any of them, that would go at least some way to working out why they were in the region.

Pushing west through the scrub at a crouch, the woman warrior's good fortune looked to hold when she came upon a dried-out waterway. Narrow and obscured by the thick vegetation drooping over it from either side, the channel ran directly in the direction she was headed. Levering herself into its shallow depth, she lay on her belly and started to crawl, the natural conduit allowing her to scramble eastward for over five hundred paces before it finally petered out.

Slithering out of the remaining depression and into the surrounding undergrowth, the woman warrior continued to crawl, drawing ever closer to the source of the smoke column, the sound of crackling wood and voices. At the outskirts of the area where the fire was located, she came across the first of the sentinels. At least two by her count, both were well hidden in the scrub but impatient enough that they moved about too much, allowing her to spot them and sidle past without being detected.

Eventually, squeezing through one last stand of fern, the Grey One reached the edge of a broad clearing and, peering carefully through the leafy patchwork of thick, green fronds, she caught her first glimpse of the fire. Given the volume of smoke being produced, she'd expected the blaze to be substantial, so it came as no surprise to discover how big it was. Taking up a large proportion of the centre of that open ground, its yellow-orange flames were flickering and licking upwards at the height of a man's head, an estimate assisted in no small measure by the presence of three bare-chested men working hard to keep it fed with a regular supply of wood.

Liath Luachra chewed on the inside of her cheek as she considered the hectic activity taking place in front of her, then slowly let her gaze drift to the northern end of the clearing. There, a separate group of five men loafed comfortably in the shade of a large rowan tree upwind of the smoke. One of those men looked to be sleeping, for he was lying on his side on a thick bed of leaf litter. The other four – presumably the voices she'd heard as she approached the clearing – were chatting animatedly amongst themselves. All five, bar a scarred individual with a close shaven skull she took to be the leader, looked to have somewhere between eighteen and thirty years on them. Despite their position in the shadows, Liath Luachra could make out that they were dressed in a variety of light furs and leathers. Judging from the array of swords, axes, and other weapons she could see on the ground alongside them, they were also heavily armed.

The group in the clearing was a *fian*. Of that, there seemed little doubt. Whether they were *Clann Morna* affiliated or not, the Grey One had no way of knowing although the presence of the previous *Clann Morna fian* meant the assumption was a safe one. Taking her time, she studied their faces closely and although none of them were familiar, she'd seen their type before. Lean, brash, full of youthful sneers and deep throaty laughter, they bristled from the pressure of pent-up violence, exuding the predatorial hunger of wolves.

They're ready for a slaughter.

Liath Luachra chewed thoughtfully on the tissue of her inner cheek. Eight men. With the two guards she'd already slipped past, that meant at least ten in total.

Her brows clamped together as her lips turned down.

That number seemed remarkably high, particularly given the presence of a second encampment and a second *fian*, which she presumed would have a similar force.

Retreating from the ferns, the woman warrior turned and carefully started back the way she'd come. Retracing her steps through the forest and the dried-out gully, she eventually found herself back before the cluster of overgrown rowan trees where Rónán was quick to emerge from his hidey hole. Ignoring the boy's excited questions, Liath Luachra hurriedly led him east, keen to put as much distance as possible between themselves and the *fianna* while it still remained bright. Fortunately, a substantial stretch to the evening remained, and if their good fortune held, they could cover that distance with enough time to find a safe refuge for the night. At first light the next morning, they'd beat a far hastier trail to An Mullán Bán, aching legs or no.

The plan, simple though it was, seemed adequate until a sudden shortcoming caused the woman warrior to slow to a halt less than thirty paces from the rowan trees. Startled by this abrupt stalling after such an energetic departure, Rónán looked at her in surprise.

'What is it, Grey One?'

Eyes still glazed in thought, the woman warrior made no immediate answer, but her right hand gestured sharply at the ground. There, even to the inexperienced youngster, the problem was immediately obvious.

The tracks.

In their hurry to seize their quarry, the original *Clann Morna fian* had made no attempt to conceal their passage and, in his haste to pursue them, neither had Bran. Later, the Grey One had covered that same ground in a similar fashion and, to make matters worse, had retraced those tracks in the opposite direction while returning to An Poll Mór. As a result of all that traffic, a well-established trail had been beaten in the earth.

And now offered the *Clann Morna fianna* a path directly to An Mullán Bán.

***

After a fretful night of poor sleep and seething impatience, Liath Luachra had them up and moving on the western trail before Father Sun had even blurred the eastern horizon. Departing the makeshift shelter in which they'd passed the night, she set a much faster pace than the previous days, conscious of the need to cover ground while also taking care of Rónán, whose smaller legs would struggle with such a pressurised stride.

Despite such potential frustrations, the travellers made good time and by noon of the second day, the smoke columns were a substantial distance to their rear. That sight was reassuring in that it not only confirmed their immediate safety from the *Clann Morna* forces but indicated those same forces were in no hurry to move east. That was a situation that couldn't continue of course. The prolonged absence of their comrades would surely be concerning them by now.

A little after noon, the Grey One noticed a great shadow of black cloud congealing in the skies to their rear. By mid-afternoon that overcast mass was already extending its bulk towards the east. Fortunately, by then the Grey One was recognising natural features from the outskirts of An Mullán Bán and knew they were finally nearing their destination.

Coming in at the lake from a slightly different angle meant it took longer to locate the narrow inlet close to where the *fian* campsite would be found. Following the lake's western shore however, they finally saw the distinctive oak loom into view. Approaching the camp, Liath Luachra called ahead to alert Bran to their presence and, moments later, was relieved to see the youth step out of the nearby bushes.

Bran was delighted and relieved in equal measure. Overcome with emotion, he hugged Rónán fiercely, a display of such unusual warmth that it caused the younger boy to regard him curiously. Too excited by their return to care, Bran turned to face the woman warrior, knowing better – even in his excitement – to attempt to embrace her. Liath Luachra however, was looking towards the oak tree where the stranger was lying almost exactly as she'd left him.

'How does the captive fare?' she asked.

Bran pulled a face. 'He's alive but he's had a fever. He's also been complaining that he feels weak.'

The woman warrior made no response to that. If the stranger did have a fever, there was little enough they could do for him. As for his weakness, that was more likely a ploy to get Bran to drop his guard in the hope of overpowering him.

'You fed him?'

'I did.'

'And he ate?'

'Not a lot. Enough.'

The Grey One grunted softly.

'Did he exchange words with you?'

'He tried when I fed him. This morning he also attempted conversation.'

'And?

'And nothing. I made no answer. As you instructed before you left, I pretended not to understand what he was asking.'

'What *was* he asking?'

'He mostly asked who I was and why he was being kept prisoner. He also seemed desperate to know where the *fénnidi* had gone. This morning, he had an anger rise on him when I continued to make no answer to his questions. He threatened me but he was too well bound to pose a menace and ...' Bran slapped the shaft of the javelin that he was holding with a grim kind of satisfaction. 'I was prepared.'

The woman warrior reflected on that for a moment.

'Did this man see you when you were captured?'

Bran looked at her blankly.

'Was he conscious when *Clann Morna* hauled you in and bound you to the tree?'

The youth shook his head.

'No.' He thought about it again. 'At least, I don't believe so. He was hanging limp when I was dragged into the camp. And he made no reaction when one of the *fénnidi* kicked him in the stomach.'

Liath Luachra nodded slowly. The youth's response seemed to align with their captive's behaviour. If the stranger truly had been unconscious before Bran's capture and his subsequent release, he'd have been understandably bewildered to come round and find his captors departed and an unknown youngster in their stead. In his place, given such a drastic alteration of circumstances, she too would have been desperate to make sense of this new situation, to learn more about his new captor and the reasons behind the *fénnidi's* extraordinary disappearance.

Exhaling softly, the warrior woman glanced up to consider the bruise-coloured sky. 'Start gathering what we need to travel,' she told the youth. '*Clann Morna* have two new *fianna* dogging our trail and they're like as not to follow us here unless that storm kicks in and washes the tracks away.'

Bran's face paled at this new revelation and, although he opened his mouth to ask a question, he caught himself in time, acknowledging the instruction with a nod instead.

'Yes, Grey One.'

Leaving the youth to carry out her instructions, the Grey One headed slowly towards the isolated oak tree at the edge of the water. Stretched on his side, the mysterious stranger was lying at an awkward angle due to the ties that bound his hands behind his back. Despite the obvious discomfort such a position imposed and the glare of the afternoon sun, he looked to be dozing peacefully.

111

Ignoring him, Liath Luachra continued to the lake's edge where she paused to examine the scuff marks she'd made while dragging the bodies of the *fénnidi* into the water. These had faded somewhat over the time she'd been away but the fair weather meant enough traces remained for an able tracker to piece the events together.

For a moment, Liath Luachra wondered whether it was worth the effort trying to obscure the various drag marks, erasing them where possible or, where not, disguising them by sweeping and scraping the earth. She decided against it. Given their location it'd probably be easy enough to work out what had happened.

You should have weighed those bodies down.

She grunted unhappily.

Perhaps. But at the time there hadn't been any reason to do that. An Mullán Bán wasn't exactly a frequented destination. Now, she could only hope the corpses had sunk or drifted too far away to be easily found.

She lingered at the water's edge, staring out at the lake and its line of islets, blinking in the smeary sunlight that angled in from the west where Father Sun continued his descent. Despite the beauty of that view however, the situation with the *fian* and the stranger had soured her mood and prevented her from appreciating it.

Turning her head, she looked towards the dozing figure, working to suppress her vexation at having been dragged into his wake even as she wondered at his reasons for travelling alone in such a dangerous expanse of wilderness. It was hard to imagine what this old man might have done to rile *Clann Morna* to such an extent, but given the enormous commitment to ensuring his recapture, it must have been substantial. Clearly there was more to that story than the fanciful 'great insult' the *Clann Morna fénnid* had spoken of.

Liath Luachra chewed thoughtfully on her lower lip as she regarded the unkempt and bedraggled figure. Finally, grasping a springy branch tip from the ground beside her, she headed back towards him, edging around to his rear to make sure his wrist bonds were securely tied and still fastened to a metal link the *Clann Morna* men had inserted into the base of the oak, presumably for that exact purpose. Satisfied, she quietly shuffled around to his front, dropping to a squat so she could face him directly.

For a time, she remained squatting in silence as she studied his face, watching his breathy exhalations ruffle the white hairs around his lips, listening to the occasional sniff and snort. When she was ready, she raised the stick and slapped it down hard on his bare upper arm.

The sleeping man lurched violently upright, his eyes wide and white with alarm. The restraints on his bound hands however, meant he almost immediately lost balance and fell over. With a strangled cry, he rolled back up onto his knees and looked around in confusion, his jaw dropping when he spotted Liath Luachra staring at him with unconcealed animosity.

Shuffling backwards in panic, he crashed against the trunk of the oak. Held in place by his tie to the metal ring however, he was unable to shuffle any further and had no choice but to remain where he was. Realising that the woman warrior had made no effort to approach him and registering his lack of a weapon, his heaving chest gradually slowed. He stared at her hard as he regained his breath and although his face was lined and fearful, Liath Luachra was struck by the fiery intelligence in his eyes.

'Who are you?' she asked.

The stranger considered her, his expression guarded. At the sound of her voice, his eyes had momentarily dropped from her face to her chest and back again. Whatever conclusion he'd come to with regard to her gender, it seemed to ease his fears for there was a perceptible release of tension from his shoulders.

'No-one of interest.'

Given the raggedness of his breathing and the throatiness of his voice, the old man's response struck her as remarkably measured.

'You're a badger rousing the bees' nest in these territories,' Liath Luachra countered. 'Your actions alone have made you someone of interest.'

Despite his earlier panic-stricken reaction, the old man's grey gaze had now settled to greater firmness. A slight tightening of the lips suggested he wasn't used to being spoken to in such a manner by a woman, however the reality of his bonds and the tenuousness of his situation was sufficient incentive for tact. The response, when it came therefore, was exceedingly polite.

'It was not my intent to …' He paused. 'To rouse the bees' nest. You have my regret for the disturbance I caused. Let me go on my way and you'll be well free of me, with my blessings to boot. I'm truly a man of no importance.'

'The men who captured you seemed to consider you important.'

That gave the stranger pause and, as she studied his reaction, the Grey One had to admire his self-control. Despite the mental grind taking place behind that forehead as he attempted to work out her connection with his original captors, his face revealed no inkling of it.

'And those who capt- ... those who sought to impede my travel. Where are they now?'

'They sit at the fires of their ancestors, keeping them company in the Dark Lands.'

That seemed to shake him.

'Who w-?' he began, then quickly mashed his lips together, as though fearful of inadvertently giving something away. His eyebrows compressed and she could see the disbelief in his eyes.

'They're dead?'

She dipped her head once.

'All of them?'

'A lot can happen during slumbers of such depth. While you dream, the Great Mother's mantle breathes on, Father Sun rises and falls ...' She left her voice tail off.

The stranger remained silent, still struggling to absorb her revelation of the *fénnidi's* passing. From the manner in which he glanced at her chest however – presumably reassessing some previous determination – she suspected he didn't truly believe her. That suspicion was supported by his subsequent question.

'And who dispatched those men to join the ancestors?' A cautious chuckle followed the question. 'You?'

'Yes.'

That response knocked the puff out of him and, this time, the Grey One saw a measure of belief flare behind his eyes. The stranger's forehead creased, causing his thick white eyebrows to knit together as he regarded her with greater attention. 'Why would I believe such a claim? That you – a mere woman – killed more than four men?'

Feeling no need to justify herself, the Grey One wordlessly held his stare.

In the ensuing silence, the old man grew visibly more uncomfortable. Finally, with a wince, he shifted his weight awkwardly and grunted as though in response to some unseen discomfort.

Unmoved, the woman warrior retained her silence, conscious that these were little more that distractions. As that long silence continued, the old man continued to eye her in confusion, struggling with the concept that a woman could overcome five able-bodied warriors.

'They're slain, then,' he said at last. 'All of them.'

This time, the statement was uttered with a new air of acceptance, but the manner in which it was delivered seemed to invite further confirmation. When it became clear that no such reassurance was going to be forthcoming, the old man exhaled heavily.

'Well, then. You've killed some hardy enemies.'

'They weren't my enemies. I had no knowing of them.'

'If they weren't your enemies then why did you slay them?'

'They threatened my charge.'

The stranger's gaze flickered momentarily across to the far side of the clearing where Rónán and Bran were busy repacking the wicker backpacks with supplies left by the deceased *fian*. As his eyes drifted back towards her, she could sense the calculation in his head, the reckoning of ages and potential linkages. 'Your sons?' he asked.

She didn't deign a response.

The white-haired man coughed gently, delicately wiping his lips with his fingertips. 'Well, given your charges are now free from danger, perhaps you could release me and I'll trouble you no more.'

The Grey One shook her head.

The stranger frowned.

'But I pose no threat to you. And as the Elders tell us …The enemy of my enemy —'

'… is no interest to me,' she said indifferently. 'I had no knowing of the dead *Clann Morna* men. As I have no knowing of you. You've dragged five deaths to my feet, and I don't care to trust you. You'll be remaining here at An Mullán Bán when my charges and I depart.'

'Will you untie me at least?'

'No.'

The old man glared at her with almost comical outrage. 'I've been beaten, I have a weakness on me, I have no weapon … I could hardly overpower … a warrior capable of laying so many *fénnidi* beneath the sod.'

Liath Luachra couldn't help but notice the caustic manner in which that last statement had been delivered.

115

'If you leave me here bound,' the stranger continued. 'Then, …
then, I'll surely die.'

The Grey One shrugged.

'You'll be dead when we leave. It makes no difference whether
you're bound or not.'

She watched as chilled comprehension slowly reached the
stranger's eyes. 'What? But … But … No! Wait! I'm no threat to you!'

His voice had leapt a full level in pitch.

'You've got a mouth. That's threat enough.'

This time, he looked at her in complete bafflement.

'I prefer no tales in my wake but two new *Clann Morna fianna* beat
a path to this place. You have a tongue and we both know a reticent
man can be turned to talk eventually.'

'Then aid me!' There was genuine desperation in the old man's
voice now. 'Aid me and I'll see you well rewarded. I have a task I'm
duty bound to fulfil before I breathe my last. If you help me evade
Clann Morna and achieve this goal, the reward is yours.'

Liath Luachra eyed him coldly, repressing the temptation once
again to deal to this *fadharcán* right there and then, to put an end to
the trail of problems he left to his rear.

As though sensing those dark considerations, the old man quailed,
and his face went white. From the corner of her eye, the Grey One
watched the two youngsters at the side of the clearing. They looked as
though they were preoccupied loading the backpacks, but she could
tell they were listening to the conversation intently.

'I beg you. Just help me travel to an old *Clann Baoisnce ráth* at
Bládhma and a great treasure will be yours. The people there will see
you well rewarded for your efforts.'

Only years of silence allowed the Grey One to keep her features
blank of expression. Once she got over that suppressed surprise, she
eyed the stranger coolly. He'd overreached himself with his slyness on
this occasion but his knowledge of Ráth Bládhma had her attention.

'They'll reward me, will they? And what would that reward be, do
you think?'

'Whatever you desire and deserve,' he answered without hesitation.

'And what is it you seek to achieve at Ráth Bládhma?'

Somehow, despite her mask of impassivity, the stranger seemed to
sense that he'd piqued her interest, for he regarded her now with a

kind of guarded hope, even as he deliberately sidestepped the question.

'Do you know where Ráth Bládhma lies?'

She sidestepped it right back. 'What is it you seek to achieve at Ráth Bládhma?'

The stranger paused and shook his head sadly. 'I regret …' His voice momentarily trailed off. 'I can say only that I'm under oath to reach Ráth Bládhma. The reasons for my trek are not my own, but neither are they ones I can share with you.'

Liath Luachra considered this response with silent detachment, surprised at the stranger's streak of resolve given his earlier distress. 'If you wish to continue breathing, then you have no choice but to share.'

The stranger's lips parted nervously as he thought through his next response.

'I travel there uniquely to deliver a message,' he said at last, his voice burdened by a tangible air of resentment. 'By all accounts, it's a critical message but one that will hold no relevance for you.'

'Ráth Bládhma is where I lay my bed,' she answered. 'It will almost certainly hold relevance for me.'

The stranger grunted as though he'd been punched in the gut. Visibly struggling with this new revelation, he stared at her more closely, giving far more attention to her short, black hair, her flat chest and worn clothing. 'Are you …' he ventured with obvious misgivings. 'Are you the daughter of a man named Tréanmór?'

The question was followed by a momentary silence, punctuated by a wild burst of laughter from the woman warrior's lips. Over at the edge of the clearing, Bran and Rónán turned to look in her direction, drawn by the rare sound of the Grey One's mirth. Even as they did so however, that good humour wilted, the laugh lines on her face fading back into an expression of stone.

'You're asking if I'm Bodhmhall ua Baoiscne.'

The stranger considered her in silence for a time, finally shaking his head as though he'd come to some important conclusion. 'You're not the daughter of Tréanmór,' he decided. 'From all that I've heard, Bodhmhall ua Baoiscne is a beauty of rare …'

Realising belatedly where that particular train of thought was going to end, he changed course with impressive adroitness.

'Bodhmhall ua Baoiscne is the person to who I've been instructed to deliver my message. My words are for her ears alone so I cannot share them with you.'

'You'd be lying cold and breathless and serving the ancestors if it weren't for my intervention,' she reminded him.

'And you've as good as admitted your intention to dispose of me.' The stranger argued, stubbornly compressing his lips together.

Liath Luachra's fingers toyed with the leather binding of her knife scabbard and momentarily wondered whether she could prise the knowledge out of him. With a burn of suppressed bitterness, she concluded that she probably couldn't. At least not before the *Clann Morna fianna* made their appearance at An Mullán Bán.

Liath Luachra glared at her captive unhappily. Despite the years on him, the hard chase, and the brutal recent ill-treatment he'd received from *Clann Morna*, he was still a slippery fish. She'd learned nothing of him or his motivations over their extended conversation. True, he'd yielded the fact that he was travelling to Ráth Bládhma, but that was something she'd already suspected. As for his claim to have an urgent message for Bodhmhall ... well, that was something he was stubbornly refusing to explain, despite his obvious fear of her and her own unsubtle intimidation.

She frowned, annoyed to realise that they were now at something of an impasse.

Drawing the knife from her scabbard with one smooth movement, she quickly reached in behind the stranger, noting how he started at her closeness and stiffened as she angled the blade down, sliding it between the cords on his wrists. Although she could smell the fear off him, his relief as the bindings fell away was palpable. Somehow, he managed to endure her proximity without pissing himself as she pulled back and sheathed the weapon, covering his obvious discomfort by staring down at his hands, frantically massaging the wrists as the blood flowed back through them.

'I'll escort you to Ráth Bládhma,' Liath Luachra told him. 'You can deliver your message to Bodhmhall ua Baoiscne, but you'd better hope it's as critical as you claim. Otherwise, there'll be more than words between us.'

Encouraged by that declaration, the stranger somehow managed to pull himself together and sit up straight. To her surprise, he abruptly reached out and offered her his right hand.

The woman warrior looked down at the proffered palm but made no effort to accept it, a snub he quickly moved to obfuscate through false, if enthusiastic, bonhomie.

'Then, a truce it is! I look forward to visiting your home at Bládhma.'

Liath Luachra tried not to wince at that prospect.

'Feoras is the name on me,' the old man continued quickly. 'And what name did you say you had on you?'

The woman warrior regarded him coldly. 'I never said.'

'Oh.' Feoras contrived to look completely confused. 'In all the excitement, I suppose I never even noticed.'

***

It was only a little later that the threatening rainclouds finally tipped their watery loads, relieving themselves over the land with all the enthusiastic excess of a drunken man's bladder. By then however, the company was already ensconced in a shelter Bran had discovered during his time alone at An Mullán Bán. A shallow cleft in a strange, semi-circular rock formation several hundred paces east of the *fian* campsite, it had an overhanging lip that protected them from the worst of the downpour and a slightly raised rock base that kept the increasingly deep surface flooding on the flat ground at bay.

It was an easy decision to delay their departure. The darkening skies meant it would soon be impossible to distinguish the route back to Ráth Bládhma. More importantly, the eroding nature of that prolific downpour would have erased any chance of *Clann Morna* following the tracks back to An Mullán Bán. Eventually, of course, in seeking out their missing *fian* they might find themselves at this location. By then, however, Liath Luachra and her party would be well gone and any evidence of their presence or any linkage to Ráth Bládhma, completely wiped away.

To mark that fortuitous change in circumstance, Liath Luachra prepared the evening meal and, within a short amount of time, had a watery stew of smoked meat, watercress and oats, boiling in a pot over a small fire. To the boys' delight, she also produced a leather satchel of *uisce beatha* – retrieved from the pilfered supplies of the dead *fénnidi* – that she made a point of first offering to their 'guest'. Bran and Rónán watched sourly as the old man took a *sliog* of the

119

sour smelling liquid, for the woman warrior had refused to offer them any. As an almost intentional slight, she also restricted her own consumption to a mere wetting of lips.

Feoras, despite his somewhat tenuous presence, proved a surprisingly gracious guest. Ignoring the Grey One's obvious limitations as a cook – the meat was too tough, the stew broth too sharp – he expounded on her hospitality and the quality of the meal with an enthusiasm bordering on excessive. Despite that effusive praise however, the woman warrior couldn't help but notice how his hand drifted to the leather satchel far more frequently than his food bowl. As a result, it was no surprise when, a little later, he'd ended up slumped back against the rock wall of the shelter, burping comfortably. His eyes glazed.

Liath Luachra dished a second portion of the stew to Bran and Rónán and poured the remaining dregs into her own bowl. Chewing listlessly on the tasteless concoction, she glanced across the fire to where Feoras had fallen asleep. His soft snores prompted the boys to stare at him in wonder.

'We should rest too,' Liath Luachra told them. 'There's work to be done in the morning.'

'Are we not leaving for Ráth Bládhma?' asked Rónán, eager to get home after so many days of unexpected adventure. He rubbed tiredly at his eyes as he attempted to stifle a yawn. 'The backpacks are full. We need only break camp to leave at first light.'

'We are,' she confirmed. 'But first there's a new task to complete.'

'A new task?'

'We'll be constructing a litter.'

This time, Rónán looked at her in wide-eyed surprise.

'A litter? Why do we need a litter?'

'Because Feoras must be carried to Ráth Bládhma.'

Both boys turned to look at the snoring figure and then back at Liath Luachra.

'He's hardly so insensible he can't walk tomorrow,' Bran protested.

Liath Luachra rolled a shrug off one shoulder. 'Perhaps not yet. But by tomorrow morning he will. I added a sleeping draught to the *uisce beatha* he's been drinking. I may have been overgenerous in my measures, but it'll do to keep him sleeping.' She frowned at the two boys. 'Potential friend or no, we'll not be offering any stranger the knowing of the route to Ráth Bládhma.'

Chapter Eight

They continued travelling west for the remainder of the day, keeping to higher ground and the dense sections of forest to reduce the risk of being observed. The raiders had been and gone and done their bloody business but that didn't mean they weren't still out there, seeking further lives to take, further corpses to desecrate. Fiacail certainly seemed to think so. Troubled by the slaughter at the farmlet, he remained uncharacteristically taciturn for the remainder of the afternoon. Having seen the raiders' handiwork up close for himself, Demne could hardly blame him.

That evening the travellers camped in a deep, moss-strewn gully where, unwilling to risk a fire, they feasted on the last of the now-hardened tubers from Trá Mór. When Demne retired to his sleeping roll, the Seiscenn Uairbhaoil warrior stayed up, sharpening the blades of *Folamh Dearg* and *Dord Fiacail*, his two long-handled battle axes. Distressed by the carnage he'd witnessed, but drained from the rigours of their journey, the sound of the whetstone against metal proved an unexpectedly soporific lullaby for the *Clann Baoiscne* youth, one that helped him drift off to sleep with surprising ease.

That night he dreamed of Inne Danu again, an almost identical replay of the dreams he'd been experiencing over the course of the previous nights. This time however, that reverie was accompanied by an odd, disembodied murmur and unrelated images of burned buildings and headless, bloodied corpses. Troubled by the nightmare, the youth instinctively plunged deeper in his slumber, sinking to that innermost oblivion where even the darkest visions do not stir. There, he slept soundly till morning.

The following day the travellers continued due west, penetrating even deeper into the Great Wild. For the most part, the character of the land remained unchanged, forest broken by occasional stretches of marsh, patches of wild grass or buckled hills that were intermittently spattered with bare rocks and stunted trees. Four days passed in a similar vein, with little encounter or experience of note and for that the two travellers were grateful.

On their seventeenth night since leaving the coast, they camped on a scrap of long grass that ran parallel to the bank of a fast-flowing river and which overlooked a narrow strand of gritty sand, a site chosen to catch the last flickers of the fading sunlight. Seventy paces upstream, the river cascaded through several rocky channels, creating a cacophony of hollow gurgles and splashes that competed in volume with the loud twitter of birdlife from the surrounding forest.

Demne listened to that discordant cacophony as he cleared a patch of verdant grass to make a fire, only to be surprised when he discovered a ring of blackened stones already in position beneath it. Fortunately, the absence of ash and the choking overgrowth indicated that a fire hadn't been made there for a very long time.

Given their limited supplies, that night's meal was a spartan affair of hard bread softened in a stew of wild mushrooms and washed down with river water. Licking the last of the sauce from his fingers, Fiacail belched loudly and proposed a hunt for fresh meat the following morning.

Demne retired to bed to find his dreams haunted once again by visions from Inne Danu. This time, however, the clearing with the silver spring was empty. There was no sign of the young woman, no burned-out buildings or bloodied bodies, but he could still hear the same drone of the disembodied murmur he'd heard over the previous nights. Too indistinct to make sense of, he simply ignored it and folded into sleep.

He woke late the next morning, surprised to find he'd slept through the emerging dawn. A thick smear of grey light already stained the eastern sky and on the far side of the campfire, Fiacail's blanket lay rumpled and empty. The javelins absent from the loops on his backpack confirmed the Seiscenn Uairbhaoil man had made an early start to the morning's hunt and had chosen to let the exhausted Demne sleep on.

Disengaging from his own snarled blanket, Demne slowly got to his feet. Reaching up to pluck a twig from a nearby branch, he used it to scrape the morning film from his teeth as he clambered awkwardly down to the little strand. There, tossing the twig aside, he undressed and waded slowly into the river. Despite the pleasant weather, the water was stingingly cold. Ignoring the icy bite of it, he eased further into the current until the water had reached his waist then rinsed the worst of the previous day's grime from his body.

The glacial water and the chill of the breeze against his wet skin eventually drove him back to shore. Regaining the strand, he found his limbs numb and clumsy from the cold and goosepimples breaking out on his skin. With nothing to dry himself, he simply pulled on his leggings and was about to shrug into his tunic when a distant sound from the forest caused him to stiffen in alarm.

The raiders!

Dropping to the sand, he scuttled forward to the shelter of the bank, concealing himself below the lip of it and listening keenly as he searched the trees for any trace of movement. For a long time, despite his best efforts, the youth heard nothing but the whisper of wind through the leaves, the gurgle of the river and the warble of birdsong. He wondered briefly whether the noise might have been caused by Fiacail but quickly discounted the possibility. If the *Ua Baoiscne* warrior was on the hunt, he was unlikely to be anywhere in the immediate environs.

As the youth continued to crouch at the riverbank, he remained alert for any noise that sounded out of the ordinary but heard nothing that sounded in any way suspicious. Eventually, after an extended period, he'd just about come to the conclusion he'd imagined it when it sounded again: an indistinct noise, so faint he had to concentrate to be certain it was real.

When the noise abruptly faded again, Demne scuttled from the shelter of the riverbank, scrambling back to the campsite where he retrieved his knife and two of the javelins from his backpack. Feeling more reassured now that he had his weapons to hand, the youth sank to a squat and listened. Once again however, there was nothing but the natural sounds of the forest to be heard.

Although he knew he should wait for Fiacail's return, curiosity drove him to follow the bank upriver, the most likely route for the sounds to have reached him, given the thickness of the surrounding forest. Negotiating the riverbank proved to be something of a challenge, however. At first, it ran smoothly enough around the bend from where the camp was located. After eighty paces or so, it quickly became clogged with a great growth of rowan trees that encroached directly over the water. Burdened by their large trunks, certain sections of the bank had fallen away entirely, creating mucky logjams that were just too hazardous to get through.

Fortunately, for the most part Demne was able to bypass them by heading inland, circumventing the obstacles until the trees had thinned out and he could return to the river. At last, to his relief, the terrain flattened out and the forest became far easier to traverse.

As he followed the river, the *Ua Baoiscne* youth regularly paused to listen and although the snippets of sound increased in regularity, some peculiar characteristic of the local terrain meant the volume and timbre fluctuated wildly. At times, the sound would wane completely. Other times it would increase to the point where he could almost distinguish voices or grunts, sharp smacking noises and what sounded like an occasional cheer.

Passing through a cluster of oaks choked with undergrowing clumps of fern, Demne suddenly found himself at the treeline of that section of the forest. Extending out from the trees was a rectangular section of grassy flatland, hemmed in on the left by a narrow lake and, on the right, by a low ridge that protruded from the treeline eighty paces north of his own position. Running parallel to the lake for several hundred paces, it had an impressive stone hillfort at its furthermost tip. Set in the base of that stone enclosure was a single gateway with a wooden gate. A steeply curving pathway descended from the gateway to the grassy flat below.

It was on that flat that Demne discovered the source of the sounds he'd been hearing in the forest up to that point; a rough game of *iománaíocht* taking place just adjacent to the lake. Encouraged by an audience of four cheering girls, eight youths were dashing about with enthusiasm, if limited skill. Wielding their *camáin* – the long, ash sticks – like weapons, they produced loud woody 'smacks' each time the sticks connected.

Surprised at the presence of another settlement so far out in the wilderness, Demne retreated into the trees and tapped his lower lip as he thought the situation through. He felt a strong obligation to warn the settlement of the nearby massacre but the general hostility with which such isolated communities tended to treat strangers meant he retained a self-interested wariness about revealing himself. There was also the possibility, although he considered it unlikely, that the occupants of this settlement were responsible for the destruction at the farm.

Undecided, he turned his attention to the game for a time, noting the subtle difference of the youths' playing style to that at Seiscenn Uairbhaoil. In age, he estimated the players ranged from between ten to sixteen years but most of the play seemed to be dictated by the eldest player, a tall, red-haired youth with a stocky, well-built frame. Watching him, Demne had the growing impression this individual was someone of authority within the community – or, more likely, the son of someone in authority. The youth carried himself with an unmistakeable sense of entitlement, arrogantly setting out the pattern of play and making the final decision on any judgements. Although he didn't play with any great skill, his size and maturity meant he was able to compete equally with some of the smaller, more competent players. On one occasion, when even this physical advantage failed him, he abused his authority to change the rules to achieve the result he desired. That created some evident resentment among one or two of the younger boys, but the other players seemed to go along with it. The girls, meanwhile, cheered his accomplishments loudly whenever he displayed even the slightest success.

Concluding that there was less risk in sharing news of the massacre with these younger players than the older occupants of the hillfort, Demne leaned his javelins at an angle against the nearest tree trunk, removed the knife scabbard from his belt and placed it on the ground alongside them. Standing upright, he took a deep breath, stepped out of the trees and started walking briskly towards the players.

Because of the participants' absorption in their game, Demne made twenty paces before his presence was noted by one of the girls. She quickly pointed him out to her three friends, and all turned to stare. Noting the girls' sudden silence, the boys looked up from their game and they too spotted the approaching stranger.

At first, startled, the players stared at the newcomer in surprise but then, as one, they advanced upon him, spreading swiftly around him in a rough semi-circle and wielding their *cammáin* in a menacing manner.

'Who are you?' the red-haired youth demanded. 'Who are you to come skulking through *Muinntir Galla* territory?' He glanced over Demne's shoulder to see if there were any other intruders hidden in the forest treeline.

Demne held his hands up, palms outwards, in a placatory manner.

'I wasn't skulking. I come only to warn you of raiders in the area. A farm four days to the east of here was recently attacked and its occupants massacred.'

To his surprise, the red-haired youth laughed openly at that. 'The day *Muinntir Galla* fear raiders is the day our tribe is done,' he scoffed.

'But, I've seen th- '

'What tribe are you?' demanded a sallow, athletic-looking youth whose hair was bound up in a top-knot.

Although irritated by the boorish interruption, Demne managed to hold his temper.

'I am *éclann*.'

The lie slipped easily enough from his tongue, nevertheless he found his anger rising as he saw the look of contempt that appeared in their eyes. The red-haired youth, in particular, seemed to find it a matter of great amusement. 'And is there anything else the *éclann* would like to say before we run him off our land?'

'I'd like to play.'

The statement, offered quietly, wasn't something the *Muinntir Galla* youths were expecting and their surprise was reflected on their features. Uncertain how to respond, they defaulted to the established hierarchy, turning their eyes to the red-haired youth to await his lead. Confident in the knowledge that he alone controlled any decision, he eyed Demne with an exaggerated air of disapproval.

'We don't allow any passing *éclann* the prestige of playing with *Muinntir Galla*. But perhaps …' He stroked his chin in obvious mimicry of some elder relative. 'Do you have any skill at the game?'

'My *camán* skills are matchless.'

The brevity and sheer assurance of the response prompted a disgruntled frown. Watching the older youth, Demne could tell he wanted no part of some stranger butting in on his personal fiefdom but, conscious that others were watching, had to go through the motions of giving the request genuine consideration. Offering Demne a magnanimous smile, he tossed the *sliotar* – the ball – up and down in one hand as he pretended to think it through.

'Matchless, is it?' he chuckled sourly at last. 'You have some gall. I'm tempted to teach you and your self-judged greatness a strict lesson. Alas, we already have two teams of four players. Your presence would make our games uneven.'

'You tell him, Abbán!' the sallow boy cried out.

Demne ignored the outburst, an exercise in arse-licking if he'd ever heard one.

'I have more skill than any two *Muinntir Galla* players combined. Take two extra players for your team and offer me two others as support and we'll still overcome you in any match between us.'

Abbán kept his smile but Demne noted a discernible narrowing of the eyes at his challenge. An eruption of giggling from the girls on the mound did little to assist in reducing the tension. The red-haired youth glanced quickly sideways in their direction and when he spoke again there was a discernible frostiness beneath the earlier bonhomie.

'I'm afraid your request is not to my liking, *éclann*. You stroll into *Muinntir Galla* territory, as welcome as a stew fart in a crowded hut, you interrupt our fun with fantasies of menace and demand to join our game as though it were your right.'

He shook his head, as though bewildered by the sheer scale of the intruder's impudence.

'Best you leave now before I have our warriors set on you.'

There was a muttering of support from the other boys but Demne looked down at the ground, shifting his weight from one foot to the other, allowing himself a lopsided smirk that the older youth was bound to see. He knew that he was overreaching, that he should turn and simply walk away. He'd done his best to alert these people, but they clearly were in no mood to heed his warnings. Nevertheless, Abbán's overbearing self-importance had irked him and he couldn't help himself from antagonising him further.

'Perhaps it's simply a game with a superior player that causes you unease. Perhaps *Muinntir Galla* can't bear the prospect of a real challenge, of losing to an *éclann* who exceeds them in skill. Play three scores to prove me wrong. The first to attain three scores can be said to have taken the field.'

Abbán's face hardened. With the challenge now directly thrown at him, he couldn't back down without losing face in front of the other players and the girls he was trying to impress. This time he regarded Demne with open hostility, all earlier pretence of amiability melted away.

'Very well, Matchless One. We'll see.' He looked towards two lean, athletic-looking boys who had their *camán* slung casually across their shoulders, one of them the sallow boy who'd called out in his support earlier. 'Dathal, Áed. You'll come join my team.'

The players acknowledged the instruction with a nod. As both moved to join him, the red-haired youth turned to face two smaller boys who were standing together off to the side.

127

'Lennán and Art. You'll play with the *éclann*. Given his matchless skills, he'll probably have no need of your support but be sure to offer your ample abilities if sought.'

A subtle ripple of laughter passed through the other boys in Abbán's team then spread to the girls sitting at the edge of the playing field. The two boys assigned to Demne sullenly stalked over to take up position alongside him. Scowling and tightly gripping their *camán*, they were visibly unhappy, although it was hard to tell whether it due to Abbán's mockery or the insult of being assigned to play with an *éclann*. Either way, Demne couldn't help but notice that both looked to be the youngest and least athletic of the entire group.

With both teams selected, they walked up the grassy stretch of the playing field, stopping approximately mid-way between the two *báire* – scoring stones. Abbán gestured towards the stone set into the grass about fifty paces north of where they were standing. 'That's our *báire*,' he said shortly. He turned to indicate the stone to the south 'And that, that is yours.'

This latter stone was far closer to the mound where the girls were sitting, a revealing decision on Abbán's part. He assumed that was where the greater part of the game's activity would take place and he wanted the girls to have an unhindered view of the outsider's humiliation.

While Demne was considering the terrain where they'd be playing, Abbán advanced to thrust a *camán* and *sliotar* into his hand.

'As newcomer, you have first possession,' he said loudly, then lowered his voice and whispered too quietly for the others to hear. 'For all the good it'll do once I lay into you.'

'*A bhroghais!* Demne snapped back. You cow's afterbirth.

With that, he moved swiftly out of immediate earshot, undercutting the other youth's ability to respond with any further comment that wouldn't be audible to the wider group. Abbán's pupils flared with anger but, conscious of the other players, he swallowed it quickly, clearly deciding to bide his time until the opportunity for vengeance presented itself.

And Demne didn't doubt there'd be plenty of that once the game had begun.

He hefted the *sliotar* in his hand to get a sense of its weight. Every *sliotar* he'd ever played with over the years had been manufactured from different materials: wood, woven straw, furze roots, leather, braided hair from livestock and many others. Those different constituents usually resulted in substantial variances in weight, evenness and other physical characteristics that tended to have a real impact on how it was best played. This *sliotar*, made from cow hair braided around some spherical core object, was impressively compact, the stitching tight, the plaited strands of cow hair dry and rough against his palm. Tossing it up and down in his left hand, he felt a decent weight to it.

Good to throw, then. Less so to kick.

Certainly, the *sliotar* was far superior to the *camán* he'd been given. Examining it closely, he gave a snort of disgust. The curved *bas* – the wide, flat section of wood at the end of the stick used to hit or carry the *sliotar* – had partially rotted away and had almost as little surface area left to it as the shaft of the stick itself. Demne dropped the *sliotar* onto it, bouncing it up and down several times to get a feel for its play.

Looking up and down the field, Demne sniffed, calculating the distances and potential angles of approach. The rules of the game were relatively simple and it was that combination of simplicity and physical prowess that had always been its main appeal for him. To score, you simply had to strike the *báire* of the opposing team with the *sliotar*. To get the *sliotar* to the *báire* you could lash it up-field with the *camán*, you could run with it balanced on the tip of your *camán* but you could also simply kick it or throw it. Anything, as long as it hit the *báire*.

The rules for interception were just as loose. Tackles, shouldering, tripping your opponent with your foot or your *camán* were equally acceptable. Kicking someone or hitting them with your hand were less so but when games became heated or frenzied, such play was inevitable. As one of the youngest players At Seiscenn Uairbhaoil, Demne had initially come off worse with respect to injuries despite a natural talent for the game. That had all changed dramatically, after he'd started to hand back some of the punishment he was being offered.

Although it was generally frowned on to strike an opponent with the *camán*, Deme suspected that wouldn't overly trouble the *Muinntir Galla* team in his case. Indeed, their unexpected decision to offer him possession of the *sliotar* to commence the game, suggested that was exactly what they had in mind.

Taking up position at the centre of the field, Demne stood facing Abbán and his sallow-skinned companion, separated from them by a distance of five paces. Both of his immediate opponents stood poised to launch into action, *camán* gripped tightly in preparation for the initial strike. From the corners of his eyes, Demne could also see his two younger *Muinntir Galla* team mates standing nervously on either side to his rear.

With a grin at Abbán, the *Clann Baoiscne* youth turned to the boy on his right. '*Hé*', he said, pretending to fling the *sliotar* towards him. As his young teammate squawked in alarm, Abbán and companion sprang into action, lunging forward at an angle to intercept the movement of the *sliotar,* belatedly realising it was a feint.

That brief heartbeat of uncertainty was all Demne needed. Charging forward, he shoulder-slammed Abbán, knocking the youth clean off his feet even as he barged past him. Through the initial line of defence, he broke into a sprint and with that head start and his natural running ability, there was simply no catching him. By the time he'd reached the *báire,* the other players were several steps behind and just to provoke them, he waited until they were almost on him before slamming the *sliotar* triumphantly against the stone.

'Hup, hup!'

The excited yells of his two team-mates, still lagging several steps behind the others, suggested they'd never been on the winning side before. Roaring and yelling, they raced into the larger group of their opponents who'd come to a resentful halt around the *báire* and leapt enthusiastically into the air.

'*Tá an báire linn! Tá an báire linn!*' We have the match!

Several paces down the field, Abbán had finally struggled back onto his feet. He stood there unsteadily, facing them with a scowl. Demne suspected it was only the presence of the watching girls that prevented him from being attacked on the spot. Such social niceties, of course, wouldn't protect him for much longer.

Somehow keeping a hold on his temper, the leader of the *Muinntir Galla* boys gruffly gestured for the teams to line up again. As they did so, Demne spotted him whisper to the sallow-skinned youth before, once again, taking up position directly opposite him.

Demne cheekily juggled the ball in his hand. 'Would another player help?' he asked. 'I can probably spare one.'

Abbán was so angry, he actually snarled. Following that involuntary outburst however, he glanced worriedly towards the mound where the girls had now risen to their feet to watch the game with greater interest. After the loudness of their earlier cheers, their sudden silence was striking.

Demne used that moment of inattention to strike the *sliotar*, tossing it into the air and then, using his full strength, whacked it with the partial *bas* of the *camán*. Despite its limitations, he angled the strike effectively, sending the *sliotar* almost vertically upwards into the air between the two teams: a small, faint circle growing even smaller as it rose towards the clouded sky.

The strike was such an odd one, making so little distance down the length of the field that for a moment most of the opposing team simply stood staring up at the steadily climbing *sliotar*. As Demne expected however, Abbán and the sallow-skinned youth had no real interest in the ball. Ignoring the *sliotar* completely, they charged straight for him.

Fortunately, the two players weren't adept at working together. Abbán came roaring in at an angle, swinging his *camán* in a manner that obstructed his companion from instigating his own assault and allowing Demne to deal with them individually. Initially pulling back to avoid a wild swing from Abbán's *camán*, he then swiftly stepped forward and thrust with his stick, slamming the thin wedge of the *bas* into the fleshy piece of skin below the red-haired youth's nose.

Abbán let out a squeal and tumbled back onto the ground, hands clawing at his face. The sallow-skinned youth tried to lunge in but found himself obliged to step around his screaming companion to line up a strike. By then, Demne had already positioned himself to sweep in with a low swing of his own *camán*, striking the second youth squarely on the left shin. This time it was Dathal's turn to shriek in pain.

Alerted by the shrieks of pain, the other players who'd been standing back to wait for the *sliotar* to fall, looked on with horror at fallen teammates. Cowed by the fierce expression on Demne's face, they involuntarily stepped back as he moved forward to get the now descending *sliotar*. Unchallenged, he caught it perfectly in his right hand and took off for the southern *báire*. This time, no-one else followed. Arriving at the *báire*, he hit it with the *sliotar* and looked back towards the other players.

Up on the mound, in an unexpected display of tribal fickleness, the girls had started cheering the newcomer's accomplishment.

'*An Fionn abú! An Fionn abú!*' Victory to the Blond One! Victory to the Blond One!

Once again, Demne watched the leader of the *Muinntir Galla* youths slowly and laboriously clamber to his feet. Struggling to remain upright, he turned to look in Demne's direction and the blood trickling down from a split upper lip only highlighted the fury in his eyes.

Meanwhile, a bustle of movement up on the hillfort drew Demne's eye to where three men had emerged from the gateway. Standing at the entrance to the hillfort, the trio were looking down at the playing field and their gazes seemed to be fixed primarily in his direction. Clearly, drawn by the noise, they'd noticed a stranger amongst the other players and were now trying to work out who he was.

Abbán too must have noticed their arrival for it incited him to a sudden paroxysm of excitement. Pointing one hand at Demne, he let out a sudden roar. 'Outsider! An Outsider. He's an *éclann* spy!'

The *Muinntir Galla* youth's bellow prompted immediate activity up at the gateway. One of the men ran inside to alert the other hillfort occupants. The two others grabbed javelins and started hurriedly down the path towards the playing field. Recognising an opportunity to make up for the grievous loss of face, Abbán pointed at Demne again.

'The warriors are coming to take him! Stop him! Stop him before he escapes!'

Taken aback by this new and unexpected development, the *Muinntir Galla* boys stared uncertainly at the youth they'd just been playing with. Whipped up by Abbán's hysterical urgings however, and conditioned from birth to tribal loyalty, they reacted unthinkingly. With a great ululation, they charged across the grass towards the *Ua Baoiscne* youth.

Startled, Demne glanced worriedly from the approaching youths to the incoming hillfort warriors, suddenly conscious of the seriousness predicament in which he'd placed himself. Coming at him from the east, the *Muinntir Galla* youths were effectively blocking his route back to the eastern treeline, the area of easiest escape and the spot where he'd left his weapons. Given the speed with which the

132

hillfort warriors were descending meanwhile, it was clear they'd intercept him easily if he attempted to make a run for the west.

The lake!

With a sickening sensation, Demne knew there wasn't another option.

Spinning on his heel, he made a dash for the shore, stumbling into the water and wading out until he was almost waist deep. Diving underwater, he swam with powerful strokes, surfacing about ten paces from shore and then swimming with a strong sidestroke until he'd put another twenty-five paces between himself and the bank. By then, the other youths had reached the water and, caught up in the excitement of the chase, were launching themselves into the lake to swim in pursuit. Propelled by his own fury and the enthusiastic support of his comrades, Abbán was leading the way, splashing wildly in front of the others, his lack of technique more than made up for through a desire for vengeance. Back at the ridge meanwhile, the hillfort warriors had just reached the flat ground and were little more than two hundred paces from the water's edge.

Pausing briefly to catch his breath and assess the level of pursuit, Demne wiped water from his eyes. Glancing anxiously towards the eastern side of the lake, he caught sight of the bend where its waters funnelled through a set of high rocks to feed the fast-flowing eastern river, the same river leading back to where he and Fiacail had set camp. Weighing up the time it would take to swim to those rocks and for the approaching *Muinntir Galla* youths to reach him, Demne knew the sensible choice would be to start swimming for the rocks immediately. Nevertheless, some mulish obstinacy prompted him to remain where he was.

Treading water, he watched the *Muinntir Galla* youths splashing towards him, their floundering and chaotic swimming styles appearing to create more spray than progress. There was enormous variation in ability amongst them, the four older, stronger youths far in advance while the four younger boys lagged well behind.

Waiting until the nearest youths were almost upon him, Demne suddenly duck-dived, kicking strongly downwards until he'd reached the lake's shallow bottom. There, he grasped hold of a rock to anchor himself, knowing that he'd be practically invisible from above with the dark lake bottom all around him. Looking up however, he could just make out four blurred and flickering silhouettes against the brightness of the surface.

Pushing off against the rock with his feet, he used the momentum to drive himself upward until he was hanging in the water just below the *Muinntir Galla* youths, who'd now come to halt and were floating aimlessly, most likely looking around and trying to work out where he'd gone. Pushing up at an angle with four strong strokes, he positioned himself below the figure he though to recognise as Abbán. Grabbing the youth's ankles, he used his own body mass to tug the boy underwater.

Panicked by the unexpected assault from below, Abbán started thrashing madly and attempted to kick free but Demne held on tight, dragging him deeper and deeper. Finally, feeling the pressure building in his own lungs, he let go and started kicking upwards, back to the surface.

He erupted from the water with a great whooping inhalation, directly in front of a startled Dathal. By then, frightened at the disappearance of their leader and the superiority of their opponent's swimming ability, most of the *Muinntir Galla* youths had already started their retreat back to shore. Dathal, who'd clearly been expecting his leader, stared at him in astonishment and was opening his mouth to call out, when Demne launched himself at the youth, grabbing him by the head and pushing him under.

Unconfident in the water, Dathal immediately panicked and struggled to break free but the *Clann Baoiscne* youth refused to release him as their combined weight continued to drag him down. Thrashing madly, Dathal's struggles grew increasingly frantic until, fearing to drown him, Demne relented and released his hold, pushing the youth away with his legs as he too kicked upward.

Breaking the surface, he sucked in another lungful of air, wiping the water from his eyes as he attempted to work out what was happening. By then, all the remaining members of the pursuing party had started back for shore, terrified at the prospect of being dragged underwater. Led by the recently resurfaced Abbán, three of the youths were already close to shore while four others had already scrambling desperately onto the bank, impeding the progress of the hillfort warriors who'd just arrived and were attempting to get around them.

As a wide-eyed and terrified Dathal resurfaced to his right, Demne took advantage of the confusion to start swimming in the direction of the eastern river bend. He'd made about ten paces before the first javelin came spinning overhead and struck the water five or six paces in front of him. Moments later, a second missile hit the water to his right, close enough for the spray from the impact to reach him.

Conscious that the critical threat wasn't from the missiles, given the small target he made in the water, Demne ignored them and focussed on swimming, increasing the strength and reach of his strokes, gasping in as much air as he could and increasing the power to his kicks. He had to reach the bend before the *Muinntir Galla* warriors for there the increased current from the narrower channel would whip him to safety. If they succeeded in attaining the bend before him however, he'd be in trouble, making an easy target in the much smaller body of water.

Another pair of javelins struck the water nearby but then the casters must have worked out what he was doing for no further missiles followed. No doubt, they too were now making for the bend, racing along the lakeshore to get there before him.

Fortunately, by then he could already feel the tug of the strengthening current and, glancing up, realised that he was far closer to the bend than he'd thought. Before he even had a chance to appreciate that fact, he felt himself being whisked forwards and, moments later, was swallowed up into a wild froth of white-water, flushed past the high rocks and sucked around the bend, out of sight of the lake now somewhere to his rear. Whipped helplessly around by the surging current, Demne was plunged underwater. Struggling to the surface, he sucked in a lungful of damp air and water, conscious that the current here was far more dangerous than he'd expected. Water emptying in from the lake and forced through a far narrower conduit, meant it was difficult to avoid being sucked under and into the churn of the current, and his efforts to remain on the surface meant he was rapidly tiring. Choking on a fresh mouthful of water, he barely had time to draw breath through his nose before he was pushed under again and in the surging white, it became impossible to see.

The next time he surfaced was by chance rather than design and the youth was greatly relieved to find that he'd been driven towards the riverbank. Kicking madly, he attempted to slide closer in order to grasp some of the overhanging vegetation and pull himself ashore. Try though he might however, the flow of water whipped him past far too quickly and those shrubs and branches he managed to catch hold of were either torn from his grasp or ripped away in his hands.

Increasingly alarmed and struggling for breath, the *Clann Baoiscne* youth was starting to panic when something suddenly caught his hair, wrenching his head back and jerking him to a painful halt. Before he could even work out what was going on, he felt himself being roughly hauled out of the water and moments later cast flat onto the riverbank. Coughing and spluttering, he stared up in bewilderment, astounded to recognise the imposing bulk of Fiacail mac Codhna.

Drawing on some inner strength, Demne forced himself to roll onto his side. Before he could try to push himself upright however, the Seiscenn Uairbhaoil man had caught the collar of his *léine* and yanked him to his feet, half-carrying and half-dragging him away from the bank and deeper into the forest. Ten or twenty paces into the trees, he was unceremoniously dropped into a clump of ferns at the foot of a twisted oak.

Befuddled and confused, Demne could only watch as the big man briefly disappeared again, returning at a run a few heartbeats later only to lunge into the ferns and lie flat on the ground alongside him. Glancing over at the *Ua Baoiscne* youth, he winked and held a finger over his lips.

Moments later, Demne heard the erratic rhythm of rapidly approaching feet, a pattern broken only by rough yells and several excited yips.

The warriors! They're on us!

Peering through the lower fern stems, Demne spotted several shadowed pairs of feet thundering past, little more than a few paces from where he and Fiacail lay hidden. Lying still, they waited, watching tersely as groups and individual warriors rushed by. At first, the pursuers moved in a single direction – downstream. After a time, unable to find any trace of the fugitive, the *Muinntir Galla* warriors started moving back and forth along the bank, beating the bushes in an attempt to flush him out.

Fortunately, the vegetation around the waterway was dense and their attempts were somewhat half-hearted. By the time they'd backtracked to the area where Demne and Fiacail were hidden, the warriors' efforts at searching had become more perfunctory and they

136

seemed to have accepted the fact that the mysterious young stranger had eluded them. Soon, they started to drift away, headed back in the direction of the grassy clearing and the ridge with the hillfort.

Two of them remained behind however, standing close together less than eight paces from where the fugitives lay concealed. Peering through the fern stalks, Demne immediately recognised one of the distant figures as Abbán. The other was an unfamiliar, scar-faced warrior with long brown hair, a heavy beard and facial markings. Despite those markings, the similar facial features left little doubt that he and Abbán were related.

Concealed within the ferns, Demne and Fiacail were able to hear everything the pair said. From the tone of the conversation, it was evident the warrior was unhappy with what had transpired, for he questioned Abbán harshly about the *éclann* who'd appeared in their midst. Abbán's evasive explanation of events omitted certain details, giving the impression that Demne had simply emerged from the forest and that it had been his aggressive insistence on joining their play that had caused the game to descend into violence.

It appeared, however, that the *Muinntir Galla* youth had a history of falsehoods, for as his tale progressed, the warrior regarded him with an expression of increasing cynicism and thinly veiled disgust.

'So, you're saying …' he interrupted at last. 'This … This *éclann* simply wandered out of the forest, demanded to be included in your game and then not only proceeded to best a superior number of players but slip through your fingers when you attempted to stop him.'

Abbán, growing conscious of the implausible nature of his tale, looked down at his feet and said no more. The warrior however was having none of it.

'I asked a question of you. I await your answer.'

The youth took a deep breath. 'Yes,' he said in a grudging tone.

The warrior made no response. Instead, he turned about and looked up and down the treeline, his gaze momentarily appearing to come to rest on that clump of fern beneath the giant oak where the travellers lay hidden. Watching the bearded man through a tiny gap in the ferns, Demne knew they couldn't possibly be seen, nevertheless it was an effort to resist the urge to get up and make a run for it.

Finally, with a sigh, the warrior turned back to the red-haired youth.

'You are my son Abbán, but even as son to the *rí*, there's no guarantee you'll succeed me one day. If you wish to lead *Muinntir Galla*, you do not have the luxury of tolerating humiliation, of losing face. You must uphold your reputation without mercy, destroy any who'd threaten to undermine it.'

He paused.

'Is it truly your wish to lead *Muinntir Galla*?'

Once again, the youth gave a grudging, almost resentful, nod.

'Then you should have dispatched the *éclann*. Bloodily. The moment he offered insult.'

The bearded man turned his head and spat upon the ground.

'Unless you weren't man enough to succeed in that task either.'

'This *éclann* was not one to be easily dispatched,' Abbán protested. 'None could have succeeded in such a task. He was fast. Unnaturally fast. I've never seen agility like it. And that blond hair ...' He paused to regard his father intently. 'It may be that the youth was *Gifted*.'

Demne glanced over to where Fiacail was grinning broadly at him, the curve of his teeth gleaming white through the gloom of the undergrowth. The youth rolled his eyes in disgust, a reaction evidently shared by Abbán's father, for when he spoke again his voice was heavy with sarcasm.

'And did this ... *Gifted* athlete offer you his name?'

The red-haired youth shook his head. 'No. Although the girls called him "An Fionn" – The Blond One.'

'Fionn.' The *rí* of *Muinntir Galla* repeated the word dubiously, rolling it around in his mouth like a berry with a bitter aftertaste. 'How did this Fionn look?'

'He had my age on him. A fit, fair-haired youth.'

The *rí* grunted without expression. 'If this Fionn shows up again,' he said. 'Then you know what you have to do.'

Shaking his head in unveiled disgust, the warrior started back in the direction of the settlement. Abbán, glancing fearfully at the surrounding forest, hurried swiftly after him.

Lying in the bushes, Fiacail and Demne watched the pair head west before they disappeared into the gloom of the forest. When sufficient time had passed, Fiacail rose onto his knees and peered about. Satisfied that it was safe, he slowly got to his feet.

'Here,' he said suddenly, reaching down to gather some implements from among the ferns and then handing them to Demne. 'You appear to have mislaid these.'

Recognising his knife and javelins, Demne winced in embarrassment, but the Seiscenn Uairbhaoil man gave no indication that he'd noticed. Still looking in the direction of the settlement, he shook his head in mock bewilderment. *'Bhfuel, a Fionn,'* he said, his voice thick with amusement. 'Chaos, violence, pursuit and threats of retribution ...' He grinned broadly. 'It's a good thing you return to Ráth Bládhma. Clearly there's little more I can teach you.'

Chapter Nine

It was early afternoon when a shout of alarm rang out from the ramparts of Ráth Bládhma. Focussed on treating an injured calf down in the central *lis*, it took a moment for the urgency of that call to penetrate Bodhmhall's concentration. Startled, the *bandraoi* twisted about, staring towards the gateway, hoping against hope it had been sounded in error. Up on the stone structure however, Cónán was gesticulating frantically for her to join him.

'Bodhmhall, come! There's movement to the west.'

Bounding to her feet, the *bandraoi* took off at a run, headed for the ladder to the right of the gateway. Behind her, the dark-haired Cumann gaped after her, hands still grasping the legs of the trembling calf. Realising that Bodhmhall wasn't likely to be returning under the circumstances, she released the animal and hurriedly clambered to her feet as well.

Scrambling up the uneven rungs of the ladder to the rampart walkway, the *bandraoi* stumbled hastily to the palisades where Cónán and the Tóla were already staring towards the western treeline. 'Where's Gnathad?' she demanded furiously. 'She was supposed to provide warning before anyone breached the valley!'

Too preoccupied and too troubled to answer, the curly-haired Cónán could only shake his head helplessly in response.

Following the young warrior's gaze, Bodhmhall scrutinised the western terrain but the uneven ground, the haze, and the overcast sky made it difficult to see anything. Finally, just as she was beginning to wonder at the validity of the alarm, she saw it: a brief flicker of movement, barely visible against the shadow of the forest behind.

Aodhán's outside!

That sudden, belated realisation made Bodhmhall feel sick to the stomach. Just a little before noon, the young man had left to drive stragglers from the herd towards the safety of the eastern pastures with some of the settlement children. The unanticipated infiltration of Glenn Ceoch and the necessity of barring the gateway in response however, meant there was no chance of alerting them in time to return to the safety of the *ráth*.

Realising that there was nothing she could do to remedy that situation, the *bandraoi* pushed the issue from her mind. With the forthcoming defence of the *ráth*, she had enough to cope with and there was nothing to be done for anyone outside the ditch. Aodhán would have to fend for himself and the children. If luck was with him, he'd realise what was happening and conceal his group in the eastern woods. If the situation truly turned sour, there was also the option of leading his charges out of the valley to safety through the secret path at Gág na Muice – the Pig's Crack.

More importantly from her own perspective however, was that his absence meant they were one critical defender short on the palisades.

Mallacht ortsa, a Gnathad! A curse on you, Gnathad!

The bustling sounds of fevered activity rose up from the *lis* where Cumann, Morag and the other inhabitants were rushing to their assigned tasks and places, some preparing to defend the walls, others sealing the gateway entrance. Risking a moment to glance down, Bodhmhall was relieved to see that, despite the obvious alarm, everyone seemed to be carrying out their duties with no demonstrable signs of panic.

Beside her, Cónán roughly yanked one of the javelins free from the rack, twisting the wooden haft uncertainly in his hands as he stared out towards the unknown threat. Bodhmhall didn't need her *Gift* to tell the young warrior was worried. As one of the *ráth's* most longstanding inhabitants, in his sibling's absence the responsibility for its defence fell on his shoulders. Combat blooded some years earlier, she didn't doubt he'd stand firm to defend his home and family, but she also knew he lacked the more visceral battle competence of his brother. More concerning, however, was his lack of practical experience in leading a defence against a focussed group of raiders.

As she watched, the young warrior glanced uncertainly to where the wizened Tóla leaned casually against the upper pilings, grey eyes staring out to the west as he chewed on a tuber with almost bovine complacency. There'd be little advice coming from that particular direction unfortunately. Completely eccentric and mute through choice rather than through circumstance, Tóla was not one to suggest or propose, although he could usually be counted on to do as he was told.

Except when he disagreed, of course.

Returning her attention to the area where she'd spotted the flurry of movement, the *bandraoi* drew on her *Gift*, pulling up that underlayer of perception that allowed her to discern the presence of life. Through her eyes, the overcast gloom of the valley dulled even further. Almost immediately, the first flame of life-light flickered into view, in this case little more than a bright pinprick due to the distance involved. A moment later, a second flame appeared, then a third and a fourth, all shivering giddily as they advanced towards the settlement.

As she released her control of the *Gift*, and brightness seeped back over the valley, Bodhmhall heard Cónán shouting hoarsely for more javelins to be brought up to the rampart. She quickly reached over to grasp his wrist, causing him to spin around and stare at her in incomprehension.

'It's not necessary,' she said. 'There are four of them. Only four.'

Cónán continued to hold her eyes, his expression of incomprehension transforming abruptly to relief, then moving to a strained wariness.

'You're certain?'

'Yes.'

Releasing his wrist, Bodhmhall turned to look west over the pilings again. The newcomers, whoever they were, had now cut free of the shadow from the forest and although still some distance off, they were easier to distinguish on the open pasture. Peering intently at one of those distant figures, she stiffened, somehow knowing that …

'Grey One!'

The words came out involuntarily, a stuttering release from the keyed up tension churning her stomach over the previous days.

'It's the Grey One. And the boys. But …' She broke off, pulling up the veil of the *Gift* again to confirm what her eyes were telling her.

'There's a fourth flame. Someone's travelling with them.'

Intrigued, the two warriors stood beside her and continued to stare, joined a moment later by Ferchar. who'd temporarily left his post on the *ráth's* eastern curve to find out what was happening. All four however, were obliged to wait until the distant figures drew closer.

'That's Rónán out there in front,' Cónán declared after a time. This time the relief in his voice was audible and he even managed a nervous laugh. 'I recognise that feisty gamble.'

He lifted the flat of his hand above his eyes, squinting as he tried to make out the others. Renowned for having the best eyesight at Ráth Bládhma, the talent was a matter of some pride to him.

'The Grey One follows after him but she's moving oddly. She's …' He broke off in confusion, unsure what he was seeing.

'She's carrying a litter,' Bodhmhall explained, her insight facilitated by the lower placement and the regular movement of one of the life-flames between two of the others. 'She's carrying a litter with Bran. That's why they're running so awkwardly. The fourth person is on the litter.'

'Who is it?' the young warrior asked aloud but the question, of course, was moot. None of them had an answer.

Realising that the settlement's occupants were waiting anxiously for news, Cónán edged to the inner ledge of the rampart and called down to the others gathered there.'

'Rest easy. It's Liath Luachra and the boys.'

Even from the pilings, Bodhmhall could hear the sighs of relief, but she paid them no mind, focussing her full attention on the approaching travellers. Now mid-way across the grassy flat separating the *ráth* from the western treeline, their features had become more discernible, the exception, of course, the individual on the litter. As she regarded the approaching party, Bodhmhall felt a flicker of unease, the sight reminding her of a similar event fifteen years earlier, when Fiacail mac Codhna and his men had entered the valley bearing a similar litter. On that occasion, Liath Luachra had been the one being carried.

Who could it be?

A stranger? Out here in the Great Wild?

A solitary traveller in this isolation?

The *bandraoi* frowned, her relief now tinged with genuine confusion. Although tempted to draw on the *Gift* again, she refrained from doing so, conscious that it would probably be a waste of time. With one or two notable exceptions, the life-flames viewed using her *Gift* were visually indistinguishable from one another and even at a closer distance its use would offer little in terms of additional insight.

The *bandraoi* continued to watch therefore, her focus latching onto Rónán, who was running thirty paces ahead of the others. Spotting his comrades staring at him from up on the rampart, the boy stumbled to a halt and waved excitedly before twisting around to

143

verify that the other members of his party weren't lagging too far behind. Even at that distance it was easy to imagine his indecision, torn between the option of giving into his excitement and rushing ahead or staying in place until his friends caught up.

In the end, loyalty appeared to win out for the boy remained where he was, holding position with visible impatience until they were almost on him. As soon as they reached him however, he was off again, running slightly ahead but making sure to maintain his pace so that they were always close behind.

Bodhmhall moved to the rear of the walkway, calling down to Lí Bán and Morag. 'Unbar the gate and get some water. They'll be exhausted when they get here.'

She could hear the sound of the heavy wooden spar being shifted as she started back to the pilings and leaned against the solid wooden palisades. Out on the grassy flat, it was now obvious that despite their efforts, the burden of the litter was weighing the travellers down. Helpless and frustrated, she could do little to assist them apart from preparing to tend to their needs once they made it to the settlement.

As the travellers finally arrived to within thirty paces of the *ráth*, Bodhmhall turned her focus back to Liath Luachra and when the woman warrior glanced up at the walls, she was shaken by her jaded and beaten appearance. The Grey One looked utterly spent. Caked in mud, her eyes were smudged, her cheekbones protruded and her usually athletic frame had gone from lean to gaunt. Although close enough now that she couldn't have missed the presence of the *bandraoi* on the rampart, the Grey One made no sign of acknowledgement, dropping her eyes instead to line up for the traverse of the narrow causeway leading across the ditch to the gateway of the *ráth*.

Just paces from the ditch meanwhile, Rónán couldn't contain himself any longer and, deserting his fellow travellers, broke into a sprint. Storming across the causeway, he disappeared from the sight of those on the ramparts, as he charged into the stone passage below.

Caught up in the excitement of the travellers' return, Bodhmhall deserted her own position and scurried around to the nearest ladder. She'd just placed her foot on its upper rung when she saw the boy burst forth from the internal side of the passage and rush past the small crowd that had gathered there, to fling himself at his foster mother, Lí Bán.

144

Sliding down the creaking rung frame, the *bandraoi* landed on the pebbled surface of the *lis*. By the time she'd turned around Rónán had already pulled back from that enveloping embrace, and he beamed proudly at the white-haired woman, eyes bright with excitement.

'A *díbhearg*, mother! We rescued a traveller from a *díbhearg* and ...'

He broke off at the muffled rustle of Liath Luachra and Bran making their way through the gateway passage, the side of the litter scraping briefly against the stones as the woman warrior appeared into daylight, visibly struggling under its weight. Emerging into the *lis* proper, her face lined with strain, she and Bran also ignored the cheers and greetings, staggering towards the now extinguished firepit at the *lis'* centre. There, drawing to a halt, they lay the litter down carefully and stood upright, wavering unsteadily as the other residents of Ráth Bládhma clustered in around them, slapping them enthusiastically on the back or crouching down to examine the man on the litter.

As she moved forward to join them, Bodhmhall noted Bran pull away, shiftily edging towards the roundhouse he shared with Tóla and Cónán. Like Liath Luachra, the youth looked completely spent but he gave the distinct impression that he was keen to avoid any interaction. By the time she'd got close enough to overhear what was being said, the copper haired Ferchar was posing the most obvious of questions.

'Who is he, Grey One? The sleepy man in the stretcher.'

Liath Luachra's response was a careless shrug and a slightly lopsided grimace, her habitual sternness softened from fatigue and relief at finally making it home.

'A captive of the *díbhearg*. As you can see, he's not a great one for words. For now, that's all I really know.'

With a grunt, the woman warrior attempted to stretch her back and shoulders, wincing painfully at the effort and then pausing mid-motion when she saw the *bandraoi* approaching.

'Bodhmhall.'

The Grey One may have intended to say more but, knowing her as she did, Bodhmhall felt it unlikely. Liath Luachra tended to turn her emotions inward and keep her personal thoughts close. Meanwhile, maintaining her own outward calm, the *bandraoi* resisted the urge to clasp the woman warrior and crush her close, to confirm beyond any doubt that the vision from the *Gift* had not come true.

She settled for reaching out to give her arm a gentle squeeze.

'Safe home, Grey One. It makes this heart swell to see you returned.'

Liath Luachra nodded, eyes shifting to the crowd around them, transferring her weight awkwardly from one foot to the other. The woman warrior inclined her head towards the fire pit.

'No fire,' she commented. 'Nothing in the hearth but ashes. You already knew there was danger?'

Bodhmhall had to make an effort not to smile at such blatant avoidance. '*An tíolacadh* made itself known while you were away,' she answered casually. 'It offered insights of a threat but, as usual, it was sparse in detail, so we took precautions nonetheless.'

She paused to cast her eyes over the unconscious man on the litter before returning her gaze to the Grey One. 'And what of this one?'

'He's not a familiar face?'

Noting the unexpected intensity of the Grey One's stare, Bodhmhall examined the stranger's face with greater attention.

'It's difficult to tell with that beard but ... No. At least, I don't believe so.' She looked sideways at the warrior woman. 'Does his presence pose a danger?'

'I don't believe there's any ... immediate danger,' Liath Luachra answered hesitantly. Bodhmhall regarded her carefully, sensing her reluctance to speak openly. Even as she wondered at its cause, the Grey One adroitly sidestepped the issue by opening the question up to the others.

'How about the rest of you? Do any of you recognise this man?'

There were a few murmurs, shrugs, shaking of heads. No-one, it seemed, had ever come across the stranger before.

'Why does he sleep so soundly?' Lí Bán wanted to know. 'Does he have an illness?' The old woman crouched beside the litter with creaking knees. Leaning forward, she made to shake the sleeping man's shoulder but recoiled in surprise. 'He stinks of *uisce beatha*. Is he drunk?'

Liath Luachra shook her head.

'No. I took the precaution of dosing him with a sleeping draught to keep the route to Ráth Bládhma secret. I needed something to disguise its taste, so concealed it in *uisce beatha*.'

The *bandraoi's* ears pricked up at that.

'You gave him a sleeping draught?'

146

The question seemed to make the woman warrior appear unexpectedly sheepish. 'The same draught I saw you use with Muirne Muncháem. All those years ago when the Tainted One sought her out. I remembered the herbs and applied them myself.'

'I ... see.' The *bandraoi* nodded as she fought to quell a mounting sense of disquiet. 'How ... er ... long as he been asleep?'

Liath Luachra twisted her lips in thought. 'Three days.'

'Oh.' Bodhmhall went very quiet, something the Grey One immediately picked up on.

'Does that pose a problem?'

'That depends on the circumstances. Mixing different herbs, particularly with *uisce beatha*, can lead to unexpected effects. Then, there's also the need to take a body's source of nourishment into account, even when the person's sleeping. Has this man eaten or drunk anything over that time?'

'He woke once about a day and a half ago. He was weak but we fed him some stew and a little water.'

'Good. Anything else?'

'Well ... we gave him so more of the sleeping draught in the *uisce beatha*.'

Bodhmhall somehow managed to stifle the groan in her throat before it got out.

'When he wakes again,' she suggested. 'We should feed him immediately. Food, but especially some water. Meanwhile ...'

She turned to address the wider group who'd been listening to the interaction with interest.

'I understand you'll all have questions for those returned safe to us, but ...' She hesitated briefly to rearrange her words. 'But given their great efforts to get home, let's first offer them opportunity to rest and recover.'

There were a few vague various murmurs of acknowledgement as the *bandraoi* turned her attention to the silver-haired woman. 'Lí Bán ... in Gnathad's absence, can I ask you to occupy yourself with Rónán and Bran, make sure they're both fed and rested.'

'Of course, Bodhmhall.' Back on her feet now, the old woman affectionately wrapped her arms about the beaming Rónán.

Nodding her thanks, the *bandraoi* addressed Cónán, now down from the ramparts as well.

'Cónán, your brother will be back with us shortly but, in the meantime, perhaps you could preoccupy yourself with our ...' She glanced at the comatose figure on the litter. 'Our guest.'

The young man followed her gaze to the prostrate figure before dipping his head in agreement. He looked decidedly more comfortable with the responsibility of such a practical task compared to his earlier charge of defending the settlement. 'Do you wish him placed in one of the roundhouses?'

The *bandraoi* turned to Liath Luachra. The woman warrior shook her head.

Bodhmhall thought for a moment before responding. 'Liath Luachra probably has the right of it. We know nothing of this stranger. He may be harmless, but I'll not risk a potential threat within our living areas. Settle him in the lean-to for now. Make him comfortable and warm but keep his hands bound and place a guard on him.'

With a grunt of acknowledgement, Cónán gestured for Ferchar to help him then moved forward to take position at one end of the litter. As the two men lifted it and started edging through a gap in the roundhouses towards the lean-to on the south-eastern side of the *ráth*, the others began to disperse, conscious that there'd be little in the way of news or revelations until their comrades had rested.

Taking advantage of their departure, Bodhmhall took the Grey One's arm and gently prompted her in the direction of the roundhouse. Sagging with fatigue, the woman warrior complied with uncharacteristic acquiescence. As they strolled slowly towards the entrance however, Bodhmhall noted that the Grey One was moving with a limp that caused her to favour her left side. The movement strongly suggested she was in some pain but, as usual, she made no complaint and gave no indication of discomfort.

It was only within the privacy of the roundhouse that the woman warrior finally dropped the façade. As soon as Bodhmhall sealed the entrance behind them, she dropped her backpack on the ground and tottered forward to the building's central roof support, using the solid wooden pole to hold herself upright. Following close behind, Bodhmhall moved in to slide an arm under her shoulder and supported her as she stumbled towards the sleeping platform.

Reaching her goal, the Grey One growled in pain as she turned to lower herself tenderly onto the wooden frame. When she was sitting securely, the *bandraoi* drew her arm free and stepped back to face her directly.

'You conceal an ache that scores far deeper than you'd have us know.'

Liath Luachra grunted softly. 'It's never wise to reveal a weakness, particularly to those who count on you.'

Bodhmhall ignored the sick quiver of worry in her stomach. Reaching out to stroke the woman warrior's cheek with her right hand, she felt the rough crease of her facial tattoo beneath her fingertips.

'I feared the worst, Grey One. With the visions from *an tíolacadh,* I truly believed you might not return this time.'

The woman warrior gave a rare smile that momentarily softened her features.

'There's no need to worry, *a Cailleach Dubh.* You are my beacon. You'll always draw me safely home.'

The *bandraoi* attempted a smile of her own but the bloody image of the body in the passage lingered in her head like an unspoken threat and the result was far bleaker than she'd intended. Releasing the warrior woman, she moved away to the fire pit to disguise her unease, crouching alongside it as she stirred the embers with a stick. 'And what of Bran?' she asked. 'He had a face on him like a hound chewing a cold turd.'

The Grey One remained silent longer than Bodhmhall would have expected. 'He's had good reason,' she said at last.

Disturbed by the sour edge to that response, the *bandraoi* levered herself back onto her feet to look back at her. By then, Liath Luachra was slumped at the edge of the sleeping platform, rubbing her feet together to scrape the grit from her soles. The beaten slope of her shoulders hinted at her exhaustion but the *bandraoi* sensed something more to the sombre mood than fatigue. Under normal circumstances, a return from the hunt or unexpected danger was an event to be celebrated or, at the very least, greeted with shared relief in the shelter of their home. On this occasion however, the vision from *an tíolacadh* and the woman warrior's own dark malaise, hung over the moment like an aggrieved ghost.

With all the subtlety she could muster, the *bandraoi* drew up the *Gift,* biting back a silent exclamation when she saw what it revealed. The Grey One's life-flame, usually a blaze of great vibrancy, now appeared greatly dampened and diminished. Bodhmhall surreptitiously let the *Gift* fade as the woman warrior began to speak, her unusually gentle voice accurately reflecting the dispirited nature of what she'd just witnessed.

'Ignore my despondency, *a rún*. Weariness weighs me down. Over these past days, I've run west and I've run east and then run west and east again. My legs ache from running, my mind from endless circling.'

Bodhmhall murmured something wordlessly sympathetic to give herself time to think. 'Well, with the first of those at least, I can offer some relief. I see you favour your left leg again.'

The Grey nodded absently, her thoughts elsewhere.

Moving to kneel by the sleeping platform, Bodhmhall helped the woman warrior remove her leggings, tugging the tight coverings down to her feet. When she finally managed to yank them free, the *bandraoi* pulled back, her nose wrinkling from the stale smell of sweat and body odour.

'You're rank, Grey One! I've encountered cattle pens that smelled sweeter. Stand up. I'll help you bathe so you can sleep in comfort.'

With obvious effort, the woman warrior rolled upright and onto her feet, listlessly divesting herself of her sweat-stained tunic while Bodhmhall retrieved a bowl of scented hot water from the fire. Using a cloth, the *bandraoi* washed the woman warrior's body, wiping the worst of the sweat and grime from her skin, resoaking the cloth and wringing it out several times before she'd finished. Afterwards, once she'd dried her with a fresh cloth, she had the Grey One lie face down on the sleeping platform while she combined oil and a collection of finely ground herbs in a small bowl from her shelves.

Pouring the resulting mixture onto her palms, she rubbed the liquescent substance brusquely together to produce a series of moist, squelching sounds. Glancing over at the sleeping platform, her eyes moved up the other woman's long white legs to her firm buttocks and badly scarred lower back, trying to decide where to start.

'A soft bed and a friendly body to warm me.' Lying face down, Liath Luachra's words were heavily muffled by the furs. 'I'll rest comfortable tonight.'

'There's no fault in comfort after days of toil, Grey One.'

The woman warrior made no answer but grunted softly at Bodhmhall's touch as the *bandraoi* bent over and slid one hand down the inside of her thigh. Intimately familiar with the woman warrior's body and its scattered pattern of welts and scars, she quickly located the cause of the limp: a knotted muscle beneath a weal on her inner thigh. Pressing her oiled fingers against that rigid tissue, she started to knead it gently.

'This wound …' said Liath Luachra. 'The one I took fleeing from Tadg's men.'

Bodhmhall looked up and considered the lean physique stretched out before her. Unable to see the woman warrior's face, it was even harder than usual to interpret her mood.

'It slows me more each year. It's never fully healed.'

'You're getting old,' the *bandraoi* teased in an effort to lighten the mood. 'As a well-versed *draoi*, I'm familiar with the symptoms: a hankering for soft furs, an incessant moaning over aches and hurts. It won't be long now before you're hobbling across the *lis* with a cane, giving out to children and complaining about the noise.'

Liath Luachra raised her head and twisted about to scowl at her.

'What's that sour puss on you?' Bodhmhall laughed as she returned to kneading the damaged muscle. 'Do you never think of the future?'

'The future's never close enough to touch,' came the muffled response as the Grey One lay flat again.

'And never far enough to elude.' Bodhmhall, edged her fingertips further along the muscle, locating a fresh knot at the point where it connected to bone. When she probed the subcutaneous tissue, it felt unusually striated. Quite possibly, it was inflamed – which explained the Grey One's pain. 'Besides,' she continued. 'Events often have their own way of overtaking us when we least expect them.'

'They already have overtaken us, Bodhmhall.' Although barely audible through the furs, the change in the warrior woman's tone was impossible to miss. '*Clann Morna* are on the rise again.'

The *bandraoi's* hands momentarily froze in place. This time, it took an intentional effort to recommence her gentle massage of the ribbed tissue. 'Was that who you encountered in the Great Wild?' she asked carefully. '*Clann Morna?*'

She paused then, recalling what she'd overheard in the *lis*.

'Rónán said it was a *díbhearg.*'

'Rónán *believed* it was a *díbhearg*. The truth is we encountered a *fian* of five *fénnidi* from *Clann Morna*. I felt it best not to correct him until

151

you and I had opportunity to discuss the matter beyond the reach of curious ears.'

This time Bodhmhall didn't stop massaging but stared down at the woman warrior's thigh, her mind whirling as she worked through the possible ramifications from *Clann Morna's* presence, even as her fingertips worked through the other woman's leg muscle.

'So close to Bládhma? Do you think they've come looking for Demne?'

She felt Liath Luachra's leg muscles clench then and realised she was working the tissue too hard, agitating rather than soothing it.

'No.' There was a catch of pain in the Grey One's voice, but it faded as the *bandraoi* eased the pressure from her fingers. 'This *fian* were chasing the man in the litter. The man who was on his way here to Ráth Bládhma to deliver you a message.'

Bodhmhall sat up straight at that, her hands dropping to her side in shock. 'A message? For me?'

'Yes.'

'What was the message?'

'I don't know. Despite my efforts, Feoras – the man in the litter – was determined to deliver it to you alone. That's why I wondered whether you'd recognise his face.'

Bodhmhall blinked, momentarily recalling the bearded visage. She shook her head then, as though to dislodge the memory. No. She was sure she'd not seen him before.

'And you say the *Clann Morna fian* were chasing him for this message.'

'I believe so. Having mulled it over for several days, that's the only motivation that makes sense to me. *Clann Morna* were either pursuing him to learn the nature of the message he carried or else to prevent him from delivering it.'

Bodhmhall caught her fingernails edging towards the skin of her palms, and angrily yanked them back before they could connect.

'Since Cargal Uí Faigil, I've had little faith in messengers.'

Liath Luachra gave a sympathetic grunt. In the ensuing silence, a sudden thought struck the *Clann Baoisnce* woman.

'Where's this *Clann Morna fian* now? Won't they be following the stranger here?'

The woman warrior raised her head, propped herself up on one arm and solemnly considered the *bandraoi*. Outside, the earlier sounds of voices and movement had diminished as the people of Ráth Bládhma went off about their own business and the resulting hush seemed to emphasise the gravity of her expression. 'Their corpses nourish the waters at An Mullán Bán. They won't be following anyone.'

With a wide yawn, she sat up fully then, shifting around on the furs to face the *Clann Baoiscne* woman.

'Two further *Clann Morna fianna* followed in support of the first but we managed to evade them and erase all trace of our interaction. It's unlikely they'll ever learn the truth of their comrades' fate. There'll be little enough to find once the Great Mother's consumed her due.'

Bodhmhall swallowed and nervously cleared her throat, shaken as much by the revelation of the *Clann Morna* presence as by the scale of the woman warrior's lethal action against them.

Five men!

'Perhaps,' she suggested at last. 'You should tell me everything that happened.'

Although visibly reluctant, the Grey One lay back on the sleeping platform and grudgingly began to recount her adventures in the Great Wild: the initial hunt with Bran and Rónán, the discovery of the tracks, Bran's subsequent departure and capture, the exhausting pursuit, her bloody annihilation of the *fian* and, finally, her unsuccessful interrogation of the stranger.

By the time she'd reached the conclusion to her story, the woman warrior's words had slowed and slurred from fatigue. Her eyes closed.

Assuming the Grey One had reached the end of her tether, Bodhmhall was about to cover her with a pair of furs when those eyes suddenly snapped open to stare at the *bandraoi* with unexpected solemnity.

'I've a weariness on me, Bodhmhall.'

'Yes, *a rún*. I can imagine.'

She made to cover the other woman again, but Liath Luachra grasped her wrist to prevent her from doing so.

'You don't understand. I'm tired of fighting.'

The *bandraoi* looked at her blankly, unsure what to say.

'I'm tired of shedding blood, of taking lives.' She grew quiet again but this time the *bandraoi* waited for her to continue.

'Before we came to know one another, back during my days with *Na Cinéaltaí* ... Back then, I slept with a damp film of gore on my hands, the echo of screams in my ears, ruddy puddles about my feet when I dreamed.'

Liath Luachra paused to clear her throat.

'When ... when I first travelled here to Ráth Bládhma with you, I'd hoped to have done with the slaughter, to have left those battle days behind me. But ...'

The woman warrior's voice cracked, and she had to inhale deeply before she could continue.

'It's true we've had years of peace together but this swirl of *Clann Morna* activity chills my blood. I can sense the tread of tribal machinations approaching, intrigues and collusions just beyond our sight that threaten to sweep us up in their storm. I had hoped that with the *fian* destroyed and all trails eroded, such troubles would pass us by. Now, my stomach aches and tells me there'll be more slaughter.'

The Grey One's eye sockets, already dark with fatigue, looked even hollower and more skull-like in the flicker of light from the fire. The *bandraoi* winced in unconscious sympathy.

'Grey One. Your weariness makes you ramble now. You truly need to rest.'

The woman warrior looked at her fiercely and for a moment Bodhmhall feared she might resist. Then, to her great relief, she gave a tired exhalation.

'Perhaps you have the right of it. Perhaps it's just fatigue or age that sets the weight on these shoulders and drives me to self-pity. I should leave such considerations to you. You're the smart one after all. You'll have a clever scheme to save us, some deft arrangement to skirt the coming bloodbath.'

'Liath Luachra, I don-'

'I have faith in you, Bodhmhall. You've always had the words to raise us when we're at our lowest, to empower us when we're at our weakest. You have the words and the wisdom to light our way out of the darkness. I'm the fortunate one to have found you.'

With that, the woman warrior reached over and patted the *bandraoi* wearily on the knee. Without another word, she rolled onto her side and dragged the corner of a fur blanket across her shoulder. Within a moment or two, she was breathing softly, fast asleep.

Bodhmhall stared wordlessly at the sleeping woman, dismayed by the display of such uncharacteristic vulnerability from the one person she held most dear. Caressing her face gently, her mind reeled from the revelation of the new dangers now confronting them.

Once again, she felt the image of the woman warrior and the bloody passage shift at the back of her head, a minute movement like a veiled threat as it wormed its way closer to her darkest fears. That bleak impression was abruptly routed by a sudden flare of pain in her left palm and, looking down, she saw blood streaming where her nervous fingernails had gouged the skin.

You're the smart one after all.

With a flush of bitter despair, Bodhmhall clenched her jaw.

Not so smart, unfortunately. She had no idea how to counter, or to even make sense of, the dangers from the visions *an tíolacadh* had shown her.

Even with the *Gift*, she did not know how or where to start.

Chapter Ten

It was the softness that roused Liath Luachra – the softness and the smell – and within the growing sense of lucidity, both were an instant incongruity. The Grey One had little softness in her life, certainly none so soothingly sumptuous. And as for the smell … well, that was something too pleasant to dare imagine it was real.

As the first glow of consciousness finally seeped in, comprehension slid in on its tails. The Grey One realised she was indoors, lying on a sleeping platform with Bodhmhall's body pressed snug against her back, one leg draped across her hip and her breath warm against on the nape of her neck. The fragrant scent filling her nostrils, had been that of the *bandraoi*.

For a long time Liath Luachra luxuriated in the comfort of that heady intimacy, drifting in and out of sleep, never truly awake until dawn's dreary light slid through the smoke hole in the roundhouse roof. Cracking her eyelids apart, she stared blearily at the blur of that muted gloom. Carefully levering herself free of the *bandraoi's* leg, she eased sideways to the edge of the sleeping platform and rolled upright onto the reed-strewn, earth floor.

Peering around the structure's dim interior, the woman warrior was struck, as always, by how spacious it was compared to the memory she carried out in the Great Wild. How warm it was. How … safe.

With a sigh, she inhaled a lungful of air scented with burnt pine from the fire and wildflower from the oil mixture still coating her thigh. For a moment she paused, wondering at the pleasant sense of lightness it triggered. It took a moment or two before she realised the reason behind it.

It was the smell of home.

Moving stiffly to the water bucket by the door, the Grey One crouched to wash her face and hands, doing her best to ignore the muted burn in her thigh. Her entire body ached. The thigh muscle still burned like the sting of an angry honeybee, but at least it was far less severe than when she'd stumbled into the settlement the previous afternoon. That injury was just one of many, of course. Years of physical effort and stress had taken their toll and left her with a collection of livid scar tissue and an accumulation of aches that would colour her old age.

She paused at that, struck by the sudden realisation that in her youth she'd never had an expectation of reaching an old age. In hindsight, it was a marvel she'd lasted for as long as she had.

Done washing, the woman warrior dried her hands and rose to pull on a fresh pair of leggings and a tunic that had been placed on a low stool by the sleeping platform. Refreshed and clean, she made for the doorway, pausing briefly to look back at the *bandraoi* still sprawled across the sleeping platform, unravelled black hair spread like a stain on the white sheepskin she used as a pillow. For a moment, the woman warrior stood there, torn between a yearning to greet the morning air and a competing desire to return to bed and curl up with the sleeping *Clann Baoiscne* woman.

Lying on her side, Bodhmhall was dribbling. Her face was soft when she slept, her facial muscles slack, wincing slightly as she responded to her dreams. Watching her, the Grey One wondered at that. It seemed odd in a way. Lying so close together, hair and limbs entangled ... You'd think they'd be able to sense some part of each other's dreams.

But that, of course, had never happened.

Make up your mind. Are you coming or going?

Unable to decide, she reached out one hand to touch Bodhmhall's foot, stroking the smooth skin of her ankle with the tips of her fingers.

The *bandraoi* did not stir.

With a sigh, Liath Luachra turned and left the roundhouse.

Given the early hour, the *lis* was quiet and occupied solely by Ferchar. Taking a respite from the task of guarding the stranger, the warrior was sitting at the only area by the empty fire pit where he could still see the lean-to, a wooden bowl of porridge on his knees. Noting Liath Luachra's arrival, he looked up at her and grinned, sharing an unintelligible greeting through a mouthful of oaty broth.

Nodding in muted acknowledgment, the Grey One made for the nearest ladder, swiftly climbing to the ramparts and approaching the northern palisades. Leaning against the blunted points of the stockade pilings, she stared across the stretch of dewy grass to the thick forest of the northern ridge. Even from that distance, the trees were visibly teeming with bird life, the upper canopy quivering from the sheer volume of movement, while the surrounding hills rang with the raucous morning chorus.

As always when she looked at that section of the forest, the Grey One shivered, recalling how more than fourteen years earlier, she'd run out from those same trees, naked and wielding a sword in one desperate, last-ditch effort to save the settlement.

Closing her eyes, she drew up the memory of those terrifying moments before she'd emerged into the open and, for an instant, could once again feel the meaty throb of her heart against her ribcage, the metallic taste of fear in her throat, the stink of terror-sweat seeping from her skin.

Opening her eyes again, she realised that her hands were clenched about the points of the pilings and a fierce tightness had gripped her chest. As the hair rose at the back of her neck, she bared her teeth in a ferocious snarl, responding instinctively to some undefined threat over the horizon, a tangible sense of menace that she could perceive but, infuriatingly, couldn't identify.

Fourteen years earlier, prior to the Great Invasion, she'd experienced a similar sense of claustrophobic constriction, a breathless intuition of danger somewhere beyond her sight but drawing ever closer. Now it felt as though all the original components that contributed to that attack were reassembling, arranging themselves in readiness once again.

With a conscious effort, Liath Luachra loosened her grip on the pilings, dropped her hands to her side and glanced down at the *lis*, relieved to see that Ferchar hadn't noticed anything amiss in her behaviour. Getting a grip on her emotions, she compressed them tightly and started around the rampart walkway.

Moving in the direction of the stone gateway, the woman warrior cursed under her breath when she realised Gnathad was at her post above it, that she was, in fact, watching her approach with interest. Drawing closer, the Grey One noticed that the *banfénnid* had changed her long, black hair since she'd seen her the previous afternoon, while arriving at Gleann Ceoch, and tied it up in a complex braid.

'I see you, Grey One.'

'Gnathad.' Liath Luachra returned the greeting with a short twitch of her head.

Both women faced each other in awkward silence.

'There were little enough words exchanged between us yesterday,' Gnathad said at last.

'True enough,' the Grey One admitted. Exhausted from days of travel and the burdened of the heavy litter, when they'd entered Gleann Ceoch her sole focus had been to get her captive and her charges to the *ráth*. Gnathad's sudden appearance had obliged them to call a grudging halt, both to acknowledge her welcome and to allow Bran a moment to embrace his foster mother. Even then, with the youth just as eager reach the settlement, they hadn't delayed long.

'What news of the Great Wild?'

'It remains wild.' The Grey One glanced over the *banfénnid's* shoulder, in the direction of the valley entrance. 'Who guards the west?'

'Tóla.'

Liath Luachra grunted but made no other response. She shifted her weight from one foot to the other, wincing slightly as the movement prompted a fresh burn in her thigh.

Gnathad loudly cleared her throat. 'This *díbhearg* that Rónán speaks of? What news there?'

Liath Luachra shrugged. 'No news.'

'Come now, Grey One. You return with an injured stranger in tow, Rónán's telling everyone that blood was spilled, Bran is evasive and refuses to speak with me, Bodhmhall is keeping her own secrets and ...' She paused, exhaled heavily and finally came to the true source of her disquiet. 'Is there danger, Grey One? Are my children safe?'

'Nobody's ever truly safe in the Great Wild, Gnathad.'

'Aaaah!' The *banfénnid* shook her head in irritation. 'Now you belittle my queries with platitudes. You know well that I speak of the stranger. Who is he? Does he bring trouble to Ráth Bládhma?'

'I don't have answers for you, Gnathad. Those are questions to be posed when he's awake and able to answer. Until then, we keep our weapons to hand, our eyes to the west and share the burden of guarding the settlement's safety.'

'Such burdens would be more easily shared with a sharing of trust.'

The resentful mutter took the Grey One by surprise. 'What's that?' she asked. 'What are you saying?'

The *banfénnid* hesitated, fearful of having already said too much yet clearly tempted to say more.

'I'm saying that there's an unequal balance of commitment and trust here at Ráth Bládhma.' She glanced uneasily at the woman warrior. 'You know I'm not one to shirk my share of the tasks assigned me. Be they menial or critical, I'll fulfil them to the best of my ability.'

'I do.'

'And yet, during your absences in the Great Wild, when it comes to the assigning of tasks, I'm assigned nothing more responsible than guard duty, repairs to the *ráth* or other meaningless tasks that diminish my standing as a warrior and defender.'

Liath Luachra frowned.

'In my absence, it's Bodhmhall and Aodhán who assign such tasks.'

The Ráth Dearg woman remained silent, conscious she was treading on potentially contentious ground.

'Both Bodhmhall and Aodhán have my trust and I have faith in their judgement. Perhaps, Gnathad, you mistake a lack of confidence in your abilities for a lack of trust. You're unblooded, after all. Unproven and untried in battle. Bodhmhall and Aodhán know this, and it'll flavour the decisions they make when assigning tasks.'

'You trained me yourself, Grey One. You know the measure of my abilities, the 'flavour' of my skill with javelin and spear. For accuracy and speed, I'm the equal of Aodhán and for skill with a knife, I'd rate myself against any other.'

Liath Luachra peeled a sliver of wood from the nearest piling, popped it in her mouth and crunched it between her molars as she considered the other woman. There was some truth to what Gnathad was saying. She did have her measure. The sacking of her home and the butchery of her friends had not only devastated the Ráth Dearg woman but exposed the horrifying reality of her own powerlessness. Seeking the Grey One's help in learning how to fight and defend her children against such a fate, she'd trained hard with javelin and spear over the years. Unfortunately, although there was no doubting the woman's commitment, the lateness of that training and her lack of real combat experience meant she'd always be at a disadvantage against those reared in martial skills from childhood.

'It's different in battle,' Liath Luachra said at last. 'No measure of training can prepare you for the stink of spilled blood, the sickening slickness of spilled innards, the piercing screams of men with hacked limbs and torn flesh, sensations and pain so visceral they leave you tainted forever.'

Gnathad responded with a cool smile, politely acknowledging the Grey One's view although by no means agreeing with it. Seeing the firmness of purpose in that gaze the Grey One understood she'd never convince the other woman. Having experienced violence and brutality at Ráth Dearg, Gnathad was convinced she had the measure of slaughter, not comprehending that coming at violence from the perspective of combat changed the experience irrevocably.

Using her tongue, she shifted the piece of wood in her mouth to the other cheek.

'Do you struggle with purpose, Gnathad?'

'With purpose?' The *banfénnid's* stance seemed to grow a little stiffer and she eyed the Grey One with suspicion. What do you mean?'

'It's not intended as a recrimination. I ask because of the importance you affix to your warrior status. That was never a subject to trouble you in the past.'

Gnathad held her stare for a moment but then, slowly, the stiffness eased from her shoulders.

'There's some truth to what you say,' she admitted at last. 'Over this past year, my girls have stopped heeding my counsel. Bran, too, has grown apart and will stand as his own man soon enough. Without my children to occupy me, I've had to redirect my focus elsewhere.'

The *banfénnid* paused, pursing her lips in thought. 'In truth, I suppose I've directed my focus to improving my physical fighting skills. Let's face it, that's probably the one physical need I can sate here at Ráth Bládhma.'

Gnathad must have caught the startled expression on the Grey One's face for she self-consciously transferred the spear from her left hand to her right. 'I know our tastes don't veer in the same direction, Grey One, but the sad truth is that pickings are slim at Ráth Bládhma. All the eligible men are taken. Ferchar is with Muirenn, Aodhán is with Morag.'

Thrown by the unexpected direction the conversation had taken, Liath Luachra bit down on the wood splinter. Struggling to cope with the sharing of such intimacy, she suspected her younger self would have shut such talk down and walked away by now. Sadly, despite her

161

own misgivings, her age and responsibility in the settlement meant she had to make some kind of effort. 'There's Cónán,' she suggested.

This time it was Gnathad who looked startled. 'Cónán is but a youth.'

'He's hardly a youth. And he's blooded to boot.'

Gnathad produced a smile that had all the characteristics of a wince. 'Perhaps. But I find I've lost my taste for unripened flavours. Besides, it's always been my intent to form a match between Cónán and my daughter Bamba. I've worked on arrangements to draw them together since the last full moon for they share much in common.'

Liath Luachra considered that for a moment then leaned over the pilings and spat the wood splinter out, watching as it arced down to hit the ground below. Try though she might, she struggled to think what the two uninformed participants of Gnathad's matchmaking might have in common. Establishing a kinship between Gnathad's fiery, copper-haired daughter and the easy-going Cónán wouldn't be an easy task. Polar opposites in character, they might have had matching hair colour but, to her mind, little else that overlapped without effort.

'Tóla, then.'

Gnathad stared at her with an expression of such appalled incredulity that Liath Luachra had to resist the urge to laugh. 'Perhaps not,' she conceded.

Even more eager now to retreat to the privacy of her own company, the Grey One was seeking a suitable means to end the discussion when a distant flicker of movement snagged her attention. Turning her gaze over the palisades towards the west, she saw a solitary figure running in the direction of the *ráth* from the western treeline.

'Gnathad, get down to the *lis*. Have Ferchar help you unseal the gateway.'

Surprised by the abrupt change of topic, the Ráth Dearg woman followed the Grey One's gaze to identify what might have triggered it, her breath catching in a silent exclamation when she spotted the distant figure.

'Should I rouse the others?'

Liath Luachra shook her head. 'One man's no threat. And it's most likely Tóla. Let's wait and see what we see.'

While Gnathad descended the ladder, Liath Luachra remained at the palisades. Studying the approaching figure, it didn't take long to assure herself that it was Tóla, a confirmation helped in no small part by the recognisably steady shamble. The eccentric warrior's unhurried pace was reassuring in that it indicated there was no cause for alarm, however his unexpected presence did nothing to allay her curiosity as to why he'd left his post in the first place.

Sliding down the ladder to the *lis*, the Grey One found that Gnathad and Ferchar had already removed the heavy strut holding the wooden gate in place and they lifted its ponderous weight aside as she approached to join them. All three proceeded through the stone passage and across the causeway, standing on the grass just beyond as they waited for the old warrior to arrive.

It took some time but Tóla eventually made it to the causeway, slowing as he drew closer and then pulling to a halt directly in front of them. Although wheezing for breath, he beamed at them in greeting, a dramatically broad, gap-toothed grin that seemed oddly out of place on his wizened features. To the Grey One's irritation, rather than reporting to her, he reached to grab Ferchar by the shoulder, drawing the younger warrior close so that he could whisper urgently in his ear.

Whatever words he had to share were quickly delivered. Patting Ferchar on the shoulder, he moved past without sparing either of the two women a second glance. Making his way across the causeway, he disappeared into the shadows of the gateway passage.

Liath Luachra watched him go with feelings of ambivalence before shaking her head and addressing Ferchar. 'Well?' she demanded. 'What did he say?'

Ferchar, always somewhat embarrassed when obliged to translate for the quirky warrior, rubbed awkwardly at his neck. 'Er, he says the turnip is coming. Accompanied by a rootlet.'

The Grey One gave an exasperated grunt. 'I'll assume we're not under attack from a warband of root crops.' She set her jaw grimly. 'Unless, of course, they're here to lay waste to Bodhmhall's *lubgort* – vegetable garden.'

Ferchar looked even more abashed at that. 'It, er ...' He paused, brushing the fringe of copper curls back from his eyes. 'It may be that Tóla's referring to Fiacail mac Codhna. He sometimes refers to warriors in vegetable terms. And Fiacail's a big veget- ... warrior.'

Liath Luachra stared at the baffled warrior.

Fiacail mac Codhna! Why would …

And, suddenly, Bodhmhall's description of the *tíolacadh* visions trickled back into her memory.

Ferchar and Gnathad stepped back in surprise as the woman warrior brushed past them and advanced several steps further out into the grass. Focussed completely on the western treeline, she ignored their bewildered stares as she scanned the distant trees for movement.

Several moments passed and then, just as she was starting to wonder if she'd got it wrong, a fresh flicker of movement drew her gaze. Shielding her eyes against Father Sun, she peered at the area where she'd seen the movement and, although it was too far away to be certain, she got the distinct sense of two separate figures moving towards the settlement.

A sudden tightness swelled in her chest and her mouth was dry. 'Rouse Bodhmhall,' she called back over her shoulder. 'Rouse her now.'

The words came out hoarser than she'd intended and, concerned, Gnathad approached to touch her gently on the arm.

'Grey One. What is it? What troubles you?'

Liath Luachra turned to look at her, embarrassed now for she was struggling to put it into words.

'*Cuairt an lao, a Gnathad!*' she managed at last. '*Cuairt an lao ar an athbhuaile.*' The calf's return, Gnathad. The calf's return to the old milking spot.

***

As news of Demne and Fiacail's return spread through the *ráth*, people emerged from the roundhouses to gather by the gateway, excited at the prospect of yet another rare return in less than two days. Discomforted by the growing crowd, Liath Luachra edged close to Ferchar and proposed relieving him of his guard duty with the stranger, an offer the warrior agreed to with immediate enthusiasm.

Returning to the eastern side of the *lis* where the lean-to and its new occupant were located, the woman warrior found a comfortable position sitting beneath the overhang of the rampart walkway. There, although hidden from sight of the central *lis*, she had a clear view of

164

the sleeping stranger, stretched on his litter amongst the stacked piles of hewn wood and kindling. In truth, the Grey One mused, Feoras didn't look like he needed guarding. He'd barely changed position since she'd seen him being carried away the previous afternoon.

Her consideration of the stranger was abruptly interrupted by a loud cheer from the direction of the gateway. Demne and Fiacail had evidently arrived through the narrow passageway.

The woman warrior pulled her knife from its scabbard and tapped the back of her hand with the flat of its blade. By now, no doubt, the other occupants of the *ráth* were swarming over the newcomers, greeting them with hugs, hearty back slaps and even more rousing cheers. Bodhmhall, of course, would be first to embrace them. The warrior woman had caught a glimpse of her running from their roundhouse, hurriedly binding the ties of a fresh *léine*, her dark, unbraided hair bound up by a simple silver headband. Flustered from being so freshly woken, her excitement at the prospect of her nephew's imminent return and her rush to reach the gateway meant she hadn't noticed the Grey One as she'd run by.

Listening to the muffled emotions of that joyous reunion, the Grey One scraped mindlessly at the earth between her feet with a knife, cutting scarlines with a guilty unease that nagged at her like a sore tooth. It was a struggle to make sense of her own reaction. She'd genuinely wished to mark her adopted nephew's return but, somehow, her natural shyness, her discomfort around people and an illogical fear that she'd somehow disappoint him, had conspired to drive her to the opposite side of the settlement instead.

Finally, encouraged by the dwindling sounds from the *lis*, the woman warrior got to her feet and started towards a gap between two roundhouses to see what was happening. Nearing that narrow aperture, Liath Luachra was pleased to see that the crowd was already breaking up, dispersing back to their own affairs. As she made to enter the gap however, suddenly the space was occupied by the bulk of Fiacail mac Codhna. Startled, both unconsciously took a step back.

The Seiscenn Uairbhaoil man was the first to recover. 'I see you Grey One,' he greeted her formally.

'I see you Fiacail mac Codhna,'

Greetings exchanged, the two considered each other uneasily, both suddenly bereft of anything else to say. The awkward silence continued.

'How is your leg injury?' Fiacail asked suddenly. 'When you escorted Demne to Trá Mór, you were still limping from your adventures with Tadg's men.'

She shrugged. 'Sometimes it aches, sometimes it doesn't.' She didn't say any more. There seemed little point in complaining about it.

'And you? You still bore the scars from that skirmish too.'

'Sometimes it aches …' This time it was Fiacail's turn to shrug. He left the rest unsaid.

The Grey One nodded in silent appreciation. Pain, at least, was something they both had in common. That unexpected sense of commonality prompted a sudden possibility. 'Fiacail, I have a service to ask of you.'

'Of me?' The big man's expression was calm but the slight waver in his response exposed his surprise.

'Yes. Come with me.' She turned and started to walk back the way she'd come, until she realised Fiacail wasn't following her. Drawing to a halt, she looked back, her lips compressed in a thin line.

'Unless you'd prefer not to, of course.'

Fiacail was looking back towards the *lis* as though regretting its now almost empty state. 'No, no.' He shook his head. 'Never let it be said that Fiacail mac Codhna shirks his responsibilities when asked.'

He started forwards with almost exaggerated nonchalance. Suppressing a snort, Liath Luachra turned to lead the way.

The pebbles of the *lis* crunched nosily underfoot as the pair approached the area where the lean-to slanted against the eastern wall. The woman warrior couldn't help but notice how Fiacail retained a consistent distance of three to four paces at her rear, almost as though he was giving himself enough space to react should she suddenly decide to attack him. When he saw the man in the litter however, any such caution was discarded as he moved forward, his eyes bright with curiosity.

'Do you know him?' the Grey One asked.

Fiacail circled around to the front of the litter to get a better look at the sleeping man's face. He blinked in surprise when he caught the whiff of *uisce beatha* but then frowned and seemed to stare at the stranger more closely, clutching his jaw in concentration.

'But that… that's … that's Dariu Mór, My uncle Dariu. He was thought to be dead for my family haven't seen him in years. Ever since he got drunk at Seiscenn Uairbhaoil and fucked a sheep during the Samhain festivities, in fact.'

Liath Luachra looked at him in shock. 'Truly? Is this man your uncle?'

'Of course not!' The warrior exclaimed. 'Honestly! Is this some new provocation of yours, Grey One? Why would you expect me to recognise every scraggle-beard old drunk, too inebriated to rise from his bed before mid-day?' He glared at her, offended by the imagined slight.

Exasperated, the warrior woman struggled to contain her anger. Few people ever succeeded in getting under her skin or provoking her but Fiacail somehow possessed a rare talent in that regard.

'So, he's not known to you.'

'Of course not. Why? Who is he?'

'I don't know. I had hoped you might be able to tell me.'

'Well, have you considered asking him?'

'That's something of a challenge. Since our first encounter three days ago, he hasn't really roused from unconsciousness.'

Fiacail frowned, his earlier exasperation now tempered by curiosity.

'Then where does he come from? I assume you didn't find him snoring beside the firepit one morning when you rose from your bed.'

'I found him in the Great Wild. Tied to an oak tree.'

This time Fiacail looked at her in open bewilderment. Opening his mouth to speak, he seemed to change his mind for he shut it again, only to open it once more a moment later.

'There are some who'd say you're a cold stone with no vein of humour, Grey One.' He sniffed. 'In truth, I'd normally be counted among their number but this …' He waved a hand from her to the old man stretched comatose on his stretcher, then back to her once more. 'This, I have to say …'

Unable to sail forth with the sentence, he allowed it to run ashore.

With a sniff, the Grey One poked at the pebbles underfoot with the toes of her right foot then scratched irritably at the side of her face.

'The stranger was hanging beside Bran, Gnathad's adopted son. The men who'd strung him up were from a *Clann Morna fian* that had been chasing him through the Great Wild for days. Apparently, he was on his way here to Ráth Bládhma.'

167

The big man looked at her without expression as he listened to what she had to say but he seemed to have nothing to add. After a moment or two, he sighed and folded his arms.

'This sounds a tangled tale. One, I suspect, that neither you nor I are a match to undo.' He pursed his lips as though considering the conundrum in depth. 'Bodhmhall however ... Bodhmhall has a mind to unravel such knots. We should bring this matter to her notice and discuss what's to be done, later this afternoon.'

Liath Luachra pursed her lips as she considered the suggestion. 'Bodhmhall's already aware of this ... matter. But why delay until this afternoon?'

'Because I've requested a gathering for this afternoon, one to which you and Demne are also invited. Untangling this knot will require time and consideration. Unfortunately, with the return of her nephew, Bodhmhall insists on spending time alone with him until then.'

The Grey One pursed her lips in thought. 'There's a faster way to untangle a knot,' she suggested.

'Oh, yes? And what would that be?'

She held up the weapon that she'd previously been using to stab the earth.

'You take a knife to it.'

***

In the end, unwilling to spend further time in Fiacail's company, Liath Luachra elected to remain where she was, guarding the sleeping stranger while the Seiscenn Uarbhaoil man returned to the *lis* with her vague promise to follow later. She was still sitting by the lean-to later that afternoon, when a slender fair-haired youth emerged from the gap between the roundhouse and sauntered confidently towards her.

The Grey One started and scrambled to her feet. Even prewarned, it took her several heartbeats before she was sure. It was Dem-

'*A Aintín!*' The youth's call reached her before she could finish that thought. 'Fiacail told me you were skulking back here.'

He grinned to disarm the comment but the Grey One couldn't help smouldering slightly. 'I'm hardly ... skulking. I'm guarding this ...' She gestured at her sleeping charge. 'Man.'

The youth halted alongside the lean-to and looked down at the stranger with interest. He seemed a little taken aback to find this unknown individual sleeping in amongst the firewood.

'Is he known to you?' asked Liath Luachra.

'I don't think so.' The youth's features tightened in concentration as he studied the stranger more closely. 'Why is he sleeping in the firewood?'

Unwilling to repeat the conversation she'd had with Fiacail, the woman warrior ignored the question. Instead, she steadied her stance and stared directly at the newcomer. 'I see you Demne,' she said solemnly.

He pulled back a little and cocked his head to regard her more closely. 'So formal, *a Aintín*? With your lurking in the shadows and your cold welcome one could almost imagine you were seeking to avoid me.'

The woman warrior shook her head. 'That is untrue. There's no chill in my heart. If anything, it swells to see you.'

'Truly?'

'You know I'm not one for great displays of emotion.'

'Yes. I'd hate to risk being overwhelmed by the full force of your greeting.'

Uncertain if he was joking or not, Liath Luachra responded with a helpless shrug. Fortunately, the youth chuckled and moved forward to embrace her. Drawn by the reality of his presence after so long apart, the Grey One gave in completely to that embrace, the familiar scent of him triggering a flurry of memories as she held him close.

It was pleasant of course, but it still seemed to be an age before Demne finally decided to release her. Quickly pulling a step back, she gestured at his hair.

'Your hair has reverted to gold again. You don't use the dye that Bodhmhall gave you?'

'I've used that dye for six years and more, Grey One. The day I left Seiscenn Uairbhaoil for good, I swore I'd never use it again. I'm done with hiding. In future, this is the person people will see, the person that I intend to be.'

Liath Luachra eyed him curiously. 'And who are you now?'

'I'm …' The question seemed to catch the youth by surprise for he was visibly flustered as he returned her inquisitive stare. As she continued to watch him however, his eyes took on a glint of fresh conviction and he seemed to stand a little straighter.

'I'm Fionn. And as Fionn, I'll live my life as I see fit. From this moment on, no-one else will dictate my restrictions, set barriers to my achievements.'

He glared at her fiercely as though anticipating a challenge to this firm declaration. When her silence made it clear that no such challenge was forthcoming, he grew quiet and looked down at his feet, as though unable to face her gaze. After an awkward silence, he raised his head and looked at her directly.

'You left me, Grey One. You and Bodhmhall left me behind at Trá Mór.'

Another heavy silence rolled out between them in the wake of that unexpected accusation and even Demne seemed a little taken aback by the force of its articulation. He coughed into his hand as though to hide his embarrassment. 'You left me behind,' he repeated, but this time his voice was far more level and moderated.

'Yes.'

Demne waited, expecting more. When nothing came, his forehead creased and he angrily pressed her further. 'But why? What reason prompted you to desert me?'

Liath Luachra frowned. 'Why do you toss the weight of such a query on me? As your blood kin, Bodhmhall's best placed to answer this question.'

'Because despite the great fondness I bear her, I've no doubt that Bodhmhall will choose her words to spare me bitter truths. With you, at least, I know the answer will bear no sweetened layers of honey.'

Liath Luachra jaw set stubbornly as she shifted her weight awkwardly from one foot to the other.

'*A Aintín*,' the youth pleaded.

'You know why,' she responded sharply. 'Even if Fiacail never told you – which knowing the mouth on him, I very much doubt – you've always been smart enough to unravel such knots of consequence.'

'Tell me anyway. I've a need to hear you say it aloud.'

Liath Luachra eyed him wordlessly, retreating once more behind her habitual mask of impassivity. The youth must have expected her to disengage with her usual reticence for she saw his surprise when she did speak again.

'Your grandfather, Tadg mac Nuadat … he gained the ability to see into our dreams – mine and Bodhmhall's. Over the years, we've learned how to keep his night visits at bay. Back then, if he'd slipped through while you were at Ráth Bládhma, there was a real risk he'd sense your presence and send further forces to snatch you.'

The woman warrior scowled then, involuntarily adjusting her stance as though to defend against an unpleasant truth.

'Your grandfather has resources that far outweigh our own. Bodhmhall and I knew we couldn't hope to resist another attack on the scale of the Great Invasion. We also knew there was no choice but to have you hidden far from us, at a place unfamiliar to us both. If we didn't know where you were …'

'Then my grandfather wouldn't know.' Demne – Fionn – nodded his understanding. 'But if you learned how to prevent him polluting your dreams, surely you could have fetched me back.'

Liath Luachra shook her head.

'There was also the matter of the traitor – the turncoat who helped Tagh set the trap when we travelled to Dún Baoisnce. To start us on that journey, the false *techtaire*, Cargal Uí Faigil, provided us with a surety based on knowledge that only a very small number of people could possibly have known. Whether the person who provided Cargal Uí Faigil with that information was based at Ráth Bládhma or Dún Baoisnce, we still didn't know. All we did know for certain was that your presence here placed your life at risk. By sending you with Fiacail, the single other person we could truly trust, you had a chance to be raised in safety, hidden from Tadg mac Nuadat's bloody gaze.'

She shrugged.

'That is why you were left at An Trá Mór.'

As her final words drifted away on the rising breeze, the youth looked hard at her. 'I missed you, Grey One. I truly missed you.'

Liath Luachra felt a shift in her chest, as though some critical support had given way.

'As you were missed, *a gharsúr*. Losing you was hard to bear. The pain of not knowing your fate cut Bodhmhall particularly deep.'

'And you, Liath Luachra? Was there any loss to you?'

The Grey One rocked on her heels as she sought an answer to his question.

'I tried not to think of you,' she admitted. 'Now that you're back you remind me that you left and my heart aches for the time lost

171

between us. Your presence here … it made me a better person. It was only when you were absent that I truly realised how much had gone with you.'

Distressed by a weight of emotion that threatened to overwhelm her, the woman warrior tried to lose such thoughts in the prosaic. 'I suppose we should accept that some things are simply not meant to be. Besides, even had you returned, you'd have tired of us eventually. One day, it would have been your own choice to depart and, frustrated, you'd simply have left and forgotten us.'

'The youth shook his head and chuckled at that. 'I don't think so. I'd never forget you, *a Aintín*. Ever.'

Touched, but unsure how to respond, the Grey One settled for clucking her tongue. 'It's true, then, that you've grown up. All men make emphatic promises. Few keep them.'

Chapter Eleven

When Demne and Liath Luachra returned to the roundhouse, Bodhmhall was poised over the workbench by her shelves, vigorously grinding a mixture of bright blue flower petals and other herbs with a stone mortar and pestle. Hearing the door shift ajar, she pulled her eyes from her task to observe them enter, her gaze coming to rest on Demne with an unexpected sense of weighty estimation.

Demne felt himself waver uneasily under that regard. His earlier reunion with his aunt had been emotionally disconcerting and he still hadn't completely recovered. At the time, imagining himself hardened and mature from his time in Seiscenn Uairbhaoil, he'd decided to mark his return with a stately indifference, a subtle if hard-edged reprisal for being abandoned at An Trá Mór all those years ago. Despite that resentment-fuelled intention however, the haughty substance of his plan had crumbled apart the moment he'd laid eyes on his aunt, the unbridled affection of her regard thawing his attempt at an icy heart. Instead of the cool dispassion he'd been determined to convey, to the youth's great embarrassment, he found himself weeping, reverting once more to the eight-year-old child who'd been deserted on a distant shoreline. To make matters worse, his aunt had then embraced him with a knowing tenderness that suggested this had been the response she'd expected all along.

Which, knowing his aunt, was entirely possible.

'There's stew in the pot,' Bodhmhall told them, turning back to her work and gesturing one-handed at a metal pot in the outer ashes of the firepit. 'Leave some for Fiacail. He'll have a hunger on him when he gets back.'

Terrified at the possibility of yet another involuntary outpouring of emotion, Demne hurried towards the fire pit, disguising his apprehension by grabbing a wooden bowl from the stack piled alongside the ashes and using the ladle to serve himself from the pot's bubbling contents. Hooking the nearest of the three fireside stools with his foot, he drew it close to the fire, sat with his bowl and spoon, and hid behind his exaggerated hunger.

Although she showed no interest in the stew pot, Liath Luachra followed close behind and settled herself on the floor at the opposite side of the fire. She sat sideways with her left leg tucked up, her right leg out straight and one arm stretched out in a kind of negligent elegance, on a short wooden bench. Staring into the low flames, the woman warrior reached one hand up, casually running her fingers through her short, black hair.

'You've spoken with Fiacail, then?' The question was directed at Bodhmhall.

'Briefly. I confess my attention was focussed on other matters.'

The *bandraoi* flashed Demne a quick smile before turning back to the workbench and pouring the ground up contents from the mortar into a clay jug. Demne watched as she carefully added splashes of hot water from a separate bowl, raised the jug in both hands and, shaking it gently, turned to face the newcomers.

'I assume you're aware of Fiacail's suggestion for a gathering. Given the events falling out of the air these past few days, it seemed a sensible opportunity to share knowledge and collate our thoughts.'

'I'm aware,' the Grey One answered. 'But where is he? There seems little point in calling for such a gathering and then omitting to turn up.'

Bodhmhall made a calming gesture. 'He's gone to walk about the *ráth*, to reacquaint himself with the settlement. I can't imagine he'll be far off.'

While Liath Luachra muttered under her breath, Demne raised the bowl to his mouth to hide a sympathetic flinch. Prior to meeting Liath Luachra, that was exactly what he'd been doing, intrigued to see if anything had changed over the years he'd been away.

Fortunately, they didn't have long to wait for the Seiscenn Uairbhaoil man's return. Just a few moments later, Demne heard the distinctive tread of heavy footsteps approaching the roundhouse. There was a polite smack of a hand against the door's heavy wooden panel, and it slowly swung inwards. Entering the roundhouse, Fiacail mac Codhna took a step forward and peered around with interest, his gaze taking in the solid roof support posts, the clothing that hung from the embedded pegs, and the shelves of herbs, the workbench where Bodhmhall was busy manufacturing her tincture. Slowly, his gaze drifted towards the wooden stand that held Liath Luachra's worn leather battle harness before settling, at last, on the curved brushwood sleeping platform and its unruly pile of furs.

He sighed.

'Oh, Bodhmhall. Your settlement has grown three-fold and yet here, in your home, you live as frugally as ever.' Moving closer to the *bandraoi*, he tossed a thumb back over his shoulder in the direction of the doorway.

'I'm pleased to see you've replaced that old flap with a proper door and added some bits of furniture after all these years but, otherwise, everything looks the same.'

Demne had to stifle a giggle as Liath Luachra glanced across the fire and mockingly rolled her eyes. Bodhmhall, preoccupied with mixing the contents of her jug, smiled politely at the warrior's observation but made no response.

The others waited patiently, watching as the *bandraoi* poured the herbal mixture into a small wooden bowl. Setting the jug aside, she stepped forward and handed it directly to the Seiscenn Uairbhaoil man. Accepting the proffered container, Fiacail raised it to his chin, closed his eyes and inhaled the steam from its contents with an appreciative smile.

'*An Gorm Géarmhilis*!' The Bittersweet Blue!

Taking one careful sip, and then another, the big man nodded as he licked his lips. 'Aaah. Now there's a flavour to shake memories from this cobwebbed skull.' He grinned broadly at her. 'Did you prepare it specially for me? Of all your herbal concoctions, this has always been my favourite.'

Bodhmhall shrugged.

'A simple enough task, Fiacail.'

Wiping her hands with a cloth, the *bandraoi* stepped towards the fire. Reaching for one of the stools, she slid it over to a position alongside her nephew. Demne automatically shuffled aside to give her more space as she sat down, striving to make himself as inconspicuous as possible. Although he had the sense he'd been granted access to this small gathering, no-one had actually confirmed that. Accustomed to the embarrassing reality of being excluded from adult discussions in the past, on this occasion he was determined to remain and hear everything that was said.

Oblivious to these stubborn intentions, his aunt was entirely focussed on the Seiscenn Uairbhaoil man.

'Fiacail, you know it always warms my heart to see you, but after everything you've done to keep my nephew safe and now, bringing him home a grown man, well ....' The sentence trailed off as she raised her palms in a helpless gesture. 'Sometimes there aren't words enough to express the gratitude.'

Demne noted that Liath Luachra seemed to have taken an inordinate interest in the roundhouse floor, for she was now staring down at it with disquieting intensity. Fiacail's grin, meanwhile, had grown even broader.

'Were I able to claim responsibility for even a fraction of that achievement, Bodhmhall, you know I'd not hesitate in doing so. Sadly, ...'

He cast a sideway glance at Demne who kept his eyes down and slurped determinedly at his stew, pretending not to have noticed the talk in his regard.

'Sadly, such credit falls squarely on your nephew. Despite my best efforts to conceal his origins, his breeding shone through everywhere from the gold strands in his dyed hair to the irrepressible skill of his sport and fighting. Look at him! See the man he's grown into. His physique is apt, his limbs are sleek, his muscles strong and his *bod* intact. All this, despite the fact that he eats with his face in the trough like a half-starved piglet.'

Although he'd been basking silently in the warrior's rare praise, this last statement caused the youth to look up with a frown, stew dripping liberally from his lips and chin. Bodhmhall and Fiacail chuckled, and his frown deepened further when he saw the woman warrior's lips twitch in amusement. With a scowl, he dropped his eyes back into the bowl and sank lower on his seat.

The *bandraoi* waved towards the last of the stools. 'Sit and join us, Fiacail.'

She waited patiently as the big man did so, although it took him some time to find a comfortable alignment for his arse on the seat's limited surface area. When he finally appeared to have settled, Bodhmhall continued.

'In truth, it embarrasses me to offer regret at the subdued nature of your welcome and the hospitality that's your due. You'll understand, I hope, this isn't from any lack of desire on our part but rather the result of ... troubling events that constrict our efforts.'

'Aaah.' The Seiscenn Uairbhaoil man gave a wry laugh and glanced sideways at the warrior woman who continued to stare fixedly, if calmly, at the ground. 'And would these *troubling events* have anything to do with the comatose individual stretched flat in your wood store?'

'They may,' Bodhmhall conceded. 'Although they may have more to do with the *tíolacadh* visions I recently experienced, one of which foretold my nephew's return.'

'Huh!' Fiacail gave a bemused grunt. Taking another gulp from the bowl, he wiped the moisture from his moustache and eyed her in quiet reflection. 'I should have guessed as much when you greeted us inside the gateway. The look in your eyes gave no sense of the great wonder I'd expected our arrival to elicit. Even then it struck me that although you mightn't have known *when* we were coming, you certainly *knew* we were coming.'

Finishing the *An Gorm Géarmhilis* with one last slurp, he smacked his lips as he rested the bowl on his right knee.

'You may find this hard to believe, *a Cailleach Dubh*, but the stretch of years dimmed my memory to the true extent of your *Gift*. Although ...' He airily held out both palms in an apologetic manner. 'I wouldn't have expected a vision from *an tíolacadh* relating to our arrival. I'd always understood it to portend elements of a more worrisome nature.'

Bodhmhall breathed silently as she returned his gaze. Watching her, Demne had the sense that a small quiet had somehow opened up inside her as a result of the big man's words. Thankfully, it was short-lived.

'And there you have the nub of it, Fiacail. *An tíolacadh* usually manifests in times of danger. Hence my concern to find it offering a vision of Demne, who I'd believed safe in fa-'

'Fionn,' said Demne.

Bodhmhall glanced at him in confusion, her train of thought uncoupled by the unexpected interruption.

The youth coughed and cleared his throat. '*Fionn* is the name I carry now, *a Aintín*. I mentioned this to you on my arrival.'

Under his aunt's silent gaze, Demne felt an anxious flush of uncertainty. At least, he thought he'd mentioned this. He'd been so flustered by emotion on seeing her that he honestly couldn't remember.

A slight wrinkling of the upper forehead was Bodhmhall's sole response to this correction. Returning her attention to Fiacail, she smoothly continued her sentence. '... who I'd believed safe in faraway territories, suddenly arriving at my gateway.'

His aunt paused then to brush some imagined specks of dust from the material of her *léine,* now stretched taut across her knees.

'Unfortunately, beyond the image of a faceless man, *an tíolacadh* offered no context to the source of that danger. Given that the visions included an image of Dem-'. She caught herself. 'Of my nephew however, that suggests some connection to your return.'

The *bandraoi* leaned forward, the sudden fierceness of her expression taking Demne by surprise.

'So, tell me, Fiacail. What lies behind your unexpected – if very welcome – return?'

Despite the singular intensity of the *bandraoi's* gaze, the big man appeared completely nonplussed and took his time easing back on his stool and mulling over the question before making a response. 'Well,' he said at last. 'The truth is there are several reasons behind our return to Glenn Ceoch. Your charming features, for example, have always drawn me like deer to the first shoots of spring. Then of course, there's my own thirst for travel and adventure, a formidable craving that has never been fully satisfied.'

Pausing to reach into the bowl on his knee, he ran his forefinger carefully around the inner curve of its rim before popping it into his mouth and sucking on it with a pleased expression.

'And the real reason?' pressed Bodhmhall.

Fiacail sighed. Taking the bowl, he leaned forward to dip it into the stew pot and scooped up a small serving. Making himself comfortable again, he wiped the meaty residue on the outside surface of the bowl with his fingers and then licked them.

'Oh, my! This is abs-'

'Fiacail.'

Amused by the *bandraoi's* impatience, he beamed at her over the flames of the fire.

'Oh, very well. The real reason for our presence is, sadly, far less pleasant. We're here because of a threat from the north-east.'

Bodhmhall pulled back a little at this response, her earlier intensity dissipating into an expression of weary resignation. She exhaled slowly. '*Clann Morna.* Yes. I suspected as much. They've already made their presence known.'

'*Clann Morna?*' Fiacail was looking at her in confusion. 'No. Further north than that. I'm referring to the *Uí Cuaich.*'

'The *Uí Cuaich?*'

Bodhmhall stared at the big man in muted disbelief. Beside her, Demne's own stare reinforced it. Like most at Seiscenn Uairbhaoil, he had some limited knowledge of *Uí Cuaich* activities, but Fiacail's disclosure was just as much of a revelation to him.

Prompted by their reactions, Liath Luachra lifted her gaze from the floor, fully alert now as her dark eyes flicked from Bodhmhall to the Seiscenn Uairbhaoil man and back again. 'Who ...' she asked, '... are the *Uí Cuaich*?'

Bodhmhall glanced sideways at her, momentarily thrown by the question. 'The ... the *Uí Cuaich* are a people occupying territory far to the north of *Clann Baoiscne* lands. There's been little interaction between the tribes because of the distance separating them across the Great Wild.'

Her lips curled down as her gaze turned inward.

'I don't remember much about them. They had little to no influence on our existence at Dún Baoiscne although I do recall hearing that they'd grown by absorbing smaller tribes through inter-marriage and inter-tribal alliances. Some people considered them a *mórtuath* – a full tribal confederation – in their own right.'

The *Clann Baoiscne* woman adjusted her position on the stool, straightening her spine and sitting upright to regard Fiacail with greater attention.

'What do the *Uí Cuaich* have to do with our situation? The last mention I heard of them – a great many years ago – was my father complaining of their growing closeness with the Druidic Order.'

'Then your father had the right of it,' Fiacail commented through a mouthful of stew. 'The *Uí Cuaich* association with the Druidic Council has warmed even further these past years. *An Ollamh*, the leader of the Druidic Council, has kinship links to *Uí Cuaich* through his mother's side. I've also heard that his hunger for greater authority over the tribes has been sated through their absorption by *Uí Cuaich*. In return, their consolidation of power receives a degree of legitimacy through the Council's blessing.'

Demne observed his aunt's grave expression as she took that in and could imagine her mind toiling furiously as she worked through the various ramifications. 'Who leads the *Uí Cuaich* nowadays?' she asked. 'When I was younger, I believe it was Aonghus Cam but he had no reputation for such ambition.'

'Aonghus Cam's passed over six years now. The new *rí* of *Uí Cuaich* is a man with the name of Conaire on him.'

'And does this Conaire have a deformed face on him?'

'A deformed face?'

'Features that are scarred or disfigured.'

Although he seemed surprised by the question, Fiacail gave it his full consideration.

'I've not locked eyeballs with the man, but if he bears such a physical blemish, it's doubtful he'd hold the position of *rí*. Besides, tales of such a deformity would surely have spread south by now and I've never heard him described in such a manner.'

Bodhmhall seemed to settle even more stiffly on her stool, visibly frustrated by the big man's response. 'If this Conaire isn't the man from my vision, then I still struggle to understand why the political machinations of such a distant tribe prompted your return to Ráth Bládhma.'

'Well, that's because the *Uí Cuaich* are no longer so distant. Three years past, secure in the backing of the Druidic Council, Conaire decided to expand the *Uí Cuaich* borders. One early spring morning, he dispatched forces north to claim *Clann Chaoch* territory for their own. In that endeavor, they were successful, for *Clann Chaoch* were a minor grouping and their resistance was quickly quashed. The survivors, the smart ones at least, wisely accepted the status of vassal tribe to *Uí Cuaich*.'

The big man paused to wipe his mouth with the back of his hand, burping softly before he continued.

'This year, emboldened by that success, Conaire turned his eye south. Since the beginning of spring, his forces have been nibbling at the northern edges of *Clann Baoiscne* territory and further east to the *Clann Morna* lands. More recently, the leaders at Seiscenn Uairbhaoil received an invitation – some might call it a veiled threat – to consider merging with the *Uí Cuaich*. It's my belief that, to avoid conflict, they will do so.

'But Seiscenn Uarbhaoil is *Clann Baoiscne*,' protested Bodhmhall.

'That may be,' Fiacail conceded. 'But you know as well as I that Tréanmór's never been particularly well liked. In Seiscenn Uairbhaoil, the people's distaste for his leadership has only grown with the savage response to Lonán Ballach's attempt to usurp him. Ever since the slaughter at Cnucha, *Clann Baoiscne* have struggled to field enough warriors to defend their territory. That infighting with Lonán Ballach has left even fewer men to oppose the seizure of *Clann Baoiscne* territory. As it is, they can barely hold the central tribe lands. The territories of its subtribes are a low priority for Tréanmór.'

'Seiscenn Uairbhaoil still owes him fealty.'

'Fealty is earned,' Fiacail answered. 'Or imposed. In this case, *Clann Baoisnce* can do neither.'

Bodhmhall's rigid stance seemed to crumple then, for she slumped back on the stool, her hands clasped tightly together. Her eyes closed momentarily as a flicker of something like pain passed across her features. 'I was aware of none of this. None of it.'

Fiacail's expression softened. 'That's hardly a surprise, Bodhmhall. Ráth Bládhma is an isolated settlement, one made even more isolated through your own efforts to conceal it. As for those developments in the north ...' He rolled a shrug off one shoulder. 'They're relatively recent and they may be substantial, but *Uí Cuaich* were effective and subtle in their implementation.'

A low growl emanated from Liath Luachra. Turning to face her, Demne felt a quiver of alarm at the frosty manner in which she was eyeing the Seiscenn Uairbhaoil man.

'Your tales of tribal intrigues displease me, Fiacail.'

The big man gave a dismissive twist of the lips.

'That's no surprise either, Grey One. By nature, you are contrary.'

Demne watched as the woman warrior returned Fiacail's gaze, her expression unreadable, her body locked in a rigid stiffness that radiated ... nothing discernible.

Except to those who knew her.

When she spoke again, her voice was unruffled but the youth could sense the tension ratcheted behind it.

'What you tell us is all well and good, but it doesn't explain your presence at Ráth Bládhma.'

Fiacail sniffed and held up his right hand to study his fingernails. 'Aaah. Forgive me, Liath Luachra. I'd forgotten your *éclann* background. An understanding of tribal dynamics isn't always so obvious to outsiders.'

'Fiacail.'

Demne almost sighed with relief at Bodhmhall's sudden intervention. Although a little daunted by her commanding comportment, he couldn't help but be impressed by the firm manner

181

in which she'd lanced the boil of mounting antagonism. Her voice had been composed and level when she'd uttered the Seiscenn Uairbhaoil man's name, but there was no mistaking the loaded warning in her eyes.

The big man sighed. 'Oh, very well!' He looked directly at Liath Luachra. The woman warrior returned his gaze with stony calm, displaying no anger at the veiled insult.

'We are here because any agreement to meld with a *mórtuath* requires a demonstration of fealty from the tribe being absorbed. That usually involves a commitment of resources to the goals of the *mórtuath*. In this situation, given the *Uí Cuaich's* hunger for expansion, I suspect nothing less than a contribution of warriors would satisfy them.'

'A warrior such as yourself,' the Grey One said quietly, her words more statement than question.

'Yes. As a resident of Seiscenn Uairbhaoil and an experienced warrior, I'm likely to find myself coerced into battles for causes I don't support. More concerning, however, is that a certain *óglach*, of suitable age and experience is likely to be conscripted in a similar manner.'

In the ensuing silence, Fiacail dropped his empty wooden bowl onto the floor. The hollow ringing sound it made only served to emphasize that hush until he moved to rupture it again.

'Having seen no evidence of a threat against Dem- ... Fionn for six years, I decided it best to bring him back to Ráth Bládhma before being presented with no choice in the matter. Either way, Seiscenn Uairbhaoil is no longer a safe place to hide.'

His tale completed, Fiacail sat back carefully and folded his arms.

'So does that satisfy you, Grey One?'

Liath Luachra shook her head. 'No.'

Fiacail's bushy eyebrows rose in gruff displeasure.

'No? Why not?'

'Because although your tale provides a reason for leaving Seiscenn Uairbhaoil it offers none for the *tíolacadh* vision. The *Uí Cuaich* hold no blood feud against Bodhmhall's family. Where's the threat to Ráth Bládhma? *Níl sa rud ar fad ach seafóid.* The whole thing is ridiculous. These *Uí Cuaich* cannot be the threat. There must be another reason.'

Fiacail seemed to give a small internal shrug. 'If there is,' he offered with flinty control. 'Then it's one unknown to me.'

Sensing the fresh antagonism building up between them, Bodhmhall moved to deflect the sea storm from striking the coast.

'We may differ on particulars, but I think we can agree that someone, somewhere, is actively aligned against us. We've had the luxury of six years of peace, and I hold no regret at having my nephew home again. That said, it'd be foolish to ignore the presence of dark forces in the shadows. The threat against Demne remains as real as it was six years ago. We must plan to ensure his protection.'

'I can protect myself,' Demne muttered sullenly, frustrated by his aunt's insistence on referring to him by his given name. In the gravity of the discussion however, his comment seemed to pass unheard.

'Yes, but from where does that threat originate?' Fiacail wondered aloud. 'Who are those dark forces in the shadows?'

That question prompted a thoughtful silence that Bodhmhall was the first to break.

'The influence of Almhu hasn't diminished in all this time. I still feel the touch of Tadg's dark hand on occasion. When he tests the edges of sleep.'

Fiacail grunted unhappily at that. 'Tadg mac Nuadat. It's certainly possible, although it's a source of great bafflement to me as to why he'd wish a violent death on his own grandson.'

'That same question's baffled us these past six years, Fiacail.' The *bandraoi* made an irritated gesture. 'I can only imagine there's some critical morsel of information Muirne Muncháem neglected to share with us in that regard. There's certainly been no let-up in her father's determination.'

'And does he still trouble you with nightly visits?'

Bodhmhall shook her head. 'Not for some years. After his first night trespass, I trained my mind to repel his incursions. Once I'd learned how to create effective barriers, I helped Liath Luachra develop a similar defence.'

Her forehead wrinkled then as she glanced across to the woman warrior. A brief look passed between them but it was a look the youth was unable to decipher. When she turned back to face the Seiscenn Uairbhaoil man again, her features were composed.

'With respect to Tadg's incursions, I endured far less than Liath Luachra. Tadg's bitterness at her thwarting of his plans meant he focussed on her with a particular malice.'

Demne cast a furtive glance at the warrior woman, but her features remained impenetrable, and she displayed no reaction to the comment. Fiacail yawned, thoughtfully tapping the wooden spoon, that he still held, against the palm of his left hand.

'Well, you'd have to say the Grey One does has a way of bringing out the worst tend-'

Demne flinched but by then Fiacail words had already run aground on the harsh reef of the *bandraoi's* glare. Abashed, he held up both hands in a gesture of contrition.

'Yes, yes. Such a comment was probably undeserved. I recognise the Grey One's achievements in foiling Tadg's plans even as I recognise the debt owed her for sparing us a violent and grisly demise. It's just …'

He tossed the wooden spoon into the bowl that he'd dropped on the ground. It rattled noisily as he floundered for a response.

'It's just a pity she didn't cut his throat when she had the chance.'

Impassive as ever. the woman warrior quietly bent forward and poked at the ashes with a stick. 'Had the circumstances allowed it, that's exactly what I would have done. Unfortunately, they didn't … and I didn't.'

Bodhmhall groaned aloud, an unsubtle warning at her vexation with the continued enmity between them.

'Not Tadg then,' she suggested, moving the conversation on from the smouldering remains of its predecessor. 'But it could well be Tréanmór. Our escape from Dún Baoiscne made him look weak and foolish at a time when he was uniquely exposed. My father's never been one to repress his feelings of displeasure and there's little doubt that he now bears us a deep measure of malice. With Lonán Ballach's challenge dealt to and his Five Friends and his Whispers to subdue any opposition, it may well be that he seeks to retrieve his heir to cement his future grip on power.'

From the stiffness of the Seiscenn Uairbhaoil man's posture however, Demne could tell that Fiacail held strong doubts with regards to this suggestion. When the *bandraoi* concluded, he made those misgivings known by shaking his head.

'Tréanmór may be keen to retrieve his grandson but with *Uí Cuaich* now testing Dún Baoiscne's borders, he'll have troubles enough to occupy him.' He scratched irritably at the stubble of his chin and grunted his conclusion. 'I don't believe the threat stems from Dún Baoiscne.'

A strained stillness filled the roundhouse as the company digested that.

'*Clann Morna*, then' Bodhmhall countered at last. 'Their bloodfeud against the male progeny of Tréanmór has lost none of its potency. *And* we know they actively obstruct any messengers travelling to Ráth Bládhma.'

Another gloomy silence fell over the company for no-one could think of an appropriate response to that supposition.

Feeling it was time to contribute something to the conversation, Demne nervously cleared his throat. 'Could it be the traitor?' he asked. 'The traitor who betrayed us to Tadg's ambush. The same traitor who provided him with physical tokens from you and Liath Luachra to allow his Dark Man to enter your dreams.'

Bodhmhall turned to stare at him in surprise. 'You retain a keen memory of events from six years ago, nephew. You were little more than a child at the time.'

Feeling a little intimidated under the keenness of his aunt's gaze, Demne nodded awkwardly. 'Yes,' he said, unable to think of anything else to add.

On the far side of the flames, Liath Luachra shifted position on the firm roundhouse floor, the movement prompting a soft hiss in response to some newly discovered ache.

'Who can tell. The identity of the traitor remains unknown to us.'

'Sadly, that's all too true.'

The beaten tone of his aunt's response caused Demne to glance towards her and, for an instant, she looked utterly exhausted, as though her earlier drive and fortitude had completely dissipated.

'I must confess, it still troubles me to think someone close could be my enemy, that one of the people I live or lived with, could wish harm on me or others I love. That's a level of deception and unscrupulous scheming I truly struggle to fathom.'

She shook her head a single time, as though divesting herself of an unpleasant thought.

'The unfortunate truth is that the four of us can trust no-one but each other. Distressing though the thought may be, the words and actions of anyone beyond this roundhouse are suspect.'

'On that subject,' said Fiacail.

Bodhmhall glanced at him, curious.

'Yes?'

'Does it not strike you as strange that we four – myself, yourself, Liath Luachra and Demne – have all gathered here at the same time?'

The *bandraoi's* gaze slipped downward and she chewed on her lower lip as she thought that through. Finally, she raised her eyes again, locking onto his with quiet certainty.

'It's an interesting conjecture but none of us could have foreseen this. Because we reside here, the presence of myself or Liath Luachra might well be expected, but as for you and Demne ...' Again, she shook her head, this time more slowly. 'None of us had any inkling of your return. When we did learn of that possibility, it was mere days before your arrival and came from a source that absolutely no-one could control.'

Fiacail nodded in silent acknowledgement of the *bandraoi's* assessment, but Demne sensed that the big man remained unconvinced. Before he could query the matter further however, a strong slap against the wooden panel of the door ended the discussion. All four turned to the doorway as the heavy slab swung inwards and Cónán was revealed on the threshold, silhouetted against the grey hue of the dusk behind him. His features were grave, but a gleam of excitement flickered in his eyes.

'My regrets for the intrusion,' he said. 'There is news.'

'Yes?' asked Bodhmhall.

'It's the man in the litter.'

'What of him?'

Cónán sniffed and wiped his nose with the sleeve of his *léine*. 'He's awake and asking for the *banfénnid*. And for Bodhmhall ua Baoiscne.'

Cónán's abrupt intrusion and a growing sense of frustration at the lack of resolution from their discussions meant there was unanimous agreement to terminate the gathering. Bodhmhall and the Grey One were the first to rise, moving quickly towards the doorway and following Cónán out into the fading light. Taking advantage of their departure, Fiacail delayed to help himself to another serving of stew. Refilling his wooden bowl, he slurped from it greedily as he got to his feet. Swallowing the last of its contents, he dropped the container onto the ground but as he made for the doorway to follow the others, Demne stepped forward to grasp him by the arm.

'You never told me.'

Fiacail looked at him, his eyebrows turning down at the youth's accusatory tone. 'I have a lifetime's worth of revelations I've never told you. Which one in particular do you refer to?'

Demne felt his cheeks flush, but he bit down on his anger.

'Of the *Uí Cuaich*. Of the threat they posed to Seiscenn Uairbhaoil or the true reason for our departure. In fact ...' The youth's features hardened as he recalled conversations between them prior to leaving the north-eastern territories. 'You told me we were returning to Ráth Bládhma because my aunt missed me and sought my return.'

'Well, the former was hardly untrue. You've seen the pleasure your presence gives your aunt.'

'That's not the cause of my anger. You never told me of the danger in Seiscenn Uairbhaoil. You were untruthful in the reasons you gave for leaving.'

Fiacail glared huffily at the youth before giving in to a harsh growl of exasperation. 'Does everyone seek to burden me with such weighty accusations? It seems that if I'm not slyly striving to conceal the reasons for our arrival then I'm attempting to conceal the reasons for our departure. Can a good man not work to aid his friends without being reproached with suspicions of an ulterior purpose?'

'I don't know, Fiacail,' the youth retorted. 'Was there an ulterior purpose for coming to Ráth Bládhma?'

'None that didn't align with the true purpose for coming here. The same one I've already declared.'

The big man scowled and although he continued to glower in affronted offence, his natural effusiveness meant he couldn't sustain it for long.

'Oh, very well. In hindsight, perhaps I could have been more forthcoming. The truth is I felt it unnecessary to burden you with the true reasons for our departure. We were leaving after all, and a predicament outrun is a predicament avoided.'

He paused as though to assess whether the response had been sufficient to allay the youth's anger, but Demne gave him no leeway in that regard. With a sigh and a shrug, the big man continued.

'When we left Seiscenn Uairbhaoil, you were still a callow youth. Over the course of the great distance we covered, however, I've seen the growing traits of the man you'll be. Everything I told your aunt was true. I admit I may have misjudged your resilience. I hope you can find it within yourself to accept this truth.'

Demne breathed deeply, conscious of the resentment still smouldering in his chest but also conscious that it was time to divest himself of it and make his peace.

'Yes. Of course.' He paused. 'But I grow weary of others seeking to protect me from the truth of things. I have to make my own way through the Great Wild. It would help greatly if my friends informed me of the true dangers associated with certain paths rather than hoping I'll never cross them.'

Fiacail eyed him with fresh appreciation. '*Go maith*! That's a mature response. One that clearly shows my beneficial influence. Shall we go inform your aunt and then listen to what the snoring stranger has to say?'

Demne awkwardly shifted his weight from one foot to the other.

'There's another topic I'd first raise with you.'

'I see. You have yet another ingredient for my stew of troubles. What is it you wish to speak of?'

'Of Liath Luachra.'

'And what of Liath Luachra?'

'You shouldn't … nettle her the way you did.'

That seemed to take the Seiscenn Uairbhaoil man by surprise. 'Why not?'

'Because she was … upset.'

Fiacail blinked and stared at him closely. Demne couldn't tell if he was genuinely startled by the response or playfully mocking him.

'She was … upset,' Fiacail repeated slowly. He frowned. 'And how could you tell she was upset?'

'Because she was quiet and said nothing.'

'She's always quiet!'

Demne hesitated, struggling to articulate something that was more half-formed instinct than fully fledged opinion. 'Sometimes Liath Luachra is … more than quiet. When that stillness comes over her … it's as though the world holds its breath. There's a … tension to the air and I never really know … I never really what's going to happen.'

Fiacail eyed him curiously. 'You think she'd pose a danger?'

Demne shrugged uncomfortably. 'I don't know.'

Fiacail sighed. 'Demne, Liath Luachra and I … Well, our natures are opposites. She reflects the dark of night as I exhibit the bright light of day. She is the fading gown of autumn while I am the blossoming spring.'

Demne cleared his throat, not entirely convinced at the accuracy of the Seiscenn Uairbhaoil man's comparisons but recognising that it probably wasn't the most appropriate time to correct him. 'I understand what you're saying Fiacail but …'

'… but you feel the antagonism between us could end in combat?'

Although his gaze had been drifting with the scattering of his thoughts, Demne's eyes now centred back on Fiacail. The big man was looking directly at him, and it took several heartbeats to form a response. When he spoke, what came out sounded far too clumsy and insubstantial to his own ears.

'I don't know. But …but if such a combat was to take place, I do know I'd lose someone very dear to me.'

Fiacail continued to stare at him but, after a moment, Demne sensed something inside the big man give way. Slowly, the tension seemed to ease from his frame and reaching out, he rested one heavy hand on Demne's shoulder. 'Rest easy,' he said with uncharacteristic softness. 'Liath Luachra and I may have our differences but you've nothing to fear in that regard.'

Moving his hand, he abruptly slapped the youth firmly on that same shoulder, his eyes once again beaming with bravado.

'But now, let us go and find our friends.'

Liath Luachra was awaiting them in the lean-to, squatting easily with her back against the inner sidewall, just out of reach of the litter. Of Bodhmhall, there was no sign but Cónán was affixing a flaming torch to the high frame that held the sloping roof in place. Flickering wildly in the evening breeze, it cast an animated yellow light on the shelter's interior.

With a curt instruction from Liath Luachra, Cónán left them, heading back to the *lis* on the other side of the roundhouses, nodding at Fiacail and Demne as he passed. Drawing closer to the shelter, the youth saw that the Stranger was still flat on his back in the litter. His face looked thinner than when he'd last seen him, as though his features had somehow lost substance in the erratic yellow light. The haggard result wasn't helped by the man's drooping eyelids and the scraggy state of his beard yet despite that ragged appearance, he was obviously alert for he regarded their approach with open suspicion.

Stepping into the shelter, Fiacail looked down at the prostrate figure. 'Well, Old Father. You've had a good sleep, but that face would make even a mother weep.' He bent down and reached one hand out to help the Stranger to his feet. Instead, the old man slapped it away.

'Get away, you unsavoury lout!'

The Seiscenn Uairbhaoil man considered the rejection with a bemused expression but stood upright and stepped back without comment. The old man's gaze, meanwhile, drifted grumpily around the others present before coming to a rest on Demne.

'You, boy. Respect your elder and help me up. That woman warrior there will assist you.'

Demne glanced at Liath Luachra. Her single nod was all but imperceptible, but he caught it all the same.

Moving dutifully around to the old man's far side, he took up a position that was mirrored by Liath Luachra on the near side. Each grasped a shoulder and an arm and Demne found himself surprised at the weight and strength in the old man's body. The Stranger may have been old, but he certainly wasn't fragile.

Grunting from the effort, they manoeuvred him into a sitting position. Once he was comfortably upright, they released him and stepped back as he surveyed the group around him. His crabby expression gave the impression he wasn't particularly impressed by what he saw.

'You,' he snapped at Liath Luachra. 'Warrior woman.'

'Feoras,' she acknowledged with admirable restraint.

'What poison did you feed me? My bowels sting and my head aches like a jagged cloud.'

Liath Luachra shrugged. 'I'm sure it'll pass soon enough.'

Feoras appear unmollified by the assurance.

'And where have you brought me? Is this Ráth Bládhma? This looks like a woodshed! Where's the person to whom I must impart my message?'

'She'll be along.'

In fact, it turned out that she was already there. The words had barely left the Grey One's mouth when Bodhmhall entered the lean-to, a leather waterskin in her right hand. Apparently, she'd taken the time to appear more presentable before their visitor for she'd managed to find a cloak that covered her *léine* and now wore a silver headband to hold her long, black hair in place.

Approaching the old man, she knelt and held the skin out towards him. The stranger looked from the skin to the *Clann Baoisnce* woman and back again. Licking his parched lips, he opted to accept the offering and took the container with both hands. Raising it to his mouth, he drank greedily, swallowing the skin's entire contents before tossing it on the ground and wiping his lips with the back of his hand. By then, Bodhmhall had got to her feet again but instead of looking at her, the old man's attention had drifted back to Demne.

'You,' he said before lapsing into a fit of coughing. Hacking into his arm, it took him a moment to recover but when he did, he focussed back on Demne once more. 'You,' he repeated. 'If this is Ráth Bládhma, then you must be the son of Cumhal.'

He peered at the youth a little more closely.

'Yes. You certainly have his eyes and mouth. And his hair colour, of course.'

Uncertain how to respond, Demne returned his stare in silence, relieved when his aunt moved in to assume control of the conversation.

'You knew Cumhal?'

The old man's gaze unlatched itself from Demne and came to rest on the *Clann Baoiscne* woman instead.

'I did.' He raised a hand to scratch at his bearded chin. 'And from the family resemblance, I'd imagine you must be Bodhmhall ua Baoiscne.'

The *bandraoi* eyed him coldly in response.

'That's the name I have on me.'

'Do you not recognise me?'

'Should I recognise you?'

'Perhaps not. We met once but that was very long ago, and you were far younger.'

The grey-haired man chewed on his lip for a moment then turned to look at Liath Luachra. 'You should take your comrades and leave. Now my words are for Bodhmhall Ua Baoiscne alone.'

Liath Luachra lips curved into a tight smile. 'I don't think so,' she said.

'Then there'll be no message imparted. I don't know or trust these others, but I now know you well enough to distrust you entirely.' He snorted. 'Bah! Poisoning my drink, indeed. I'll have you kn-'

'I trust her,' said Bodhmhall.

The Stranger glanced towards her, irritated by the sudden interruption.

'I'll have y-'

'Just as I trust those present far more than I'll ever trust you,' she continued, stomping roughshod over his attempt to speak. 'If you have something to say, I suggest you spit it out now. Past experience leaves me with little patience for messengers and false claims of friendship so don't waste my time with such games.'

From the corner of the lean-to, Demne watched enthralled as his aunt ground the Stranger's obstinacy underfoot. Realising this was a verbal battle in which he wasn't going to prevail, Feoras allowed his eyes to slide off to one side, sly and furtive.

'If we're not alone there can be no message imparted.'

Bodhmhall however, was not to be dictated to.

'Then that's how it will be. I'll ask you to direct your eyes to Liath Luachra. She now bears a second skin for you, one with a second serving of the draught she used to bring you here.'

Feoras glanced towards the woman warrior who held up the skin in question, shaking it briefly so that he could hear the contents gurgling inside.

'When you're senseless,' Bodhmhall continued. 'You'll be transported into the Great Wild and deposited very far from here. When you come to – if you come to, you can then go your own way. But know this ...'

The *bandraoi* leaned forward over the Stranger with a striking sense of menace.

'Should you ever pass this way again, should I or one of my people ever cross paths with you again, your demise will be quick but extremely painful. That much, I promise you.'

Pulling back, Bodhmhall spun on one heel and started to leave the lean-to. Behind her, Feoras gulped silently, one hand unconsciously moving up to clutch at his throat.

'Wait!'

Bodhmhall paused, slowly turning her head to look back over her shoulder.

'You should not try me,' she warned.

'I'll do it!' he said quickly. 'You give me no choice. I will deliver the message.'

Sensing the sincerity in his voice, Bodhmhall shifted about to face him, an impatient frown on her face. 'Well …' she demanded.

'Do you not wish me to offer a surety?'

Bodhmhall shook her head. 'The last surety I was offered turned out to have less value than a lie. No. Deliver your message. I'll know whether you're telling the truth or not and the consequences will be yours to accept.'

'Very well.'

Although he was clearly shaken by the *bandraoi's* uncompromising bluntness, Feoras hurriedly closed his eyes and started to inhale deeply in a rhythmic fashion. Demne watched in fascination, recalling a description of *An Dord Rúnda* – the vocal technique used by the false messenger Cargal Uí Faigil to both memorise and deliver his message. On this occasion however, the process seemed far less contrived.

Taking another deep breath, the Stranger exhaled with the slow chant that he'd use to relay the memorised message. Soon, a steady drone was rolling up out of the old man's lower chest and he released the message into the air as a chesty intonation.

Listen to the words for Bodhmhall ua Baoiscne, daughter of Tréanmór, sister to Cumhal and Crimall.

All power to you, Bodhmhall ua Baoiscne.
Trust this man for he speaks for me.
So says your beloved brother Crimall.
Who hopes to lock eyes with you soon.

The droning murmur of the old man's chant continued wordlessly for a time, but it soon became apparent that the delivery of his message had been fulfilled. Finally, as the droning chant faded completely, he opened his eyes to stare at the *bandraoi*. Bodhmhall was staring directly back at him, her eyes cold, her manner unimpressed.

'That's it?' she said at last. 'That's the extent of your message? A concocted communication purporting to come from my long dead brother?'

Feoras looked at her uncertainly.

'You misunderstand, *a Cailleach Dubh*. This message is no false concoction. Your brother Crimall is alive and in hiding to the west.'

He coughed and paused to nervously lick his lips.

'But his life is now in mortal danger, and he urgently requests your help.'

This adventure concludes in FIONN: The Betrayal

Historical and Creative Note

Fionn: Stranger at Mullán Bán commences a second arc in the Fionn mac Cumhaill Series that builds on the various plotlines established over the previous books (and the Irish Woman Warrior Series – although that won't be so obvious as yet). One of the main changes you'll see in this arc compared to the earlier books, is the growing role of the character Demne/Fionn – no real surprise given that he's the titular protagonist and the vast amount of Fenian material relates predominantly to his adventures.

With *Fionn: Stranger at Mullán Bán,* my adaptation of the Fenian stories continues to align with the original narratives (including the lesser-known ones), although I have amended one element of the established plotline relating to the naming of Fionn. As a general rule, I approach any change to the original material with caution as its important that any ancient Irish cultural constructs aren't be diminished, rendered meaningless, or used out of context. In this case however, I've been obliged to adapt the original material as much of it is unclear. For example, if we take one of the more common English translations of the story (from Macgnímartha Finn), we find the following description of how Fionn got his name:

One day, he (Finn) went out alone until he reached Mag Life, and a certain stronghold there; and he saw the youths hurling upon the green of the stronghold there. He went to contend in running or in hurling with them. He came again the next day, and they put one-fourth of their number against him.
Again, they came with one-third of their number against him. However, at last they all went against him, and he won his game from them all.
"What is thy name?" they said.
"Demne," said he.
The youths tell that to the man (chieftain) of the stronghold. "Then kill him, if ye know how to do it - if ye are able to do it," says he.
"We should not be able to do aught to him," they said.
"Did he tell you his name?" asked he.
"He said," said they, "that his name was Demne."
"What does he look like?" said he.
"A shapely fair (finn) youth," said they.
"Then Demne shall be named Finn, (the Fair-haired One)," said he.
Whence the youths used to call him Finn.

He came to them on the next day and went to them at their game. All together, they threw their hurleys at him. He turns among them and throws seven of them to the ground.
He went from them into the forest of Sliabh Bládhma.

Then, at the end of a week, he came back to the same place. The youths were swimming in a lake that was close by. The youths challenge him to come and try to drown them. Thereupon he jumps into the lake to them and drowns nine of them. And after that he goes to Sliabh Bládhma.

"Who drowned the youths?" everybody asked.
"Fionn," said they.
So that henceforth the name Fionn clave to him.

Obviously, without the background cultural context (some of which you'll have picked up if you've been reading the series), it's difficult to make sense of the above description. The fact that the Old Irish – in which the original manuscript was written – was rendered into English of the time, also makes it more difficult for a contemporary audience. The adaptation you'll find in the book is contextually correct and it does work within the framework of the established narratives, so, I can honestly say – hand on heart – that …

No authentic Irish cultural constructs were harmed in the production of this book.

You'll also see in the above description that 'Fionn' is spelt 'Finn'. This – and the name 'Find' – were alternative spellings used for the name when it was originally written down in Old Irish. Most of the Fenian narratives translated to English from the 18th century onwards however, tended to use the name 'Finn' as educational entities in Ireland of the time were controlled and run by English institutions. Many of the people managing these institutions (with some important exceptions) couldn't speak Irish and didn't really have any real interest in Irish culture beyond its study as a conquered culture.

Much of the subsequent English translations were generally made for the purpose of entertaining English-speaking people and, as they struggled with the pronunciation of 'Fionn' and 'Find', the name 'Finn' was used instead. Consequently, 'Fionn mac Cumhaill' was also anglicized to the execrable 'Finn McCool' – a figure that's little more than a sanitized and anglicized caricature of the original.

Where to next?

The fifth book in the series (**Fionn: The Betrayal**) will be **available in 2023** and released through the **Irish Imbas Bookshop** some time before going out to the larger ebook stores. If you'd like be alerted when this (or any other Irish Imbas project) becomes available, you can sign up for the **New Release Notification** at the Irish Imbas website. This simple email is sent out 2-3 times a year (solely to notify people of a new release – there is no marketing).

Alternatively, readers who are interested in slightly more regular updates, aspects of the creative process, bits and bobs on new Irish Imbas projects and other articles, can sign up to the **monthly newsletter** (**Vóg**), which can also be done at the Irish Imbas website. This comes out 10 times a year.

As always, my thanks to those of you who've taken the time to read this book or who've made the effort to support my work through the Irish Imbas Patreon Page.

Brian O'Sullivan

Wellington, October 2022

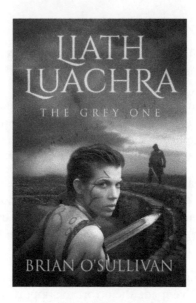

Liath Luachra

[The Grey One]

Ireland 1st century A.D. A land of tribal affiliations, secret alliances and treacherous rivalries. The young woman warrior, Liath Luachra, has survived two brutal years with mercenary war party "The Friendly Ones" but now the winds are shifting.

Dispatched on a murderous errand where nothing is as it seems, she must survive a group of treacherous comrades, the unwanted advances of her battle leader and a personal history that might be her own undoing.

Tribeless and friendless, she can count on nothing but her wits, her fighting skills and her natural ferocity to see her through.

Woman warrior, survivor, killer and future guardian to Irish hero Fionn mac Cumhaill – this is her story.

Liath Luachra: The Grey One [A Sample]

Liath Luachra, the Grey One of Luachair, watched the raiders slip in before dawn. Blurred figures barely distinguishable against the shaded grey background of the surrounding forest, they slid through the grass at the edge of the clearing like wolves on the hunt.

Wolves.

She considered that for a moment. It seemed ... apt. This particular band of raiders styled themselves in the manner of a wolf pack to the point of naming themselves *Na Madraí Allta* - The Wild Dogs. Their leader, a big man with black hair and a distinctive black beard, even went so far as to insist on being called *An Mactíre Dubh* – The Black Wolf.

As she watched, the Grey One chewed quietly on a stale slice of oat bread. The texture of the loaf was tough and leathery and she could feel pieces of the original kernel when she crushed it between her molars. Her belly twinged. She hadn't eaten since noon the previous day and her stomach, flat at the best of times, had recessed even further into her torso. Fortunately, the morsels she was chewing would keep the worst of the craving at bay, hold the hunger weakness off until she had a chance to eat again.

Or didn't need to eat again.

With that depressing reflection, she resumed her scrutiny of the raiders. Sprawled on her belly, she was lying in the treeline on the forested southern crest of a high, U-shaped ridge. The ridge formed a natural enclosure around a wide clearing and from that height she had an unobstructed, if murky, view of the little settlement situated directly below. In all, the settlement consisted of three rectangular thatched buildings and a number of lean-tos lying off to the side. The larger buildings formed a rough semicircle around a well-established fire pit located at the centre. Low flames cast a dull orange glow onto the mud and straw-daubed walls.

A herd of about fifteen cattle milled about the buildings and out around the pasture in the rest of the clearing. A squat figure was silhouetted against the fire. A sentry for the cattle, he'd proven unforgivably lax in his responsibilities. Overly confident in the security offered by the settlement's relative proximity to the *Uí*

Bairrche stronghold and the natural concealment of the encircling ridge, he'd simply left the cattle to fend for themselves and retired to the fire to doze.

'One, two, three, four.' A pause. 'Five, six … shit!' Another pause. 'One, two … three.'

The Grey One turned a sideways glance to Canann an Súil – Canann the Eye – who'd paused in his counting to scratch an itch through the thick fistful of whiskers enveloping his chin. Foiled by the bushiness of his facial growth, he settled for a quiet curse instead. The Grey One made no comment. Something of a simpleton, Canann was one of the least effective members of their *fian* – war party. He rarely said anything worth listening to and was beside her uniquely because of his exceptional night vision. Canann, it was claimed, could make out the contours of a pig's arsehole at the end of a deep mine shaft. There was no pig to be found anywhere for any great distance – except, perhaps, in the settlement below – but that claim would be sufficiently tested by his ability to identify how many raiders they faced.

'By The Great Father's testicles, shut your gob, Canann.' An infuriated whisper, laden with venom, this time originating from her left.

The Grey One frowned as she considered the darkness beside her. Bressal Binnbhéalach – Bressal SweetTongue – of the *Uí Loinge*, was usually the most articulate and self-disciplined of individuals. Almost completely obscured by the shadow beneath the forest canopy, she struggled to make him out.

'Calm, Bressal. They approach from the northern gap. They're too far away to hear us.'

'They'll hear us if that cretin doesn't stop counting out loud.'

The Grey One left the discussion at that. As *rígfénnid* – leader of the *fian* – Bressal could demand what he liked of its various members. For the most part a reasonable man, his current belligerence belied an intelligent mind and a superior facility when it came to sheer rat cunning. Despite his intellect however, she'd noticed a recurring pattern of abominable hostility over the course of the current season. Usually just before a fight.

It was the tension of course. Bressal was no fool. It was he, after all, who'd organised this particular action, who'd conceived and developed the plan for taking down the raiders. Now unfortunately, just prior to the battle, his behaviour was becoming a dangerous liability.

Liath Luachra reached across and placed a hand on his. The slim man's forearm was greasy with nervous sweat, the skin about his wrist warm and slimy. She forced herself to hold it there for a moment or two. As a general rule she avoided close physical contact with others and particularly with Bressal for the man had been seeking her caress for almost two years. Over that time, she'd done everything in her power to discourage such interest but right now he needed to be distracted.

As she anticipated, he started at her touch and with the shock of that contact she sensed the tension gush out of him. The leaves crackled softly as he shifted his weight and she pulled her hand back before he could interpret it for something more than it was or, worse, respond in kind. To prevent any further interaction, she turned away to face Canann. The keen-sighted buffoon was still counting but at least he'd reduced his voice to a muted whisper.

'Nine, ten, eleven … eleven, twelve.' He was silent for a moment. 'Twelve,' he declared suddenly but with obvious satisfaction. 'There are twelve men, Liath Luachra. Twelve men.'

'Are there twelve men or is it that you can only count to twelve?'

A momentary silence passed between them.

'There are twelve men,' he insisted, an aggrieved tone to his voice.

'Good, Canann. Good. She tossed him the compliment thoughtlessly, much as she'd toss an unwanted bone to a hungry dog. Despite the fact he was more than twice her age, the warrior lapped the praise up like an excited puppy, moaning softly and nodding to himself as though in confirmation of his count.

Ignoring both men, Liath Luachra turned her focus back to the approaching raiders. She didn't have Canann's keen eyesight but she still managed to catch glimpses of movement in the moonlight as the raiders spread out from the clearing's northern entrance and formed a rough arc along the treeline on either side. When they were ready, they'd swarm out around the settlement in that formation. For the moment however, they seemed happy enough just to sit and observe.

The guard should have been waiting at the entrance. Not warming himself by the fire.

That simple negligence irritated her, which was unusual. Few things roused the Grey One's emotions one way or the other but acts

201

of carelessness in a combat situation occasionally worked their way under her skin to provoke a stir of anger. She frowned, placating this uncharacteristic indignation with the knowledge that the guard would probably be the first to die. For the settlement below however, she felt no particular sense of sympathy, no empathy. By ignoring the most fundamental of responsibilities, they'd brought the consequences on themselves.

Crawling forwards, she edged out of the enclosing shadows until she could look down on the base of the ridge where the other *fénnid* – the other members of the *fian* – were concealed. Like the raiders, the settlement's inhabitants were unaware of their presence, an instruction from Mical Strong Arm who'd also shown them the secret route up from the far side of the steep ridge. Her *fian* were spread out down there, having formed a similar half-circle sometime after nightfall.

My fian.

She felt a momentary twinge of frustration at that. Bressal's *fian*, she corrected herself. *Na Cinéaltaí* of the *Uí Loinge*. Even their name – The Kindly Ones – bore Bressal's typically caustic sense of humour.

Raising her head again, she looked across the clearing to the trees where the incoming force was assembled.

Twelve raiders.

She bit at her fingernails. *Na Cinéaltaí* had seven *fénnid* in total, eight including Bressal. Two of these – Senach and Sean Fergus – were concealed off to the right. Three more – Murchú, Conall Cacach and Biotóg – off to the left. Although numerically inferior to their enemy, the odds didn't overly disturb her. *Na Cinéaltaí* would be working with the element of surprise. Absorbed in their slaughter, the raping of women and the pillaging of property, any possibility of opposition would be the last thing on the raiders' minds. She was also comforted by the fact that each of the *fénnid* carried two metal-tipped javelins. With the initial volleys, any numerical advantage would quickly be countered.

She experienced a small sense of satisfaction at that. The javelins had been her suggestion. Bressal, who'd laid out the *fian's* original placement, had made a big deal of humming and hawing as he'd considered it but he'd approved it in the end, as she'd known he would. Over the previous season of engagements, he'd increasingly deferred combat responsibilities to her. Despite his agreement, he'd also made a point of letting the other men know that he was accepting it only because it aligned well with his own plan.

And that his own plan was a good plan.

Liath Luachra wasn't too sure about that. It certainly wasn't so good for the settlement. A sub-branch of the *Uí Bairrche* tribe, its people had been cruelly sacrificed as bait to ensure the destruction of *An Mactíre Dubh*. Mical Strong Arm, the *rí* – king – of *Uí Bairrche* had even gone so far as to increase the likelihood of a raid at that particular settlement by spreading false rumours of a treasure cache hidden within one of the buildings.

Liath Luachra had initially been surprised by Mical Strong Arm's callousness towards members of his own tribe until Bressal, always well connected, had informed her of reasons behind it. According to one of Bressal's many cousins, the leader of this particular branch was a potential rival to Mical's son for the future leadership of *Uí Bairrche*. By allowing the settlement to be destroyed in the course of the raider's destruction, the *rí* was killing two birds with a single sling shot.

Liath Luachra tried to wipe the fatigue from her eyes. Following reports of *Na Madraí Allta's* incursion on *Uí Bairrche* territories, it had taken two days of frantic travel to get here in time for the raider's assault. There was little prospect of rest any time soon.

With an effort, she turned her focus to the distant trees. Now that the movement of the raiders had ceased, the clearing had taken on a derelict, deserted appearance. Settled comfortably in place, they'd most likely wait for dawn to have sufficient light to launch their attack.

The Grey One pulled her grey wool cloak about her shoulders. The autumn season was upon them and this would be the last *fian* action before the pre-winter dispersal. If they survived the next battle, the *fian* would travel back to Bressal's home place at the *Uí Loinge* stronghold where any loot would be distributed and the *fian* would disband, some members drifting back to their tribal territories for the winter, others *éclann* – tribeless – like her, finding alternatives to pass the frozen months.

She shuddered at the thought of winter. For her, the cold season would involve a return to Luachair, a desolate valley by the marshes far to the south-west. She'd spent the previous two winters in a small cave there. With a flap over the entrance passage and a low fire, the cave could, on occasion, feel relatively warm but mostly the cold would drive her to her blankets to sleep like a hibernating animal. In the heat beneath her furs and blankets, she'd nibble on *Beacáin Scammalach* – Cloud Mushroom – to smear her mind and avoid any chance of self-reflection. Most of her time would pass in an incoherent blur and, on occasion, she would not see daylight for days.

In the past, Luachair had contained four separate families, scattered in small farms along the length of the forested valley floor. A band of passing marauders had put paid to most of them. Nowadays, an old couple – the only other survivors and the last occupants of the valley – would come up to the cave every three days or so to leave food at the entrance: vegetables, broth and if she was lucky some kind of meat. The smell of food would eventually rouse her from her blankets although, once or twice, absorbed in her dream oblivion, she'd managed to ignore hunger for periods of up to four days.

Later, sitting beside the fire, she'd gobble the food down until she felt strong enough to venture outside and walk the valley before returning to the warmth of her blankets.

As a child, Liath Luachra too had lived in that valley. Now, with sixteen years on her, it was the only place that retained any semblance of home although 'home' was already a concept she no longer truly believed in. The old couple had been friends of her mother from a time before she could truly remember. Nowadays, she rarely spoke to them and avoided their attempts at conversation. The interaction she wanted with them was simple and very limited. In exchange for the food, firewood and privacy they provided over the course of the winter season, they received her share of booty from *fian* activities: the skins, the goats, metal, anything of value. It was a relationship very much stacked in the old couple's favour and although she was aware of this she didn't really care. The arrangement was a means of surviving the winter and prolonging her existence for another year, although the ongoing futility of the latter was something that was never far from her mind. All the same, it wasn't as though she had any realistic alternative.

Apart from an offer to share Bressal's bed.

She shivered.

Stop thinking. Focus on your enemy.

She looked across the clearing to the northern trees.

Soon.

***

The raiders made their move shortly after dawn, just as Liath Luachra had predicted. The attack was faultless, carried out with methodical coordination and precision. The twelve men rose from the trees as one, in response to some silent, predetermined signal. Advancing at a crouch, they moved forward in a wide semicircle, creeping purposefully towards the unsuspecting settlement.

By that time, Liath Luachra, Bressal and Canann had already worked their way down the ridge, using a slight dip to conceal their descent. Rejoining the others, Bressal had the *fian* form a curved line just inside the southern treeline so they had a clear view of the raiders' advance, unobstructed by the bulk of the buildings.

Crouched behind the bulky buttress of an ancient oak, Liath Luachra could feel the hunger for violence building inside her, the physical and emotional 'stretch' as her nerves pulled on her muscle tendons, twitching for release.

At Bressal's insistence, Murchú – their most recent and inexperienced recruit – was crouched alongside her. The *rígfénnid*'s nephew, he was a handsome youth of fifteen years or so but inexperienced and overly nervous. He repeatedly twisted the javelin haft between the palms of his hands and every now and again he'd raise the weapon as though preparing to cast it then quickly lower it again.

Patience tested by that irritating repetition, Liath Luachra released a feral growl from deep within her throat. Startled, the boy looked toward her and, noting the fearful widening of his eyes, for the briefest of moments she wondered what he saw. A girl in faded leathers, no doubt. Probably bigger than most girls he knew, lithe as a whipcord and strong.

She knew that most young men like Murchú didn't really know what to make of her. Her fine features and lack of facial hair revealed her gender for what it was but the contrast of those austere features with hair cropped close to the skull, the mass of white scars along her lower back and the tangible ferocity in her smoky grey eyes often left them confused as to how they should act with her.

'Breathe,' she instructed him and although it was expressed in a whisper it lacked no authority for that. 'Breathe in, breathe out. Focus

205

on your breath and try to relax your muscles until I tell you what to do next.'

In the colourless light of dawn, Murchú's face looked pale but he dipped his head in acknowledgement. Satisfied that he wasn't going to panic, the Grey One turned away to check her weapons, making sure that the sword pulled freely from its scabbard, that the metal tips of the javelins were firmly affixed and wouldn't break loose under pressure. She also slid the leather sling coiled around her left arm further up towards the elbow to make it sit more securely. A small bag of stone bullets lay inside her tunic but she doubted she'd have opportunity to use them in the coming engagement.

With that, she focussed on her own breathing for she could feel how her body had grown rigid from the mounting tension, the muscles of her neck and shoulders involuntarily cramping to the point where they felt as taut as deerskin on a tanning frame. The sensation was one she was familiar with but no less uncomfortable for that. Her body always reacted in this manner before battle, tightening up like an enraged but restrained hound just prior to being unleashed.

In a strange sort of sympathetic symmetry, her mind also seemed to coil tighter at such moments, as though her intellect was battling to repress the animal bloodlust inside her. Ironically, she always felt that her mind never functioned as well as it did leading up to that point of release. Just before battle, her thoughts were pure, crisp and as sharp as the finest blade. At the surrender to that physical action however, all reason was discarded as she reverted to a slavering force of violence.

A hand tapped her left thigh and she twisted on her heel to find Bressal regarding her with mute intensity. A slender, sallow man with a narrow face that was always freshly shaven, his misleadingly benign appearance gave no hint to the depths of fury that could erupt if he was obstructed or displeased. He jerked his head towards the settlement fire pit. Following the gesture, her eyes locked onto the indistinct form of a large man with a black beard, crouched in the shadows near the sleeping guard, a long knife in his right hand.

The Black Wolf.

She nodded her understanding. Bressal was instructing her to mark the man, to prevent him from escaping in the turmoil to follow. She repressed a quick flicker of irritation at that. If he'd followed another of her suggestions – concealing one of the *fénnid* by the clearing entrance – they could have effectively sealed the battleground. Fearful of the raider numbers however, he'd insisted on having all of his force to hand.

With these last instructions transferred, Bressal hissed, held her eyes then abruptly made a sharp passing gesture with his hand to alert the others that he was turning combat leadership over to her.

She stared at him, but Bressal simply repeated the gestures with greater insistence and turned back to study the raiders.

The Grey One breathed deeply as she attempted to absorb what had just happened, but looking down to the settlement, she saw that she had little time to do so. By now, had he been awake, the guard would have been alerted by the uneasy shuffling of the cattle as the dark shapes moved towards them. One or two of the animals began to low quietly but the dozing guard slept on. Liath Luachra watched in silence as the black bearded man crept up behind him. Moving forward with ruthless efficiency, he clasped a hand about the guard's mouth, yanked his head up and sliced his throat open from ear to ear.

Disturbed by the smell of freshly spilled blood, the cattle started moving again, this time crowding towards the southern side of the clearing, obstructing both the *fian's* proposed route of attack and their view of the settlement. Liath Luachra hissed in frustration. Through the milling of the frightened cattle she could see the raiders cluster around the entrances to the dwelling where the settlement's inhabitants still slept soundly. This would have been the perfect time to launch their initial javelin volley but now the opportunity was lost, the field of casting ruined by the position of the shifting cattle. On either side, the men glanced towards her, waiting for her lead. She, in turn, looked to Bressal but he completely ignored her. Scowling, she made a pressing motion with her right hand. They would have to wait.

There was a sudden roar from the settlement as the raiders surged into the various buildings, a roar echoed almost immediately by shrieks of agony or the screams of women and children as the settlement's population awoke to their fate.

The screaming did not last long as *Na Madraí Allta* once again upheld their fearsome reputation for ruthlessness. Soon, the only cries were the victorious yells of the raiders and an occasional scream of pain. Frightened by the noise and the violence, the cattle had shifted position once more, this time stampeding off to the grassy area beyond the buildings, closer towards the entrance of the clearing.

Na Cinéaltaí waited, concealed in the thick undergrowth just inside the treeline. They watched in silence as the raiders dragged bodies from the buildings, piling them in an untidy heap by the fire. The Black Wolf had settled himself on a low grassy hummock, laughing and talking loudly with two of his men while he watched the others rummage through the buildings and ransack the little settlement.

The Grey One forced herself to unclench her javelin, conscious of the fact that if she continued to grip it too tightly the tension would strain her arm muscle, throwing off her cast when it was time.

And it wasn't yet time.

Despite the tempting proximity of the Black Wolf, too many of his men were still scattered in places she couldn't see, inside the longhouses or out of sight on the far side of the buildings. For the javelin volley to achieve the effect she wanted, it was essential that the raiders were clustered more tightly together. They would have to bide their time.

As she continued to watch, a high-pitched scream came from the nearest building and, a moment later, two females were dragged through the doorway and into the open. Both were skinny, fair-haired girls, dressed in loose wool shifts. The older girl looked to have no more than seventeen years on her, the younger less than fourteen. Both were almost out of their wits with fear.

Their captors dragged them to where their leader was sitting and cast them onto the ground to cower before him, weeping and clinging desperately to each other. The Black Wolf scratched his beard while he looked them over. Slowly, he rose to his feet.

With surprising alacrity, the big man reached down and ripped the shift from the eldest girl, provoking a cheer of delight from his men. The girl screamed and desperately tried to shield her breasts from the guffawing raiders who'd started to gather around, eyeing her with undisguised hunger.

From the corner of her eye, Liath Luachra noticed Murchú turn his head to look at her but she ignored him. Further along to her right, she heard an evil chuckle and a whisper from one of the *fénnid*. 'There's a pair of beauties worth waiting for.'

Conall Cacach. No surprises there.

Her lips compressed as a snicker of laughter repeated down the line. She made a sharp hissing noise and they settled down.

'Where is it?'

The Black Wolf's voice carried surprisingly well in the stillness of the clearing, his deep, bass tones reverberating loudly in the windless morning air. Petrified, the girl turned her head away and wailed and he had to slap her across the face to get her to stop.

'Where is the treasure?'

Given the absence of any treasure, the girls' stricken confusion was understandable, from Liath Luachra's informed perspective at least. The raiders, lacking her insight into the matter, were less generous in their interpretation.

The Black Wolf sighed. With menacing deliberation, he lifted a heavy wooden club, hauling the head up from where it rested on the earth beside him. A brutal but effective weapon, it looked to be about the same length as his arm and terminated with a large knob carved into the shape of a mallet with a short metal spike indented at its centre. He hefted it threateningly in his right hand then poking it under the girl's jaw, he forced her head up so that her eyes met his. He bent down slightly. 'Where is it?'

'Grey One!' Murchú whispered urgently. She flashed him a furious glare and he flinched, hurriedly lapsing into silence. Turning her gaze back to the settlement, she refocused her attention on the position of the raiders, counting them out in a silent whisper.

'Your final chance. Where is the treasure?'

The panic-stricken girl released a terrified wail, provoking a flash of anger in the big man's eyes. Swinging back the club, he brought it crashing down.

The sound of the smashing skull carried clearly across to the trees and caused even the battle-hardened members of the *fian* to flinch. The warriors watched wordlessly as the girl toppled to one side, hitting the ground with a heavy slap, the left side of her head a broken, bloody mess.

'Well, that's a waste!' A bitterly disgusted whisper from Conall Cacach.

Liath Luachra would have turned on him, but she was too preoccupied with her count of the raiders. The black-haired leader, meanwhile, had turned his attention to the second terrified girl who, traumatised by the sight of her murdered sister, sat soundlessly clutching herself, staring at the body with a blank expression. The raiders closed in, curious to see what happened next.

'Javelins,' whispered Liath Luachra. Taking a fresh grip on her weapon, she stood and raised it, drawing the haft back until her right hand was well behind her ear. She held it there, noting the action reproduced down the line of waiting men. '*Scaoiligí!*' she hissed. Release!

And cast.

The whistle of the incoming hail must have alerted the raider standing closest to them for he turned around and looked towards the treeline. A puzzled expression had barely formed on his face when the first missile stuck him in the chest, the downward momentum of the metal head punching it through his sternum to emerge two hand-widths from the base of his spine. The other raiders had no time to register what had happened for the other javelins were already falling in amongst them.

The second volley hit them before they had time to react to the first. Six raiders were down, three unmoving, three screaming in agony as though in counterpoint to the screams of challenge from *Na Cinéaltaí* charging out of the trees towards them.

Surrendering completely to the battle frenzy, Liath Luachra led the charge, literally frothing at the mouth as she stormed across the open space to where the shocked survivors were gathered. Her throat was already raw from roaring, her vision reduced to a blinkered red haze. Consumed by her desire to reach the raiders, she was barely conscious that she was running.

By the time she bowled into the remnants of *Na Madraí Allta*, they were over their initial shock but she could almost taste the despair that filled their eyes. They knew they had no hope of survival, that no quarter would be given, no mercy spared. In a retaliatory surge of desperation and fury at the unfairness of it all, they brought their weapons up to bear, intent on going down fighting.

A skinny man with a face coated in black tattoos lunged at Liath Luachra with a metal-tipped spear but consumed in the throes of her battle frenzy, to her he seemed to be moving ponderously slow. Even as the wicked looking metal point came up to take her in the gut, she'd dropped to the ground, hitting the earth with her haunches and sliding forwards on the dewy grass. The warrior attempted to change his grip and jab downwards but she'd already slid past his left leg, gouging a vicious gash along the rear of his knee. Even as the hamstrung warrior toppled, the rest of the *fian* broke over him and his comrades in a violent wave of screaming violence and sharp-edged metal.

The Grey One used her remaining momentum to regain her feet, her eyes flickering around to locate the Black Wolf. Unlike his comrades, the bandit leader had not frozen in shock at the first volley of the javelins but responded with impressive instincts of self-preservation. Recognising their predicament, he'd bolted, ducking behind one of the buildings so that he was not only hidden from sight but sheltered from any further javelin cast. By the time Liath Luachra caught sight of him, he'd already cut around the corner of the longhouse and was galloping at full speed for the gap leading out of the clearing.

Good plan, Bressal!

She took off after him, leaping over the body of a raider with a javelin through his skull, careering past a protruding lean-to. Finally on open ground, she yelled and waved to scatter the startled cattle who once again had gathered to obstruct her path.

Because of his size, the Black Wolf would most likely have outrun her if he hadn't been hampered by the wicked gash in his arm, the result of her first javelin. She had hoped to hit him in the chest but because he'd turned at the last moment, the missile had streaked past, ripping a deep streak of skin from his arm. The resulting wound wasn't lethal by any means, but it was enough to upset his usual running gait, slowing him down.

She pursued him through the gap, in her excitement releasing a bloodthirsty ululation.

Glancing back over his shoulder, the Black Wolf now realised his sole pursuer was a single female. This seemed to provoke some misplaced sense of outrage for he suddenly slid to a halt and twisted about to confront her.

'You threaten *me?*' He roared as she drew towards him. 'You threaten *me*, little girl!'

With this, he lunged for her, swinging the wooden club with wild force. Once again, her swift reactions vastly exceeded those of her opponent and she slid into a crouch, driving forwards with *Gléas Gan Ainm* as the club whistled overhead in a poorly calculated overextension. Realising the danger that he was in, the big man

211

belatedly attempted to pull himself back from the swing, but he was too slow. The sword plunged a full finger length into his gut and the twisting movement he made as he attempted to pull back caused the blade to slice along the skin, opening his belly even further.

He pulled back with shock even as the Grey One was reversing her hold on the sword. She smashed the hilt into his face, so savagely that he tottered backwards and tripped over a fallen branch. And then she was on him, stabbing and stabbing, repeatedly, sinking the metal blade deep into his chest.

She was still stabbing when the blood haze finally cleared and she became conscious of Murchú and Bressal standing nearby, observing her with shocked expressions. Straddling the corpse, her hands were coated in a thick sheen of blood and entrails, her clothing and face drenched with blood. Pushing herself off the body, she rose on trembling legs, her chest heaving.

'She's cut him to pieces,' Murchú looked up from the shredded carcass to her blood–stained face but, cowed by the insane venom of her glare, dropped his eyes again almost immediately.

Bressal shrugged. 'She's left the head. That's all we need.' He turned a glance towards the panting woman warrior. 'Good work, Grey One. You've saved the day.'

***

After the earlier shrieks and brutality, the settlement seemed relatively calm when she returned although it was hard to ignore the iron stink of blood, the smell of gore and shit and the corpses strewn about in contorted poses. *Na Cinéaltaí* had come out of the battle exceptionally well, the single casualty a simple gash on Senach's arm. Their victory was substantial.

Unhampered by the wound, Senach – a lean, dark-haired *Uí Loinge* man with more than thirty years on him – was down on his knees, working with Biotóg to rifle the corpses, looting both raider and settler alike. Sitting off to the left on a pile of firewood, Sean Fergus – Old Fergus – watched them with an exhausted, worldweary expression. The eldest member of the *fian*, his grey hair was tied up in braids and he sported a heavy moustache – also grey – drenched and dripping from the bucket of water he'd just immersed his head in.

Conall Cacach and Canann were standing by one of the longhouses with the troubled young girl. They had her up against the wall and Conall, a big muscular streak of malice with rotting teeth and greasy black hair, was groping her small breasts through the shift as she stared blankly into open space. With a brutal twist, Conall ripped the hindering garment to shreds. The girl displayed no reaction.

'Uncle!' Murchú nudged his uncle and gestured angrily towards the scene. Bressal slowly shook his head. 'No survivors,' he said quietly.

A sample of what the reviewers say:

"Dark, dangerous and strikingly original."

"A fast-paced traverse through bush trails and battles with a female heroine who is commanding and fascinating."

"In the legends of Fionn mac Cumhaill, Liath Luachra is an intriguing name with minimal context, but in Brian O'Sullivan's adaptions she becomes a most fascinating and formidable character in her own right. Her backstory is a great read; brigands and bloodshed, second-guessings and double-crossings. This is an Ancient Ireland that is entrancing and savage, much like Liath Luachra herself."

"The plotting is riveting – full of twists and turns – and the action is full on, hell for leather. If you like Games of Thrones style dramas with a strong splash of Celtic culture, this is a book you'll enjoy."

"For the first hundred pages, this was a 4-star for me. I really felt myself lost in the world of 2nd century Ireland due to the authenticity of the writing and highly descriptive prose. Some historical fiction can be very accurate but a bit dry and heavy-going. Definitely not the case here. At about the 100-page mark though, it really yanked me in and moved to a 5-star. I stormed through till the end, having one of those days where you just have to tell the kids to sort themselves out. Couldn't put it down."

More Books from Irish Imbas

Beara: Dark Legends
[The Beara Trilogy – Book 1]

Nobody knows much about reclusive historian Muiris (Mos) O'Súilleabháin except that he doesn't share his secrets freely. Mos, however, has a *"sixth sense for history, a unique talent for finding lost things"*.

Reluctantly lured from seclusion by a mysterious religious corporation, Mos is hired to locate the final resting place of legendary Irish hero, Fionn mac Cumhaill. Confronted by a thousand-year old mystery, the distractions of a beguiling circus performer and a lethal competitor, Mos must draw on his knowledge of Gaelic lore to defy his enemies and survive his own family history in Beara.

Beara: Dark Legends is the first in a trilogy of unforgettable Irish thrillers. Propulsive, atmospheric and darkly humorous, *Dark Legends* introduces an Irish hero like you've never seen before. Nothing you thought you knew about Ireland will ever be the same again.

A sample of what the reviewers say:

"A great tale with all the elements of a "Who dunnit" all woven into modern and ancient Irish history and mythology."

"Fantastic book - couldn't put it down. A 'MUST' read! original Irish thriller, historical novel, mystery novel, best book I've read in years."

"O'Sullivan has done an amazing job of introducing a culture that many would say is dying and using it as the basis for a unique and exciting thriller. I think I've learned more about Irish history and the Irish language in this one book than I have in many years of school and television, without it once feeling forced or jaded."

"A great mixture of a strong story and strong characters, dark (some very dark) themes and wonderfully evocative descriptions of the wild Irish landscape, interspersed with ancient Irish lore running throughout the book."

"Excellent story, very well thought out, many twists and turns that weren't expected. Thoroughly enjoyed the main character Mos and his no nonsense-take no crap attitude to life, he says what most of us often probably think but are too polite to say, highly entertaining!"

"O'Sullivan's cast of international characters enliven this tale of archaeological intrigue, magic, murder and sex, set mainly in West Cork, Ireland. Dual story lines, across different time zones, reveal secrets of Irish spirituality, ancient lore and language."

9 780995 107915